Running On Sand

LINDA ANNE ATTERTON

Copyright © 2016 Linda Anne Atterton.

All rights reserved. No part of this book may be reproduced, stored, or transmitted by any means—whether auditory, graphic, mechanical, or electronic—without written permission of both publisher and author, except in the case of brief excerpts used in critical articles and reviews. Unauthorized reproduction of any part of this work is illegal and is punishable by law.

ISBN: 978-1-4834-5056-8 (sc)
ISBN: 978-1-4834-5057-5 (e)

Library of Congress Control Number: 2016905987

Cover Image by: Edward Hopper

Because of the dynamic nature of the Internet, any web addresses or links contained in this book may have changed since publication and may no longer be valid. The views expressed in this work are solely those of the author and do not necessarily reflect the views of the publisher, and the publisher hereby disclaims any responsibility for them.

Any people depicted in stock imagery provided by Thinkstock are models, and such images are being used for illustrative purposes only.
Certain stock imagery © Thinkstock.

Lulu Publishing Services rev. date: 04/29/2016

Contents

Dedications vii

About The Author viii

About The Book ix

Imprints x

Acknowledgements xi

Prologue—Sand xiii

Rock - Paper - Scissors 1

House - Tree - Person 11

Stars 17

The Sea Wall 27

Spot The Difference 37

Reflections 49

Blowing Out Candles 63

Solitaire 71

Sand Dunes For Beginners 78

In The Mirror 90

Upside Down 101

Happy Families 107
Tennis 119
Robert 127
Truth or Dare 137
Are You Ready? 144
Changing Shape 157
Drawing Circles 164
The Only Way Out 173
Undercurrents 183
Someone To Turn Back To 198

Epilogue—Stepping Stones 225

Dedications

For my son Christopher and my parents

About The Author

Linda Anne Atterton was born in Scotland near Glasgow.

She studied at Aberdeen, Oxford and Cambridge Universities, qualifying as a Clinical Psychologist before moving to work in Norfolk in 1991. Her specialism is brain injury.

At seventeen, she was winner for her age group of Lallans magazine competition for a Scottish poem. Since returning to creative writing after a long break, she has published poetry in the UK and Ireland, in Abridged, The Moth, and Far Off Places, as well as being included in several anthologies. Her sonnet *Banished* won Litro's Shakespearean Sonnet competition in 2014.

Running On Sand is her first novel. It began as a short story, *Are The Stars Hot or Cold*, which reached the semifinals of Carve Magazine's competition in 2014. The idea came from a flash fiction piece (*Sea Defences*, published in Litro) and from a poem, *Toy Suns*, published in Abridged. She lives in Norwich, about twenty miles from the seaside village where the book is set.

About The Book

There comes a time in your life, which feels like a storm, and after it you are never quite the same. You have to put the pieces back together and they will never quite fit. Some are lost and some are new. There are holes and cracks you try to hide. The scenery is different too; you could be looking through a window, standing on a balcony. Are you stronger or weaker? You are both yet neither. You will learn you can feel broken but be whole. This story is about how you do that, about learning to run on sand when nothing quite feels solid, how you can feel safe with sand when you adjust to it.

 I am not the girl in this story and her story is not mine. But when you're looking out a window after the storm you can get stuck and doors can be too hard to get through. You find the exits in your mind instead and that is what I did while writing this book. When you emerge you will have changed without quite knowing how.

 I chose Sea Palling as a setting for the story simply because it felt right. I have rearranged the scenery a little. All the characters are fictional. But the beach, the seals, the doughnut shop, the amusement arcade and the sun and storms are real.

Imprints

This story is about how people we meet and things that happen to us leave an imprint on our lives. I have therefore chosen to dedicate specific chapters to the people who have made a special imprint on my own story and the story in the book.

'*Drawing Circles*' is dedicated to Chris Gray my editor who taught me to be truthful to what I felt and supported me when being truthful was also painful. Without her belief in me this story would never have been told.

'*Reflections*' is dedicated to Nesta who knows me as well as any mirror!

'*Stars*' is to Gemma because she is one, and my friend as well as my niece.

'*Solitaire*' is dedicated to Sam whom I thank for never leaving me to play it!

'*House-Tree-Person*' is dedicated to my husband who now knows 'finished' is author-speak for 'soon'.

'*Sand-dunes for Beginners*' to Katrina Plumb for her help in editing and her inspiration and intelligence.

'*Truth or Dare*' to my son for helping to write it!

'*Stepping Stones*' to Hayley Millins who stopped me looking as if I'd been up all night when I had!

'*Someone To Turn Back To*' is dedicated of course to someone!

Acknowledgements

I'd like to thank my family for their patience and support.

A special thank you to my mother for being who she is and all the English Literature she helped me learn!

To my editor Chris Gray for her huge kindness in guiding and supporting me and for pulling no punches!

To my special friends Nesta Reeve and Samantha Metcalfe for always being there.

I owe a huge thank you to my cousin David Wilson, the artist in our family, for leading me to the painting by Edward Hopper which I used in the cover and to Yale University Art Gallery for allowing me to do so.

Prologue

Sand

July 1972

He runs faster than me. I will never catch him up. I follow him across the beach, half blind from wind whipping hair into my eyes. The sand is warm and deep here, soft and golden, perfect except to run on. I am knocking over sandcastles, jumping over sunbathers, trying to reach him before he gets to the hill leading back to the village. The hill is sand at this side, climbing steeply to the top then turning into road and hurtling you to the bottom. By the time I'm halfway up he disappears. I start to cry. I freeze the tears into an ice-lolly, tasting the orange one I always choose. Chris never says they cost too much. I force my legs to keep on going, finding that if I lean my body to the slope I do not slip. I know that at the top the sand runs out, the road gets flatter. Catching my breath, the sand burning my feet, I tumble down the hill and he is waiting for me, smiling. Smiling back I run to throw myself into his arms. He grins and starts to run again, the ice-lolly melting as he dashes past the ice cream stall, the doughnut shop, the miniature arcade. I dodge the tourists, push into the wind, and glimpse him turn the corner near the playground. Speeding up I chase him through the streets until we reach our own. He suddenly stops without looking back. I could catch him up but something slows me down. I shout, he doesn't seem to hear. He breaks into a sprint that I try to copy, seeing all he sees a minute later, pictures in slow motion drawn in crayon then pen. The children next door stand like statues turned to stone while playing football, I can see the ball forgotten in the road, see their mothers at their doorsteps, empty speech bubbles where there should be talk. An ambulance with the engine running sits between our house and number six as if confused to be here on such a sunny day. Two men are carrying a kind of bed along our path. Chris is talking to it, blocking their way. A tall man cuts across the grass and puts a hand upon his shoulder, saying something which makes my brother shake his head, shake off the hand and run inside the house. The man belongs to somewhere else not here: a calm, clean room, the taste of syrup hiding something else. Somebody on the bed, the man who any minute should be home from work. The body is my father's. I know that he is not inside. I bend to him. Whatever words Chris said, I can find none. I touch his cheek, as he touched mine to wake me up on holidays and Sundays. I shut my eyes and know that if I glued them shut I would still see him there. I run to find my mother. The word is caught inside my throat, a different shape when carved by fear. She is draped in shadows in the kitchen. When the word breaks free she never hears it. She is holding onto Chris. The word means nothing said by me not him.

I wait for him to come, to say the words that will explain this, hating her for stealing him. I want to kick the football hard, to run until I'm back upon the beach. I wonder if I climbed the hill again, didn't cry, ran faster, it might change back so nothing happened, so father would come home from work as usual. When Chris comes out I want to ask him but he seems too far away.

Mother seems to forget to send us to bed. We go when it's too strange to stay awake. I lie and wonder how I'll get to sleep. I wake and don't know what has scared me. Then I hear Chris crying. Climbing into his bed I put my arms around him like he does when I'm upset. He pulls me closer, strokes my hair.

"I'll look after you now dad's not here. I was proud of you today Grace. You kept on running even when you couldn't see me, you made it over the hill and didn't cry. I remember something Dad said once about the dark. When I was scared. He told me to imagine what was in the dark, the very worst thing I could see. What do you think I saw?"

"A monster?" I guess.

"Nothing but him. So I reckon if we turn it round the very worst thing is he isn't here. Nothing can be worse than that, the very worst has happened."

I wish that he'd been right. That the worst was not still out there. Worse than we could ever have imagined. Something we would only see too late. I hold my brother tighter. If I had known the future, would I ever have let him go?

He runs faster than me. I run in his footprints, we only leave one set. He makes me faster, pacing me. He teaches me; I learn much more than he suspects. The day my father died I found out how to run on tears, that when you think the ground is solid it returns to sand.

Rock - Paper - Scissors

June 1972

My father was forty when he died. A heart attack, the kind that turns your heart to stone. He had loved my brother and me without favouritism. He had loved us completely, taught us how to crab and fish, how to paint and draw. He had loved my mother too, tolerating her airs and graces with humour and understanding. He had married the younger sister of his childhood sweetheart. Once they outgrew sweets she outgrew him. The story in the village told of how she broke his heart and their engagement, setting herself free to marry someone else. A doctor's wife, she moved to Cambridge, a hundred miles away. Like any story the village told, there were different versions. I have heard that he was offered a more ambitious position there and I have also heard that he took it only out of fear my father would win her back. Either way she became my aunt. My father told me love makes the real decisions, all people make are plans and most of our plans will crumble as easily as sand. He rarely spoke of it so if his heart was broken then he must have joined the pieces well. In wedding photos my aunt and her husband sit smiling at my mother. She was only eighteen, still at that stage where vanity and selfishness are considered youth not character. The photos show a charming face, the most demure expression. I suspect she wore it till she won him from her sister's shadow, then the patina wore off. Where understanding and kindness mix with proximity one can find a kind of love. So it was for my father. He put away the love he lost and took her hand to build a family. They could have complemented each other. Many marriages in the village grew from less. The sandy soil needed strong roots, the will to bend. She was never swayed by love or shaken by compassion. Her fragile beauty hid a core of iron. Her fragility was fear; she hid from storms, from darkness, illness, hugging fears without a name. My father was a kindly giant, a tree who sheltered. Joined by love the union could have grafted, made a tree no storm could break. Instead she resented his strength, but drank from it greedily. Her roots drew from his, touching, never tangling as one. She held his branches for support without any intention of embracing. She waited for the apples to turn to gold and blamed the tree when they did not. For my father the ordinary magic of an apple was enough,

Acquaintances would describe it as a useful marriage. Friends would use the word 'lucky', the partner benefiting from this luck dependent upon whether the friend owed the bond to my mother or my father. There were no friends they shared. The older people would use luck to refer to the fact that two healthy children had been born, the luck being the greater due to the firstborn being a boy, and because however much I disliked it I looked like mother.

It was impossible to deny she was beautiful but it was not as a flower blooming in a meadow or in gay abandon on a tree in spring. Her beauty shone like a China rose in a glasshouse and shone brightly only when reflected back at her, in the gleam of men's eyes as they fell on her, in the mirrors she had my father place to best check her hair or to dress in front of. She did not like solitude, or books, or even music, except to dance to.

My father found joy in all of these things. He was a boat-builder. With opportunity he might have been a painter or sculptor. He was a wonderful craftsman but too modest to charge enough for his work. He made most of our toys until he died. Secret boxes, puppets that danced, wooden crabs that walked, and even a ballerina captured forever in a carved pirouette. She circled on top of a box if you wound the key to the tune of Clair de Lune. Her rigid posture in the dance and the cool, smooth texture of the wood reminded me of my mother. I loved the toy the more having made the link, but solely because it was a link only I saw, another proof of how well my father and I understood each other. It amused me to realise that my mother was innocent of the knowledge that she was the model for the carved figure. The eyes were the same topaz blue, painted to echo the same shape. The carved fall of long, curling hair, tucked behind one ear, was hers.

It is raining. Not a passing shower from a cloud with somewhere else to go, but a heavy drizzle from a flock of clouds that has not shifted all morning and seems perfectly at home. June was my month, Chris said, "two scoops of sun and one of clouds". It was Saturday lunchtime but mother seemed to have forgotten lunch. This was not in itself unusual, except my father was home, which normally reminded her that my brother and I might be as wild as she complained but not wild enough to hunt our own meals. We had planned on swimming. Drizzle was not a deterrent but, after finding towels, guiltily retrieving yesterday's wet costumes from beneath the bed, the rain began to pour as if the grey sky was a sponge being squeezed. This had lasted an hour now.

So we half lay on my bed, playing rock-paper-scissors, although Chris always won. I had grown up losing to my brother, forever taller, faster, neater, even blonder. I had never minded. That would be to covet a cat's grace, a falcon's speed. It simply was.

"You lose because you give yourself away," Chris said.

It was not in Chris to delight in beating me. If I lost to him he made sure I lost to no one else, teaching me, daring me, never letting me fall so far behind that I gave up, never waiting long for me to catch up either. Always round the next bend, treading water, urging me on. At thirteen I was faster than most fourteen year old girls in the village. If this meant I was secretly disliked, befriended only by the few content to come second, I would not hang back. I watched the other girls deciding who would be queen and who princesses, knowing that the crown was like the ones in glass boxes in the amusement arcade. You paid to see the talons close around a plastic toy. You bought more tokens, lost more than it was worth. You wore it for a day or two before it caught the sunlight, then they mobbed you. I made my crowns of daisies, roamed my kingdom with my brother, made my father's lap a throne.

"What do I give away?"

"What you're thinking. Most people do it. In card games they call it a 'tell'. Your body or face betray you. Like a cat's tail moving as it waits to pounce on the bird. I can tell by now what move you'll make next. Before you are 'paper' you put your tongue out as if you're drawing. Just before your left hand turns into a rock, the right will tense, as if it knows the shape you're seeing in your mind."

"So how do I not tell?" I demand.

"You keep your face a mask and your body a statue until the last moment. You forget I am your brother. Like when we race. You overtake me. Then you spoil it. You turn your head to see how close I am. I know you will. Then I overtake you."

"So what are your tells?" I ask, practicing the word.

"You tell me," he smiles, wickedly.

We play again. I watch his hand as it shapes to scissors in the air, then pours to paper, sculpts to stone. I can read nothing. I try harder. Minutes slide away, the rain tattoos upon the roof, we are reflections of each other, peeled apart by nothing but the movement of a hand in the shadows, glued together in my mind's eye. For I am blind to what it is my brother tells. Too close to see.

I give up guessing, bored and hungry, wondering why father has not come to find us, the clock has chimed two to itself, the three a pendulum away. Our father's time at home is told in laughter, treasured all the more for being rationed. When he goes, the laughter disappears. We need to make it by ourselves. Ours tastes of cooking chocolate. Spread too thin it cracks. I want my father's chocolate, dropped in kisses, drizzled on the stale day. The afternoon is running out.

I shut my eyes and I am there. From the outside our house looked like any other in the street. We lived at the end of a row of terraced houses. A row that only added up to seven, a street that only had one row. From the front the houses looked like narrow cardboard boxes holding one another up. Each stretched backwards, deep inside. The door opened to a steeply climbing staircase. Veering left, the hallway took you to the lounge, on to the kitchen at the back. The only bathroom was beside the kitchen. If you took the stairs you found two bedrooms, back and front. My parents' bedroom was the back one, bigger than the one I shared with Chris. The rooms were dark inside, regardless of the season or the sun, because the windows were so small. Our front door was the only door, as if the doors ran out when number six was built. You reached the garden by going round the path that led behind the house. Each garden was divided from the next by a hedge or fence. As the end house in the row we had the biggest garden, stretching around the side and to the back. At the bottom trees made a thicket, flowers fought with weeds. The flowers must have won in the beginning: our address was 7 Flower Row.

Our house hardly held itself up and felt as if the wind could blow it down. We barely knew the people, never knocked except to hand in letters posted by mistake. Our neighbours went in and out of each others' houses as often as their own, their children almost siblings. They were kind, they noticed Chris and me and drew us in. My words could draw the house, not invite you in. My mother never let a single child in to play, a single parent in the door without a reason. She never found a reason good enough.

I know now how I would decorate that house. I would paint the walls in sunny yellow, or the butter yellow of English roses. I would replace most of the mirrors with pictures framing places I had been. I would make the ceiling sky, the carpets grass, the floorboards sand. I would tear down the net curtains which always looked like cobwebs.

Would it have mattered? What matters is what happened there and what did not. If there is laughter in a house walls can be grey. Love will never care. Forget to close the curtains moonlight paints in silk. The furniture can be old and shabby, worries sink. If you are a child the bedroom can be pitch black, wind can shake the windows, rain bombard the roof, talk floats in bubbles up the stairs and you feel safe.

I wish that memory stretched further back. So that I could reach a time our house was like all the others in and out. I wish those places I would frame were real.

When you have lived in a house long enough the house becomes alive. You fall asleep inside its hands and wake to hear it breathe. As a child a house seems solid, fixed when everything else is moving, changing, even you. A child does not measure time in years or months or much at all. Time is tied to things that happen, when to where. A child's day is like a cuckoo clock, figures pop out to show the time. Their comings and goings become clockwork. Close your eyes, imagine pictures, listen and the echoes rhyme. My parents didn't rhyme. Today the house felt wrong again. So I let the walls turn into paper, sink through floorboards till the sounds have shapes. No swish or clank of lunch. Instead a silence, broken by jagged edges. Voices rise in anger, drop like stones. I beckon to Chris, place my hand behind my ear.

"I don't want to listen," he says.
"Well I do. I'm fed up with them fighting," I throw.
"It's just like rain. It will be gone by tomorrow," he says, refusing to meet my eyes. Today's rain was the shaking tail of a wet week.
"You starve till tomorrow then!"
I open the door, ajar enough to hear; if heard, enough to pretend it accidental. My mother's voice is cutting words into angry shapes that need no tell. They curl into a fist and punch a hole inside me. My father's words are flat and hard to catch; he speaks in a voice I have never heard before, as if it's kept for her.
"Alice, I'll go a long way to make you happy but not somewhere else. Can't you just be happy here? With what we have ?" There is true bewilderment in the shape of his voice.
"I hate it here. You better than anyone know why. And tell me what we really have? A house no bigger than a sandcastle and a boatyard you hide in making toys." The words are bait.
"What do you want to have?"
"People I fit in with. Roads that go somewhere."

"Cromer is bigger, busier."

"Why not Norwich?" Her voice is too sweet now, the one she uses when she wants something you don't.

"And the children?"

"Would forget this place and have chances instead of dreams."

"Forgetting isn't that easy ."

"They'd have each other, Lawrence. Make new friends. That's what children do."

"Where do I fit in? Or don't I?"

I shrink inside as father casts the words, a net deep below the water, into a pool he thinks he knows. Sometimes when you fish you catch nothing at all, sometimes what you catch you wish you could throw back in. For my mother spares him nothing, lets him look into a net her words jump out of, gasping for air.

"I never wanted children, you knew that."

"I knew the girl didn't. But you were young and girls grow into women."

"When we made them which woman did you see? Lucy?

"I saw my wife. Your sister was to me what I was to her. Kisses in schoolbooks, names on sand."

"You stole my children. I carried them inside me, you carried them as soon they came out. You picked them up each time I put them down. Now I hardly count to them."

"They were more down than up to you, Alice. As for count; be honest. Count how many times you let Grace cry to cuddle Chris?"

"Are you so sure you want honest? I picked Chris up because I wanted him. I counted one and was content. You said one didn't make a family. It did for me. All the love I had when James died I gave to Chris. You look at Grace and think because she looks like me I should love her.

"You could love her if you really looked at her. We could be happy if you stopped looking back."

"I look at you and all it does is pull me back there. Do you know why I agreed to marry you?"

"I was not blind Alice. If it was not for love I thought there'd be time to find it."

They are walking too fast for me, the steps so big I have to jump. I feel her lead him to a cliff and sense he's blind.

"The child we buried was never yours to cry for. I needed your name, not you. Chris is your first born son, James was mine."

"Who was he?" His voice sounds wrong.

"The father? Not worth the telling. An accident. You picked me up, that's all."

You can push a man so he will fall and still he'll choose the words he drops. My father was big and when he fell, he fell hard. Even in his fall surpassing her.

"You could have told me. I loved him anyway. A name is just a name, not who you love."

I never heard her answer, if she found one. An eavesdropper shot and fallen to the ground, I escape and slam the door and without explanation get into bed and pull the blankets over my head. I feel Chris sit upon the bottom of the bed and when I start to cry I feel him move and pull the covers back to let him in.

"If you don't stop crying I'll fall out!" he whispers. My arms go round him tightly. While my face is hidden in his sweater I work out what to say.

"Do you ever wish I was a brother?" I ask, half wanting to make him ask me what I heard so I can halve the hurt, half knowing he can't make this right.

"Is he bigger or smaller?" he teases.

"Less trouble. Doesn't cry on you."

"No. He'd never let me do his hair."

I laugh, relieved but at the same time ashamed because I daren't tell him what I heard and risk becoming less important to him. I sit up and pass the hairbrush to him, turning round so he can pull the hair into a thicket down my back to find the tangles. Even when the brush snags I bite my lip and make no sound. He brushes till I want to let him pull the secrets out as well and bite the harder. I remember him teaching me to count like this, from one stroke to twenty, adding on more strokes each night to fifty, brushing to a hundred, making me promise never to tell how I had learned so fast in case his friends found out. The brushing flows in long strokes until the static buzzes, then he divides my hair into three ropes and plaits it. When it's for school he can do this in minutes, when the plaiting is to tidy up the day he goes so slowly I lose all track of time. He seems to get lost too, to want to stay lost. Time moves in flitting shadows. By the time I pass him a ribbon to tie it with the sky is full of them, like pink and violet rainbows that have come undone. The clouds have silently moved on, to find another place to rain on.

It was supper time when father called us down. I couldn't look at him when he tried to smile across the table. In my head their words went round and round until I could have rhymed them back out loud. We sat propped up by our chairs, the polished wooden table he had made more alive than those around it.

My mother gaily waved away the missing lunch.

"The cupboards were empty, darlings, so father went to meet the boats and got some crabs. Such a mess to dress! I picked some asparagus, Chris. And there are strawberries especially for you, Grace. A feast instead of lunch."

The easy way she hung a tablecloth as scenery, knowing what lay behind it, angered me. I let her serve me then looked at the plate, reluctant to be her puppet.

"Aren't you hungry, Grace?" she asked. I itched to say 'Aren't you too late to care?'

The warning flickered in my brother's eyes.

"Just tired," I drawled.

My father was no longer made of rock. He was a paper bag blown up into a balloon, held tight and punched until it burst. My brother would always come first no matter how fast I ran. I loved him too much to tell him he was really second.

The crabmeat was rich and sweet, the bread still warm in the middle. The strawberries needed no sugar, the cream a pool of silk. I ate and watched my brother's face relax, my parents move like cardboard pop-ups in a child's picture book. I ate it all and wondered how part of me could feel so full and leave the rest of me so empty.

That was the day I found out my mother never wanted me, that I was less than a ghost to her. I did not realise it was also the day I learned to keep a secret from my brother.

House -Tree - Person

Not far from our village is another that lies beneath the sea. The storms relentlessly pulled it in. For years the church tower stood alone upon the dunes until it finally sank. For a decade when the tide was out the wind would sometimes sweep the sand away and bare the skeletons in the graveyard. Then they built the rock reef and the sand grew deeper, burying them for good. If you look hard when you walk along the beach you can find jigsaw pieces of the tower and hold the flint inside your hand. The fishermen say if the tide is right you can hear the church bell ring.

Childhood is a land we only borrow. That is how it should be. What we remember later is a story, the one we want to tell, the version we can live with. The land is under water now, all we have are echoed lullabies and blurry pictures, souvenirs of somewhere we once lived. Our minds have polished smooth the parts that cut too deep, concealed the images that hurt too much to see. The original story has become a palimpsest, we overwrote it as we grew. A child begins to build with shapes and colours, turns them into pictures. Words come later, but as footnotes, chapter headings. Words are only labels, names for what we feel, or see or hear. If we know the names, or dare to pin them on, the labels make things real. The pictures are different sizes, some are black and white, some colour, some are only outlines. There are pages we linger on, the corners dog eared and sticky. There are pages we flick over, so bright they brand the eyes, so dark you squeeze them out. It is a land of dreams and nightmares with no borders in between. To touch the paper is to swim and feel a current pull you down, to catch an echo that instinct warns you to drop. Your mind can glimpse the land below the water, read the imprints in the sand.

In Latin, 'imprint' simply means to print. When you grow up beside a beach you think of prints as footprints. An imprint is the trace of what has made it. In sand a footprint leaves the person's stamp, as large as they are big. as deep as they are heavy. Trace the footprints and you may find a path, find out whether they walked or ran, ran towards or to escape. In memory imprints are arranged in order of importance, meaning has no logic. Unless you find out why the prints are there. Until you discover why the person tried to rub them out. To go back to childhood you start where you began. With pictures.

They say that by asking somebody to draw three pictures you can see reflections of childhood. The pictures should be drawn in order, a house, a tree, a person. All are drawn in pen or pencil, then in crayon. Some houses have no door or windows, look as if they're falling down. Trees are friendly giants or slender elves. Some are twisted monsters. The person can be tiny, so faint it almost disappears. I will never draw the person first. The person that I draw will not be me.

My father told me when I was a child that some types of birds will follow the first living thing they see on opening their eyes, resulting in a bond so strong it is impossible to break. My mother told me that when I opened my eyes the first thing I saw was Chris. She would add that he happened to be standing there bewildered by the noisy stranger in her arms. Chris would add that it was lucky he was there as birds will imprint on inanimate objects. Being human, little did we learn in trying to break the bond except that the impossible was true.

I am five and he is almost seven. It is my first day at school. I let my mother dress me in my blouse and pinafore, tie up my shoelaces, too confused by what she's telling me to fidget, knowing that questions make her cross. I'm sure she said my class is full of birds. I imagine brown and yellow balls of feathers lining up outside the classroom, I remembered Chris telling me about the lines, he'd never mentioned birds. I shut my eyes and picture goslings following the teacher to the classroom, softening the pain each time she pulls a rag out of my hair, not seeing why she hadn't let Chris plait it. Then using brush and fingers she turns the curls to ringlets, says I could be pretty if I smiled. Chris patiently explained as mother walked us to the clutch of buildings making up the village school. There were six classrooms named for different birds. The first was Goslings for the five year olds. His classroom was called Fledglings, then came Geese. The older children were Seagulls and Sandpipers and ended up as Owls. I became more confused the more I heard. My mother bent to kiss us on the forehead, promised Chris macaroni cheese for tea. I wondered why he smiled when her kisses stung so. I looked around me, heard the screech of voices and wanted to go home, but Chris was here. I felt him squeeze my hand.

"Be brave Grace, I'll wait for you at playtime," he said and ran to fill the gap his friends had left for him.

I could be brave except with ringlets. I could hold my head high with a ponytail, or hide between its curtains had she left it loose. I looked along the waving line of children, checking all the girls. None of them had ringlets.

Inside the teacher smiled kindly, wrote her name upon the blackboard, told us to put our hands up as she called out our names. My hand rose as the gaggle turned to stare. The ringlets were forgotten, they could be brushed out. As long as A began the alphabet, I would be the one she picked on first, Atwater left no choice.

The five-year olds were scared like me. Even the boys were smaller. There were four six-year olds, left behind to let their brains fill up their heads. The two boys were about my height. The more she called on me the more I shrank inside. My answers were correct but wrong. Outside I looked for Chris and when I couldn't find him found a bush instead.

"Your hair looks like worms."

I turned around to find the voice and saw that the boys had watched me hide and now an older boy was with them. Surrounding me they pulled me deeper, out of sight. One put his hand across my mouth. When I bit it the smallest grabbed my hair and pulled it hard to pin me while the oldest boy wove back the branches making it a trap. The cries froze in my mouth: he was dangling a worm and smiling.

"Let's see if worms like her hair."

He stepped forward to drop it. I felt it land and squirm to hide, the wetness find a piece of me between the strands of hair. They were too busy watching me to keep their guard, the hand had gone, the scream escaped.

My head was freed. I looked up, surprised the scream had worked. Chris was standing over them, his hands clenched into fists, his blue eyes burning.

"What did you do to her?" He focused on the tallest boy.

"Can't she talk?" he said stubbornly.

"Yes, but you will. I don't care who your father is. Tell me why my sister screamed."

"He put a worm in her hair," the smallest boy accused. The other nodded.

"I only pretended." He opened his hand, the worm curled inside. He dropped it to the ground.

"You're all worms," Chris said in disgust "You can't even stand up for each other. If any of you come near my sister again you'll wish I'd killed you now. Come, Grace."

He wouldn't let me tell our father. By the weekend I could cradle worms in my hands. Not because the imprint of the first was smoothed, because I only felt his smile.

When I was five even Chris agreed that the one thing I was better at was drawing. I would draw our world for him, he would colour it for me. Our father made the picture come alive. I would draw him just to make him stay there longer. I drew our mother only if Chris asked me to. Only he could make her smile. She always loved him more. I could have understood if loving him the more meant she loved me less, there was so much more in Chris to love. Instead of less it left me nothing, left him nothing he could do to put it right. The further she withdrew the closer he and I were drawn .

We saw her differently. Partly because she loved us differently, partly because we were different too. Chris always saw the best in those he loved, refused to draw the parts that made them whole. I drew their faults in black and white and gave them colour only if I cared. The more I loved the less the colours tended to be true. If I draw her for myself she is dressed up like a ballerina, her face is chalk white, her lips are red. Her eyes are blue, blue tears run down her face. She is standing on one leg; the other one lies broken on the floor.

I draw him and he is never all he was. How do you capture what makes someone unique to you, the sun and moon, the other half of you? I can picture him in my mind at any age, I can draw well enough to hint at speed, at the grace he got more of than I did, use crayon or watercolour: all you will see is a reflection, never him. A slim figure, always growing away from me, half caught between looking for me and looking into the distance. He looked at the world, I looked out at it, caught up in a world of my own. He would be smiling, me frowning, if I smiled I echoed his. You would not guess for I will never draw us both together. If I do I am a shadow. I rarely draw him or any other person that I love. Drawing makes them disappear.

I will draw the house that I grew up in. In the background I will draw the sea. I will usually draw the house at night. The house makes no connection with the ground. It stands alone, I will forget to draw the street. The windows will be small, the curtains cobwebs. The house is darker near the top. You must look carefully to count the bedrooms, the back two are only sketches. One of these is started then crossed out. Inside the third bedroom the door is smaller than the others, yet more definite, a key is perfectly detailed in the dark. In blue are outlines of two beds. Two children are fast asleep on one, the boy is clearly drawn, his figure almost hides the girl's A black square is full of stars. I will draw the staircase, make myself invisible, then run out the house and cry. It does not matter if I make mistakes, the drawing is for her, she is the reason I never went back. He is the reason I stayed so long.

My tree is a pine tree growing in the sand. Below, the roots go deeper than the tree is tall, reach further than its width. The ends are waved, like plaits that came undone. The tree will bend not bow. I see the apple tree my father planted with his father, bright with blossom in the spring. The branches spread like arms. I used to lean against the trunk, a feeling of safety warm inside, my feelings light as butterflies, without the words or need to pin them down. Chris and I would climb it in the summer, sit and talk or play 'I spy'. We only saw so far, we thought the view we had was all we'd ever want. We thought our paths would always match.

There are always two pictures in your mind that you have to find to draw. Your mind will draw them for you somewhere you will never see unless you sleep. The first is the dream you could have made come true, the path you drew then drew away from, left the sand to cover. The second is the nightmare you cannot stop, the path you were drawn into, that the sand itself will shrink from and leave it for the waves to hide. We forget our dreams, grow out of nightmares, leave childhood behind.

That is how it should be.

This is how it was.

I touch these dusty pages you will turn. I peel them open. Strange how all the time the lakes were pools, the forests thickets. Now storms are echoes, screams are wind. Yet thumbing through I listen, deafened, bruised by sand, stung by salt. The sticks are driftwood, stones are pebbles. Yet still I bleed. I follow the footprints to the water's edge and let the waves reach out to pull me in.

Stars

The village is ours again in winter. From the towns the roads spread like ribbons, becoming narrower until they reach the coast. From above, this corner of England looks like a patchwork quilt. There are squares of green field, and darker diamonds and triangles of forest. Golden squares shimmer as the wind blows through the corn, and in June there are red squares where poppies paint whole fields scarlet. About ten miles inland, one long ribbon of road winds and curls, loosely following the contours of the coast. Smaller roads taper from it, point towards the sea. They cross each other in an intricate pattern like a net cast over everything belonging to us. The villages dot the coastline edged by marshland. Parallel to this a tangle of gilt and green embroidery fills in the sand dunes and seagrasses. Looking down, a strip of golden sand a mile wide in some parts and a mere sliver in others curves unbroken east to west. Finally the land runs out. A band of sea is backstitched to the sand, the colour chosen suggesting the water is only body deep. From there the bands change hue until they blend with the sky, to disappear into nothingness. They have the glow of shot silk, dancing as it moves, or with the seasons, sometimes taffeta like the seals, or milky silver at the quiet edges of the day. Truly blue silk is rare here. The sea nearly always has a greyish tint. Inland, irregular circles of rich green or grey satin dot the quilt to show small lakes or pools. Further east and south stretch the wet silver ribbons of the Broads, the rounder, man-dug lakes. It is a land stolen from the sea, dominated by water, imitating her costumes, her moods, and her voice. The towns and villages are inconsequential, almost completely merging into landscapes and seascapes.

For the older people in the villages, the towns don't merge at all. The ribbons to them are lines carefully crossed, marking boundaries and social differences as distinct as cracks. Most folks only went to Norwich once a year but that was enough, a trip planned with wary precision, clutching rail or bus tickets in their hands like talismans. They would discuss the experience for weeks before and for a few days after their return, describing it in the post office as if they had visited a foreign land: enjoying describing the challenges they conquered, losing their way, nearly missing trains, as if they had disappeared down a rabbit hole.

The old folks met as children in Lilliputian school classrooms, married childhood friends and foes. The swirling winds will sculpt their faces, the sun and rain enamel them to shiny pebbles on the beach. Even their small houses sit as alike as sandcastles they once built and couldn't bear to leave behind.

As the ribbons carry you along you go faster, you can't help it. The sea waits like a womb, wet and warmer than the land. You are traveling backwards to childhood: to eating crab sandwiches from the hut at the quay, hiding in sand dunes, and paddling in rock pools, and on those rare, sun glazed days, running into the water, salt stinging sun pink legs. The borders and ribbons are semi-permeable. Like membranes they allow some things to move backwards and forwards as often as they want while others enter and then never leave. The borders recognise those who enter and leave, knowing who to let pass. Then, very rarely, they make a mistake. Someone slips through who should never have been let in, and danger slips in behind them like a shadow.

Chris and I rush past the old folk in the post office to the other queue to stand there laughing, waiting for our turn. We watch the shopkeeper's wife peel the cardboard from the yellow brick of ice-cream, cut two smaller bricks and fit them into cones. She smiles, and fills a bag with cola cubes we know will cost us nothing. We sit upon the wall and watch the tourists going home and never wonder where that is. My brother and I are still too spellbound by the sea and by each other to wonder where the ribbons wind if you go the other way. Too young to know that it is harder and easier to leave than we imagine.

There are reasons why those born here rarely leave. Everything is designed to keep you here. The tourists flocked in, learning on the way that in meant slow, that roads looped round the landscape and not through. If they asked for the shortest route the villagers scratched their heads and sent them on the scenic route, bewildered that anyone would ask for short. The newcomers learned that scenic left you out of petrol, slip roads left you stranded, signposts left you lost. They never learned that roads to us were hopscotch lines we skipped across, that cars were toys. Real cars were for people rich enough to buy them or too busy to do without them, people who had somewhere else to go. Buses were rare except in high summer, trains a fairground ride.

In sunshine the mood of the village completely changed, became a buzz in busy shops, a hum of laughter from the beach. City people might take the crotchety train to London, jerked from Suffolk's green tunnels to lines hemmed in by concrete towers, strapping on wings to fly abroad: they were nobody we knew or met. There is only one city in Norfolk. Even Norwich people mostly took the small train or buses to Sheringham or Cromer, seaside towns pebbled with hotels and guesthouses, popular summer playgrounds since Victorian times. Wide bands of antique gold sand and iron piers that walked into the sea on stilts. At night the strings of coloured lights hung like glass beads. Streets became a jumble of smells: fish fried in batter, crabs alive an hour ago, stripy peppermint rock, hoppy local beer. The visitors came to us for day trips, overdressed in hot weather, underdressed for days when the sun lit the room when you sat down to breakfast only to disappear a moment after you stood up. So they sulked inside the café, asked for weather forecasts with their hot chocolate and bribed their children to be quiet by feeding them coins the slot machines devoured. The café and the amusement arcade were joined by design, the weather accidental. If the sun emerged they asked for fancy ice creams on sticks our shops didn't sell, buying rings of doughnuts in brown paper bags instead, licking fingers clean. On hot days we watched them fight with deckchairs, drape themselves in towels to squirm into swimwear, put up windbreaks for a breeze. We shared our ribbon of beach reluctantly, laughing at their antics in the sea, the flapping arms and fleshy legs that never moved in tune to swim. Their children candy pink from sunburn, running in and out the water, scared of waves. The slightest drizzle melted them away, to scurry over the sand like crabs.

The villagers smiled more, learned summer songs from the wireless, tunes they whistled as they walked without remembering any words. Their teenage children sang instead, as if they heard a new language in the words. In village halls lights flashed, a needle spiralled on a plastic floor. In three minutes you could hide, get lost, be torn apart or fall in love.

There were other visitors, shiny cars arriving, strangers spilling out. Exotic butterflies, long liquorice legs in black tights, denim princesses poured into pipe cleaner slim jeans, smoothing long hair in imaginary mirrors. Their boyfriends preening, stealing glances at the village girls.

By the end of August cooler winds returned and blew them all away. The waves swept up their footprints, darkness sealed the holes they filtered through and shut us in.

Darkness is not what folks think about when they hold the word seaside in their mouths. They are licking a stick of seaside rock with the word sunshine that goes all the way through as you eat it. They are seeing pink and white candy floss clouds in the blue sky. This place is only sunshine somewhere in the middle, after you've sucked that candy stick for months waiting for it, or at the end of a wet day when the sun punches a hole in the grey cardboard sky just when it's time to go inside for dinner. It's bitterly cold here most of the year. In winter the sky begins to darken around three o'clock and the black pools in the morning sky don't empty until at least eight o'clock. The grey sky can cover this coast like a tent all day.

Darkness is safe and invisible. Here, the dark is true dark: you can count the streetlights in the village on one hand and they flicker out like candles when the rain pelts down, or the wind gets up. They only bother to fix them for the tourists. When the amusement arcade is boarded up, the caravans lie empty, no one needs them. Darkness tucks you in. Chris would leave the curtains open so we could lie in bed and see the stars framed in the window, almost close enough to touch. Our father used to promise he would teach us how to read the moon and use it as a calendar to tell the date.

I stand with my father, my brother asleep in his bed. I had had a bad dream and he had heard me crying, tuned to wake. Unusually Chris slept on, my father holding me until the tears stopped.

"I hate the dark."

"It will be dawn soon, child. Look at the moon. It is lighting the way for the sun, as she passes slowly under the night's belly, to return every morning, when the stars go out."

"Where does the moon go then?"

"It orbits us, takes a trip around the world. It is closer to us than the sun. But the sun is brighter so we look at her instead. The moon is not a star, what light it has is borrowed from the sun. Like a mirror. That is why we sometimes see the moon as well, before it leaves."

"But if the stars are lights, are they hot or cold? They look like snowflakes, or pieces of ice."

"Stars are sometimes hot and sometimes cold. If you see them shining in someone's eyes, you can tell."

"How?"

"If you look into someone's eyes and the stars you see there sparkle and you find warmth in that darkness, they are the hot sort. Other eyes you will look in and feel the stars pierce through you, cold as a winter sea. Yet those eyes may be beautiful and can dazzle you. Those stars are a trick to hide what lies behind. Those are cold stars. But you should fear the eyes or the soul they shelter, not the dark."

That was how my father taught us. He would not take a fear away, dismiss or banish it. He would take your hand and wade into it, he would teach you to swim in it, to open your eyes underwater, watch you dive into a whole new world.

My mother left us to him and when he wasn't there she left us to each other. If she was in the mood to talk she talked to Chris and nailed the sentences into place with smiles until they made a fence to keep me out. Chris and I had an unspoken pact not to mention this or let it come between us. Since her talk would leave no room for conversation he soon found a reason to escape. So mostly she left us to our own devices. We no longer questioned this or expected anything more. We two had long before created a separate world and reflected a single image. We were divided in years by two summers but as alike as two flowers from the same plant. We shared our mother's blue eyes, her fair hair. On us the hair was straight, refused to curl.

Our similarity was such that people immediately took us for twins, Chris the taller by virtue of gender alone. He was taller than his classmates too, a slender birch surrounded by stocky oaks. Most tall boys tumble through a puppet stage of tangled strings before the brain untangles them. My brother never did. If deer took human form he would have been a fallow deer, a buck whose lightness gave him speed. You looked at him, then he was gone. His voice was quiet, yet if you listened his became the only voice. His hair was silver blonde not gold like mine, his eyes were lighter too. Swiss topaz eyes, my mother called them. She simply called mine blue.

When I think of being a child, there is no image my memory paints that does not include my brother. His delight when I began to talk, turning a doll to a playmate: his pride when he first swam with me and the waves swallowed me up, to spit me out laughing. We were as complete as a full moon. He shared a room with me, as our small house had no third bedroom. He, not my mother, brushed my hair; I would wriggle away if she tried. So it grew long and wild. She chose my clothes in the town; he fastened the tiny buttons. I sometimes overheard my parents as they talked.

"It is funny if you let it be, Alice. The Thompson girl was pulling her hair. Miss Graham says he asked her to play a new game at break, took her to the janitor's shed, told her to count to a hundred, and locked the door. She won't be tormenting Grace again."

"She sticks to him like sticky-willow."

"There's nothing he won't do for her," reminded my father.

"If that means stealing a doll from the shop, we cannot afford his devotion," she said bitterly.

I never saw my father throw words back. But I can see him closing his mouth tightly, as if they might fly out like crows.

I took the doll back to the shop. I remember my skin under my clothes burning with shame. I sat it down on the shop's glass counter, where its gold ringlets shone, the blue satin dress spread in rippling folds. The shop was quiet and the shopkeeper kind.

"I would have bought it, but mother says it's too expensive except for a birthday."

The doll cost three pounds. Far more than a birthday was worth in the village. My thirteenth birthday present had been a jewellery box my father had made. I had no jewellery but a ring that Chris had won in the arcade, the diamond glass, the silver plated. Mother said jewellery would be real when I was older, older seemed so long to wait. In secret I had dreamed of unwrapping her, but this doll was just a dream. The tourists were the only ones who could afford her. Even so the shop was lucky to sell one of these dolls in a summer. I had never bothered much with dolls. The few I had had matted hair and faded clothes, were naked more than dressed. She was different. I had looked to see if she'd been sold each time I passed the window, never looking long or going in. It would have hurt too much to get too close. It was the beginning of September. The sun had gone, the clouds had chased the tourists home so I was standing looking in the window when he caught me, half relieved she wouldn't get sold, half forlorn I couldn't buy her.

"You're not turning into a girl on me are you?" Chris teased. "Here Grace, go buy the biggest bar of chocolate you can find. That should cure it." He handed me some coins. I didn't count them: I didn't need to. It was Friday afternoon. Chris had given me the last of his pocket money. Saturday was pocket money day. I ran onto the post office before he changed his mind.

That night I got into bed and felt a bump below my pillow. I pulled out hair that felt like mine and touched the satin I had never felt.

"I can't keep it Chris."

"Well I can't take it back!"

"How did you manage to steal it?" I whispered, wondering if I could put it back and not get caught.

"That was easy. I said I wanted bleach because they keep that on the top shelf. While he was climbing the ladder I got the doll out the window and stuffed it inside my jacket. Being quick enough was the hard bit."

Putting her back was out, then: I was far too slow to get away with it. Leaning down I found my torch beneath the bed and switched it on below the sheet to dim the light the way I did for reading so I could admire her. I had been right - without the glass the longing stabbed me. Already taking back had changed to holding on. My mind was crawling over ways of keeping her, the shoebox I could hide her in, the wardrobe she could live in if she lay behind the clothes. Then like a beetle toppled on my back I knew that I was stuck: to take her back uncovered Chris as the thief, to keep her covered stole her magic.

"What happens when he notices it's gone?"

"I'm the last person they'd suspect."

The trouble was he was the only person to suspect. When the knock upon the door came just after dinner time on Saturday my father answered it. We didn't need to wait to know who it would be. Nobody else had been in the shop all afternoon, the shopkeeper told him, torn between proving his case and proving someone's son a thief. Chris and I were sent up to our room. We heard the voices go into the lounge, the sound of mother making tea. We sat on our beds and waited till the voices moved into the hall, then listened for the car driving off, for father coming up the stairs. I automatically moved across to sit with Chris.

I let the words I'd planned rush out and left no room for either one of them to get in first or interrupt.

"I talked Chris into taking…I mean stealing it. So it's really my fault. He said it was stupid to want a doll that much. He was right."

"That tells me the truth better than the truth would," father said wryly. "You'll take the blame for him stealing something you wanted. The shopkeeper said you weren't ever in the shop, Grace, just stuck onto the window. Well the two of you can decide which one takes it back. I told him you would want to make it up to him. So after school I hope you'll like stacking shelves. Until he decides you understand that people in a village have to stick together. Not just you two."

I took her back. Chris argued but I won. The shopkeeper hung the closed sign up as I unwrapped her from the tissue paper I had found. I hadn't looked at her again until I laid her on the counter. As he went to put her back I somehow knew I wouldn't look in the window tomorrow. Suddenly he stopped and held her out to me.

"Keep it, gel. I'll not sell her now."

I shook my head and hoped the tears would tell him what I couldn't say. I could take her home but she would never feel like mine. I would keep her spotless, scared to mess her hair, afraid to hold her in case I dropped her, even to touch her and get her dirty. Maybe love meant a face that didn't always smile, a hand that found yours in the dark. I walked home the long way, past the playground, breaking into a run when I remembered it would be fish and chips for tea. I sat between Chris and father, holding laughter in as mother put the plates down, smoothing out her skirt and picking up her knife and fork. The three of us were eating with our fingers. She looked exactly like the doll.

I had found out that Chris would steal for me, that I would lie for him, that wanting something too much made you someone else. I was careful after that to never let him see how much I wanted something. I learned to hide how much things hurt until I was broken, when no one else but him could feel the cracks or pull me from the darkness.

I knew the day I took the blame for Chris that father wouldn't say so but secretly he was proud of how we stuck together. I remember how he never really punished us, he made a wrong a lesson. He taught us to walk in the dark, not knowing how soon he would need to. He taught us to look after one another, never thinking how important it would be.

I can taste the bile of guilt in my mouth as I stand with my brother when the black men lower my father into the ground. It whispers what I cannot say, even to him: why not her? I daren't look at her lest she reads the thought in my eyes. Now I realise she knew and never forgave me.

If you grow mostly in the dark, and sunshine is something that warms your body for a day and hides the next, you quickly learn not to rely on it for warmth. You learn to move well in the dark, to open your eyes under water, to bathe in moonlight. When I look at the stars I remember my father but it is not his eyes I see. They are dark pools and the stars that pull me in gleam like ice.

The Sea Wall

September, 1972

We are used to strangers here. Whatever they take they only borrow for the summer; what we care about they cannot buy. We are used to danger too. We look towards the sea and watch the sky. We do not look behind us to the borders, do not lock our doors. If you look for danger, do not pierce the darkness, think that you will hear it come or keep it out. It will slip in through the hole that loss has left behind.

My father was twenty-one the year they built the sea wall. In late January the previous year the Great Storm had fallen on this coast and lifted the waves until they crashed over the sand dunes. The sea poured through the village, invading fields and farmlands. Seven people were killed. Through the centuries the sea had reached out to take back the land once water, leaving villages islands and tearing down houses as if they were no more than cardboard. Giant waves mocked what men had built, consumed what women bore. The villagers turned their backs upon their brooding neighbour and put up a wall. Yet the sea will never be tamed. The villages cling to the low-lying land, reduced to souvenirs, pawns to be surrendered to the sea, their war too expensive to fight.

My father's death was a storm repeated daily as I wormed out of sleep. The deeper layers had not absorbed the memory. Memory only sank so far down. Each time I woke he was alive, his heartbeat stopped by blinking. A childhood in the country breeds an intimate relationship with life and death. We learned that calves emerge from one end of the cow as the other end eats grass: a mess of blood their mothers licked away to suddenly stand on gawky legs. Our hands had felt the final dance of fish, and slit their sequinned skins. My father was not lost or gone away, but dead. And yet he did not feel dead. I burrowed into the quilt and longed for sleep to readmit me. The door was stubbornly shut. For thirteen-year olds will slip through the door of sleep without knocking, not beg to get back in.

When the waves creep over the dunes and lap around you, there will be no warning when the storm is death. No flags change colour, even the sea is blue. The wind will lose her voice, no thunder drumbeats on the sky. When someone you love no longer exists your kingdom looks the same. The waves will lap around your feet as they are skipping through the day. The day will feel like any other day. Each time you forget for a moment you would give anything to stay there.

My father's hands were gentle giants. They learned the shape of things where most of us rely on sight: a shell, a leaf, a flower. He touched our faces drawing smiles where sulks had been before. It was a time when fathers saw their children as most male animals see their young: invisible. It was unthinkable to produce no children; this aroused suspicion of a hidden problem. Equally, openly shown affection was frowned upon and mocked. Our father touched us both as if to check that we were real. His hands reached out to comfort, to warm, to calm. I think he would have liked a wife who did not run or hide from touch. I only ever saw my mother back away as if his touch would burn. I felt the echo of my father's arms and gasped as if for air. I turned my body to the wall beside my bed and sobbed until the pillow was a sponge. Chris would stroke my hair until I fell asleep then somewhere in the night I'd wake and cut across the dark to slide in next to him. He started giving me his sweater when he tucked me in. Perhaps he remembered father doing this or simply thought of it. He always seemed surprised it worked.

I traced the shape his blankets sculpted, I listened for his breathing if I woke. I followed him from room to room. Another fifteen-year old boy would have been overwhelmed. Chris accepted all of this as if an extra shadow stuck to him. His gift was healing, be it animal or human, a broken bird or a broken heart. At ten he once amazed my father bringing him a bird the cat had got. The wing had been sewn on again, the stitches neat. He made a broth from seeds he crushed in milk and somehow coaxed it in the tiny beak. After three days the head fell limp and he tucked the bird into the hole my father made. No flowery words to sweeten death; Chris looked into the sky and simply said it must be great to dodge in and out of the clouds. Then he filled the hole and put a stone on top to thwart the cat.

My mother gave up trying, silently removing plates of untouched food.

"Grace, you must eat," Chris pleads. "Eat a little, leave the rest."

"It's cold," I say. He takes it away. Another bowl appears beside me. Vanilla ice-cream.

"Ok," he says. "That's meant to be cold, Grace. No problem."

I look up at him, surprised, the voice is not the Chris I know.

"You expect me to eat ice-cream, when father's dead?"

"No Grace. I want you to try. I expect you not to behave like a brat," Chris says. The words are firm, leave ripples in the air.

The ice cream is collapsing, an island melting into sea. I watch entranced. I hear his footsteps leave the room. The silence takes his place. I wait for him to come and scold me. When he does not, I pick up the bowl and hurl it at the wall. I let it waterfall down the wallpaper, running through the flowers, then I run.

I lie upon my bed and hate him, wondering how long he'll manage to leave me here. Chris always caves in first. I wake, the shadows flit like bats. It must be after eight o'clock, the window filled in ink. He is not here and suddenly fear is everywhere. Because what takes one thing you love will never count, just take. I swallow the scream and sobs replace it.

I turn the pillow over, finding somewhere dry to cry. I hear the door scratch upon the floor, soft padding on the wood. My brother fills the room, cuts out a shape in black beside my head.

The pit of anger glistens, fades away. "Where did you go?" I ask the pillow. Chris reaches for my hand, I turn to meet his eyes, intense blue flames.

"I'm not immune you know, Grace," he says. "I feel what makes you cry, I could eat all day and still be empty." Sadness trims his voice.

"Then what's the point?" I ask, a whisper.

"We have to find one. We have to swim and make it out the other side. Pretend the sea's a swimming pool with waves." His voice is sure, a current pulling me with him.

"Like learning to swim again?" I venture.

"Like pushing through the water, Grace," he answers. "You can swim."

I thought my mother's distance was a wall, a grown up version, made of glass not stone. Behind the glass I waited, picturing the waves of grief she kept at bay to stop them drowning Chris and me. The weeks passed, the glass so thick she never seemed to see us. I wished the glass would crack, spit out the anger choking me, at least to mirror what I felt, to see the pain that cut across my face each time another memory surfaced. Even the women in the village shops would tuck their sadness beneath their mottled feathers and fold me in their arms. I began to make Chris go in instead. They filled his pockets up with sweets, toffees and Cola cubes we stuffed into our mouths as if filling a well. The emptiness was never sated, the sweetness tasted wrong.

Chris and I decided if only she would cry some kind of magic spell would right things, without imagining how. The weeks blurred, she was still sealed. I sat in my room one morning, hypnotised by the clockwork dance of the ballerina, lulled by the tune, as the clock hands skipped past the time to leave for school. The door broke open, my mother marched in, her face carved from ice not wood.

"I thought you'd gone with Chris. I know you can't be trusted on your own but..."

I'd told Chris I'd catch him up, knowing when he met his friends he'd forget about me until there wasn't time to do anything about me. I ignored her, I would take the telling off from him.

"Your father's dead Grace. You're not. We have to move on. You're turning this room into a coffin."

Her voice is cold. Shocked out of my trance, I look up and hold her eyes.

"It's easy for you to move on. You don't miss him. You never loved him anyway."

"I'll forget you said that, Grace."

"You forget us anyway. Even Chris hates you now."

My words are stones. They drop and I remember the game we'd played the day I'd learned how much damage words could do. These stones could not be covered up.

For a moment I waited, satisfied to see anger crack her face at last. Then, with no warning, her arm flew as if to slap me, dropping and sweeping the music box to the floor. I dived after it, already knowing that the thin carpet wouldn't save it before I turned it over, looking at the broken ballerina, the leg no glue could ever set, the tune unwound forever. Wishing she'd hit me instead I swallowed hard, determined not to cry in front of her. She wouldn't have noticed if I had. Without a glance she left me beside the toy and closed the door, I opened it and listened as she telephoned the doctor.

"There must be pills you can give her to stop this, she is wild with grief." I sat upon the bed and waited, calmer than I had felt inside since father died.

Dr Jolly knocked softly on the door. I had never liked him. He used long words like needles. He had a nasty knack of telling when a tummy ache was caused by sweets. I had no idea how an empty heart was cured but I would listen.

"Come downstairs, Grace," he said. I went. He had read her well enough to know she would not leave us to talk alone, so spoke to me, making sure she heard.

"Grief is a storm, Grace. A storm that tosses you from anger back to emptiness. Winds will howl and only you will hear them, silence drowns you. You float in numbness, cling to sadness, sink in blame. If I could invent a pill to stop it I would not. All it would do is trap you in there. Storms must run their course. You will hurt as many days as he loved you. You will miss him as long as you live. One cannot be separated from the other. That is what love means."

He looked hard at my mother, "Love will do what pills cannot, madam." She pinned a smile on and nodded, taking out her purse, as if the gesture was an insult. He waved the note away and, smiling at me, left. I went upstairs, brushed my hair and went to school. Too old to try to glue together something that would never hold.

Until then we had never realised we lived in parallel to people, less connected to others than the paper dolls I played with. For they at least were tied by strips of paper, family ties torn but rarely cut. Surrounded by houses, rows of strangers went about completely different lives from ours. Our closeness to our father, mother's clear dislike of her neighbours, drew a borderline. Since our grandparents died long ago, the only blood tie remaining was our aunt.

"I don't understand why you won't move to Cambridge, Alice," she said. I knew my mother's smile wasn't real. Lucy would always be my father's first love. My mother had twisted that into a thorn and punished my father with it. The second thorn she kept for Lucy. If my aunt felt it she didn't show it. She took the scone Chris told her I had made.

"Don't you think you could drop the 'Aunt' now Chris," she laughed. "Look how tall you are! And Grace, you too. Aunts are for children."

Chris blushed. For Lucy was charming. In her my mother's eyes were pools to fall in, smiles not drawn in crayon.

"The children would never settle in Cambridge, Lucy," my mother said. For never would she admit that money was the reason, lack of it the truth. Our father left the house free of a mortgage, leaving little else. There were no savings. Renting out the boatyard bought us time. Now time was running out, our mother's pride was not. Unspoken the rules might be but Chris and I knew them well enough, I'd never tell our aunt scones were cheap to make and Chris would never tell her I did all the baking. No matter what we called her she would wave goodbye never guessing that I cried every night, that Chris would haunt the boatyard father left, a wooden figure pulled to somewhere safe to cry.

"Grace, go home," he whispered. "I'll come soon."

"Where is home now?" I threw at him. "Where she pretends she cares or here where father isn't?" And Chris would bite his lips to stop the answer flying out.

"Don't make me hate her, Grace. Pretending is better than nothing."

I see the tears that swim inside his eyes. I fish for them. For mirrored there they swallow mine. They look like stars.

I learned to comfort him not pull him under, blot his tears with hands that found him in the dark. He pretended, I learned to let him find his hiding place, then leave him to come out.

A paper boat we starboarded, rudderless. Our mother was a figurehead, no more. Home had become a boarding house, the kind that nobody stayed in but tourists with nobody to warn them any better. Meals arrived late or not at all and nothing complemented what it shared a plate with. The milk was sour, cheese and bread a biology lesson. With no choice but to look after ourselves we began to teach ourselves. We learned washing machines were a case of trial and error, cooking was a series of experiments, a mixture of triumphs and disasters. As we grew more adventurous we needed more ingredients so Chris talked mother into letting him do all the shopping and did it better, saving money in a honey jar for a rainy day. The rainy days fell on days he'd blot my tears with teenage magazines for girls whose broken hearts would join like jigsaw pieces in a week, whose nightmares could be trapped in plastic dream catchers. Or he'd take me to the arcade where tears were trumped by flashing lights and jangling tunes. The autumn rustled in, the rainy days were real, the arcade was closed for the year. We muddled through, until our mother felt more absent than our father.

She built a wall we couldn't penetrate. I had been half right; mirrors showed a face, she only saw her own. What had been silence was a gulf. What had been distance was a sea.

I found out death made you an island. You had to live there to understand its storms, fathom its hiding places. There are waves that swallow you and sometimes the water will slip over your head and make you wonder what it would be like to just let it. The hush between storms where you rest to discover the silence cuts more, longing to hear the wind again. The waves will settle, surge in when you wake, you clutch the edges of a dream. It will not cover up death's shape. It will not hush its truth. You navigate back without knowing, until one day the sun comes out. You wonder what it is.

We might well have imagined my mother stranded when my father died, not by grief, by fear. Instead she seemed transformed, as if emerged from a cocoon. She went out for tea with smiling strangers wearing younger clothes. She flew off in evening dresses, leaving a shadow of perfume. She was bright yet distant as winter sun. She waved goodbye but never said where good was or how long bye would be. On nights when bedtime came and only clocks kept time, Chris would let me sleep in his bed and tell me stories I never heard the end of. In the morning she was rarely up for breakfast, if she was she only wanted coffee, scarcely said a word.

She spoke of father only to remind us why we couldn't have new clothes, or why we couldn't have coppers for the arcade. Father had spent too much time standing still, she would tell us, he had lacked ambition. Coppers weren't loose change anymore.

"Are we poor now, Chris?" I asked. We sat on a huge stone on the beach, wrapped in towels. The stones make good seats but are there to break the waves up, to shield the sand dunes, guard the village against the sea that wants the land we stole. I shiver, what had been a breeze before we swam is now a wind that pulls us close together, sharing warmth.

"Poor? Did someone say that, Grace?"

He looks so angry I wish I'd left the question in my head.

"Ivan. I went in for chocolate coins, he asked if I had any real ones. He said when dad died he owed money to the shop."

Ivan's dad owned the village post office and newspaper shop. But in reality they sold everything, from sweets to light-bulbs. My mother never went there, preferring the town. Ivan helped his parents in the shop at weekends, weighing sweets like butterscotch was gold. He hated me and was afraid of Chris. At school he'd captured me once playing Kiss, Cuddle or Torture and when he'd asked which one I'd have I'd asked him what the difference was. Chris had rescued me, scolding me later for thinking with my mouth open. So knowing I still do I cut the story short. If I tell him Ivan said a kiss might buy a coin I'll have to tell him my exit line: no amount of chocolate coins was worth that much.

"Poor means different things, Grace, to different people. But I guess Dad wasn't planning to die." He sounds bitter, not like Chris. Through the towel I feel his body turn to rock.

"We're poor compared to Ivan, not most of the village. We're poor to mother when it suits her. We're poor because I'd like to go to grammar school and she says it doesn't matter what I'd like. I always wanted to be a doctor. Chocolate coins won't buy that, Grace. One day mine won't melt. I don't ever want to have to swim this hard again."

"We're poor not having Dad," I remind him, try to change him back. He just looks into the distance as if the words don't touch him. I pull away from him and when he leaves the space I drop the towel and run across the sand towards the sea. He calls my name, wind calls it back. I don't know what I feel, I only know the sea will rinse it out. I swim until the shore dissolves, a blur of sand, across the shelf to where the water turns cold, so deep the grey is almost black. I turn around but he has turned to sand. I float upon my back. The sun is just a dust of glitter on the clouds. I wonder why I ran when all I care about is back there on a beach I cannot see. I dive beneath the surface, into nowhere, until the world above me disappears, the one I swim in real. Time swirls. I feel my head go light, my lungs are empty, legs and arms so strong before refuse to move in time. The undercurrent takes control. Waves take my body, dance with it, they kiss me, fill my mouth with salt. I gasp and water floods my throat.

There are fish beside me, blue fish flicker, flash a signal, telling me to follow them. I lose sight of them then see his eyes and wonder why he's woke me up, I want to sleep. I feel him lift me, panic rushing in as sense returns. I feel his strength take over, flow between us, mine until I find my own. It takes so long to reach the top. The first gasp of air stabs inside me. I force the second down, my lungs are bursting, wanting more but full of sea. He holds me as I heave it out. The sky is grey, the water thick as tar. We struggle through it, crawl to reach the sand. We lie too tired to stand, to talk of what we have escaped, still drinking air, our eyes too stung by salt to see the sun appear. It turns the sand to silver as we wrestle clothes on, turns the stones to lumps of gold.

    Tears burn my eyes as we walk home. I know now that what is still a home to me is not the same to him. It is a box with me inside it, a box that soon will be a cage. I take his hand, a silent vow. I promise him before that happens I will let him go.

Spot The Difference

Spring, 1973

The storm will growl and go, and leave a hush too strange to trust. When the sea is silk not steel, the morning does not look like night, you start to mend the sky. A thousand jigsaw pieces will become a hundred, fifty, grey will change to blue. You look for corners, join the blues together, place the grey ones far apart. For touching they may join by themselves, turn the whole sky grey. There are some pieces you never find. You never make a fairy-tale blue sky. Your eyes will skip the grey, forget how blue the sky was before the storm. Without the grey you cannot have the sky.

    A child by instinct knows what adults learn, that one storm heels the boat but two will roll it over. She will sail a ship in puddles, build her castles, laughing when the rain pelts down. For sand and paper she expects to lose. Yet gales will shake the windowpane she makes a cave beneath the quilt. If I had listened to the wind I might have heard it whisper to the sea. For summer has storms too.

    April cracked to May. The clouds were dipped in yellow, spilling into blue. The sun came out as if to promise summer would be early, and this time did not take it back. We tried on last year's summer clothes and nothing fitted. Chris suggested going into town to buy new clothes, perhaps have tea. Chris could make suggestions as if the words were sprinkles on ice cream. Mine would be the ice without the cream. As if spring had confused us with the plants the two of us had suddenly shot up. If mother had looked away from her reflection long enough she might have seen we were no longer twins. We now had different shapes: Chris was one head taller, I curved gently in and out. For her we seemed to shrink the more we grew and blur the more we changed. If she looked for me she looked because I made a path to Chris.

Today had to be different. She looked and only saw a fault.

"Grace, not that rag again." It was my favourite dress, a faded blue I wore because my father used to say it matched the colour of my eyes.

"Go and take it off. We're going to a party. Find a pretty dress."

"I have no pretty dresses," I protested. Already she had turned away to smile at Chris. I wondered why this hurt, why I could fade for her and she could not for me. And since I could not hate my brother, anger swelled like fizz bombs unable to explode.

"You never go to parties anymore," Chris said.

"I'm not invited," I threw back. It cost a lot to say this so anger shone like coins.

"Well, glowering like a cat I'm not surprised." He smiled and all the coins were chocolate wrapped in foil.

"Whose party is it?" I said. "No one in my class got asked."

"Dr Jolly's son is sixteen, Grace. I don't know why we were invited. Robert goes to boarding school in Norwich."

"Does he have sisters?" I asked. No doubt they would be spoilt.

"Robert has no sisters or brothers, Grace. His mother died when he was born."

His words choked up my throat, my own squeezed out. "Do I have to go?"

"Yes you do. They asked us all, I won't insult them by turning up without you." I hid a smile, the tone was father's, brooked no argument.

I knew the house. It sat alone behind the sand dunes, as if the wind had dropped it there; I'd seen it when our father took us walking. I'd asked who lived there, curious why anyone would build a house on sand. Father said the sea and wind could make good friends. It had been Chris who'd told me it was the doctor's house. Mother had ordered a taxi. Her dress was long enough to trail the ground, her hair swept up. I wore a skirt and sweater she had picked. Chris as usual got away with wearing what he liked, a shirt and jeans.

I remember looking out the window as we waited for the taxi, squeezing in, the strangeness of her body close to me, the warmth stealing into me from Chris. It was the first time either of us had been in a car at night and I clutched excitement to myself. I knew in front of mother Chris would make it nothing. The trees made strange shapes in the dark, the roads swung side to side so fast they felt like tunnels, mist appeared then vanished, made the drive a ghost train ride, one that stopped too soon. I tumble out and hear the breathing of the sea, can taste the salty whisper of the waves. Approached, the house is bigger than I thought. Chris rings the bell, footsteps seem to come from far away. The door is opened by a boy. He laughs.

"Dad says I'm a rotten host. I don't remember any names."

So this is Robert. I laugh back.

"I'm Grace," I offer. "This is Chris." I wait for mother to introduce herself and realise she's gone inside.

The house is upside down. The living areas on top are reached by spiral stairs. The bedrooms must be downstairs leading off the hall. Robert shows us to the lounge, a throng of people I don't know. He finds a space beside the window and suddenly I understand the strange arrangement of the house. The window makes a giant frame; the only thing inside is sky, a giant moon, and stars as big as sugar lumps. A balcony is outlined through the glass. I realise that my brother and Robert are no longer talking. Robert is watching me instead. I hope the envy is not written on my face.

"Would you like to look from outside, Grace?" he asks. "Chris?"

"Grace can if she likes. I'd like a drink first. Behave, Grace!"

I glare at him. He goes. I watch as Robert slides the glass apart and follow him. Embarrassment flickers, swallowed by the night. He pulls the door completely shut, the voices silenced, sea and wind the only sound.

"That's got rid of that lot," he grins. I open my mouth, remember Chris. "He won't know if you misbehave. Unless he's telepathic too."

"Too?"

"As well as super confident and bossy."

"My brother reads me like his books. Like all I do or say is tattooed on my face. But this is your party. Why get rid of? Don't you like them?"

"Honestly Grace? There's more candles on the cake than friends here. I was up to half a dozen when you came."

"Then why...?"

"Have a party? I really don't know. It's not like Dad at all. He even invited teachers. They're eating all my cake." He mimes despair.

"Why ask us?" I dare.

"I don't know. He told me he thought I'd like you. He never told me you looked so alike. You could be twins. I'm rather glad Chris stayed out there though."

I smile at the way he turns the house inside out. "He's not usually so bossy. Or maybe I'm just used to it. We're only twins on the surface, he's much more well-behaved."

"How else are you different?"

I smile. "This feels like 'Spot The Difference'."

He calls my bluff. "Let's play, then."

"How?" I ask, confused.

"Okay, these are the rules. I'll make a guess. I get two points if I'm right, you get two points if I'm wrong."

He dives straight in while I'm still wondering if I want to swim.

"Chris likes to be liked. You don't care if you're liked at all."

I am down two points already.

"He smoothes things over, you stir things up." I nod.

"Chris sees the best in people, you see the worst."

"Ok, your points."

"You don't mind losing, he does." My smile tells him he's right.

When he has twenty points and I have two I am more interested in how he's doing it than playing on.

"It's not magic, I just watch a lot. Only-children do. Like always looking through a window or looking from a balcony. You always need an invitation or a ticket, you're more out than in."

I listen, thinking that it sounds a lot like watching Chris and mother.

I realise I'm hungry, glad when he offers to go fetch some food. There are too many people. He comes back quickly, precariously carrying a plate of sandwiches. He's brought some cake too.

"Who's Chris talking to?"

"My Dad. Your mother's with the wolf."

"Who?"

"Paul Taylor. He came here with a doctor friend of Dad's. Dad adopted his dog."

"How do you adopt a dog?" I ask wistfully.

"You'd have to ask Dad. It was before I was born. He's more the other guy's friend than dad's. They're alike except Paul's dark. They both like fast cars. They both like blondes. They usually have one each. Like Sindy dolls but not as bright."

I toss my hair and glare at him. "Not all blondes are stupid."

"Present company excepted naturally," he smiles. I feel too blonde to answer.

"Peace, Grace. It means not you. And they arrived without the dolls tonight. I guess that's why Paul zoomed in on your mother. Bob is hunting by the watering hole. Beside the drinks." I laugh, relieved he doesn't underline the explanation by teasing like Chris does.

"Maybe Sindy was busy washing her hair." I wipe my hands upon my skirt and peer through the glass.

"You won't see him, he has her cornered. Trouble is the minute she gets hooked he'll get bored and walk away. Or so I've heard. When no one saw me listening."

He winks. "Invisibility. The cloak around the only child. You can disappear as long as you keep quiet."

I know that cloak. Except I disappear when I don't want to. Just by being next to Chris.

"Why wolf, why not something else. A jackal?"

"He looks more like a wolf. A hungry one. Don't worry, women never get time to get attached. He won't stay around long enough."

I decide mother can look after herself. "What else?"

"He's the richest guy here. Apart from me of course the most charming. Apart from Chris the most good looking."

He says this without jealousy and of course he's right. Compared with Chris all other boys fell nowhere near. I looked more carefully, finding Robert no exception yet knowing something made him one. He shared his father's shape and height but that was all. The smile was different, the nose was, too, the eyes a greener shade of brown, an almost heart shaped face. If life had not been so unfair I guessed his face would match his mother's. I wondered what was underneath his smile. Had Robert cornered me to make friends or just been bored? While I scarcely knew him I had nothing to lose.

"Are you a wolf too?"

"No, and neither will I walk away. Which is what you meant."

The same serious look beneath the teasing. Sad? I don't suppose he knows it's there. I glance at him and sense a puzzle, places where the pieces don't quite join, in the cracks are darker colours, shades that do not match sixteen. The teasing only half a game, the jokes to fit in, not show off. I wonder what cracks and missing pieces a mother leaves when she was never there to see the first piece laid.

"How did you know so much about us?"

"I'm very good at guessing. If you have no brother you have no one to fight with, no one teaches you to trust. Every boy you meet could be a enemy in disguise. No sister fills the dark with stories, says it's okay to be scared. You learn to figure people out. I get the rest from dad. My dad is not a pills and potions doctor. Country doctors don't just deal with bodies. They don't just put things back together. Half the people dad is asked to fix are broken inside here." He pats his head.

"Not in there." I put my hand across my heart.

"Hearts can't break, Grace," he argues.

"Mine did," I say. "When father died."

"How could you tell?" It feels too late for me to back away.

"Because it hurt every day, I couldn't make it work, I couldn't make it care about anything."

"Then how did you know when it mended?" He asks.

"When it does, I'll tell you," I whisper.

"Grace I'm sorry. I wanted us to be friends and all I've done is upset you. Should I get Chris?"

I wonder how he knows or guesses I don't want mother. I look inside. The crowd has closed around him. I shake my head. "This is just like rain. I never know when I'll cry, or where, or who it falls on."

I drop my head. It should be real by now yet sadness always catches me off guard. I know so many ways to hide it, none will hide the pictures in my head. I grip the railings and blot the tears with wind until it blots the pictures too.

"It's so peaceful here. Like falling into sky. Do you ever get tired of looking at it?"

"Can I tell you a secret, Grace?"

I nod. He hesitates, then lets go.

"I'm frightened of the dark." He turns his face slightly so I can't read his eyes.

"Robert, it's pitch black out here. How can you say you're scared?"

"Because this really *is* my balcony. Dad built it for me. He says fear we keep in cupboards grows until it squeezes out and fills up every space you have. He told me if you name a fear your voice will steal its power. He built the balcony so I could step into the dark and name each thing I see and feel until I learned that dark was not the same as fear."

"Did it work?"

"It all depends on how dark it is," he laughs, "and if I have somebody with me. Dad says that's cheating. Do you think so?"

"It depends how often you cheat," I smile.

"Not often," he says, "I'm usually here by myself." He says this as a fact, not something wished away.

"It's kind of weird when I come home. In Norwich street lamps shine all night and when the train is nowhere near you can see the city glow."

"Why?" I asked wanting to be on that journey but hardly able to remember what a train felt like.

"Because some buildings don't switch off their lights at night."

I have only been to Norwich in the daytime, when father took us to the castle. I remember feeling small, not letting go his hand until I nearly wet myself and Chris having to take me to the toilet and how he'd made me laugh by putting on a girl's voice. The memory is so real

I can feel the wetness leaking with the laugh, the shame I couldn't tell so had to pull up and wear. Imagination needs something to build on, feelings are the bricks and people are the frame. I can only paint the glow of moonlight not a place that doesn't sleep.

"Why not?" I don't really want to know just to block the memory. Memories don't make anything now but hurt. Tears just rub it in.

"There's lots more buildings. People do different things there. They stay up late. Or don't go to bed. Some people work at night. The hotels and cafés can be open well past midnight."

"You can eat fish and chips at midnight?" I ask, still hungry.

"You can eat lots of things and drink all night. But not at boarding school!" he grins.

"The weird thing was when I went away to school I missed the dark. At first it felt all wrong. But even when it is dark there I don't get scared. Just here." He glances at me as if he thinks I'll laugh.

"I don't think that's strange. The dark and fear are not like twins. Something made you link them. Somewhere else the link is weak or broken. Monsters don't wander far from where they live. Just their shadow."

"You seem much older than thirteen. Most girls I know would giggle. Boys would change the subject."

"How many girls do you know?" I smile.

"None, if know means secrets. Sisters of school friends."

"My mother says I need a lot of work to be a girl and not just look like one."

He bursts out laughing.

"I like you how you are."

"When do you go back to Norwich?"

"Tomorrow afternoon." He breathes out to hide the sigh. He looks like Chris when he is trying to fix on something happier than what he feels inside. And suddenly I want to tell him about the castle trip but Chris would hate it and though he wouldn't know I'd told I can't.

"There's still tomorrow morning. Meet me in the café for breakfast when it opens? In six weeks time it's summer holidays. If we play it right Dad will fix some weekends home till then."

The door squeaks open, noise comes pouring out with Robert's father in its wake.

"Your friends are leaving, wondering where you are. Go say goodbye even if you hardly said hello." Robert looks at me.

"She won't fly away," his father says.

"I hope not. She likes the dark."

I move as if to push him in.

I like the way his father doesn't try to make me talk. He lets the silence close around us, shell not glass. I glance at him. The corners of his mouth tuck in a smile. The face is satisfied, as if a plot is hatched and safe to grow.

I wake up and the smile draws itself, remembering the dark, the we in Robert's 'if we play it right'. Like upside down is right way up. I shake Chris till he growls.

"We're meeting Robert. It's half past eight Chris." I dump his clothes upon the bed.

"He meant you. Why must I go?"

I fix him with a smile. "Because I won't insult him by turning up without you."

I watched the doughnuts cooking, swimming in the oil. a shoal of ring shaped fish, the bubbles breaking on the top. Robert poured the tea, laid out the plan as Chris sat half asleep. If school agreed he would come home on Saturdays, to save time his father would drop him off at lunchtime, take us back to his house for supper, leaving Sunday mornings for the weather to decide. If it was wet we'd stay indoors. I listened mutely knowing mother was the only cloud that mattered, that indoors would never happen in our house. If I tried hard enough I would still taste the sugar on the doughnut, not feel the hole inside. I couldn't try that hard, it hurt too much. Robert watched me sit the doughnut back upon the plate, push the plate across the table, saw my brother lift his head. He caught the look I shot at Chris, the code he flickered back that meant 'don't talk'. I shook my head. It only mattered Robert saw, that telling him would make him understand. It was the first time keeping someone mattered more than pleasing Chris. I felt him burn.

"Your house is fine, Robert, our house is not."

"Don't, Grace."

"Why not? If he's going to be our friend he might as well know the rules."

"There aren't any rules."

"Then I can say anything I like. Mother puts up with her children, not riffraff they bring home. She'd rather see us left out than let them in. That's why we have no friends and you know it Chris!"

Without a word Chris pulled his chair out so sharply it grated on the floor. He walked straight out, not looking back.

Chris and I never had to patch or make things up. Patches were for tears and making up for cracks. Quarrels to us were waves that left us drifting never more than waves apart, till distance left us lost and currents tugged us back. The quarrel would sink and vanish into grey. I let Chris ask mother by himself, knowing it made no difference. Her answer would be silent, given when she closed her face. 'No' needs no reasons when reasons wear to nursery rhymes. To my amazement when he ran into our room he wore a smile.

On Saturday mother dallied over breakfast, told us she was meeting friends for lunch. She handed me a box of chocolate biscuits, told Chris to brush his hair. She went upstairs to change and came down an hour later wearing a gauzy wrap dress and running out without her coat. At noon I made the sandwiches, put the biscuits on a plate, the orange foil the brightest colour in the room. Chris watched the window, glancing crossly at the clock. Eventually the car drew up at three o'clock and he jumped out. Chris's smile was dipped in chocolate, mine was shy in daylight, Robert's lit the room. I would learn timetables were guesses made on paper, weekends melted in your hands. I knew the train would carry him off but Robert would not walk away.

Two weeks before the summer holiday Robert had exams. Tired out from swimming, Chris and I settled to get lost in books. A car disturbs the silence. Chris turns the page. Unpeeling from the bed. I look outside, Robert's father's car, the shadow walking up the path familiar. I have stopped thinking of him as the doctor, not yet found another name. He is an outline in my sketchbook till I decide what colours fill him in. I run to welcome him and reach the door just as he knocks, unlocking it and masking my surprise: it is Sunday evening, sunset burnt to dusk.

"I hoped your mother might not think it late to chat?" His words are careful, etched in copperplate, inflected with a tone I cannot read. This man has trained his face to show no tell.

"I'll fetch her, I'm sure it's fine." I'm sure it's not. My mother does not chat. Her visitors are pens not pencils, telephone calls several days before, not Sunday raids on doors. I show him in and try to work out why he's here. I find her in the lounge, explain. She tuts, I follow to the hall, embarrassed to have left him waiting there. She waves her hand, dismissing me.

I hear the door swing shut, the tea I was about to offer swilling in my mouth. I wonder why he left without goodbye. We had to wait a week for Robert to come home to learn why his father came. We tried to think why Robert was so keen to meet upon the beach when wind was stinging in our eyes.

Robert only knows the outline. His father, prompted by the headmaster at the village school, had put Chris forward for a scholarship at Robert's school. His school grades and the doctor's statement of support had swayed the panel into offering him a place dependent on an interview. Our mother had refused to take him there, rejected their offers to go with him instead. She argued she did not believe in boarding school.

"She must love you very much if she would miss you so," Robert says, unable to imagine anything but good in what he does not have. I close my lips to stop the anger squeezing out.

I run ahead to thank his father where he meets us in the car park, wanting to wrestle back some hope.

"I'm glad you tried and so is Chris. I know he wants to go, He will never make a boatbuilder or a fisherman. Whatever he does will never make him happy, only frame what might have been. There must be some way to persuade her to change her mind?"

"I'm sorry, Grace. Perhaps if Chris told her how much it mattered she would listen to him. Perhaps she just needs time. She's too afraid she'll lose him."

"It's always about what she needs, never about us. You built Robert a balcony in the sky so he could face the dark and fear and tell the two apart. She builds Chris a cupboard, calls the darkness love. Soon he will not know the difference."

"Maybe it's the only way she knows how to love," he said gently. "Darkness lies inside as well as outside Grace. What hides behind your eyes is harder to rub out than shadows in the night. When Robert went away to school the balcony shook a lot. I never let him feel it. Your mother has a room of fears, you have a drawer. You share yours with Chris, she opens hers alone."

He waited for me to answer, saw the tears before I turned my head. My eyes would match the sea and not the sky. Chris and I shared too many things we couldn't talk about. I knew his biggest fear was being stuck here. He knew the only darkness I was afraid of was the one without him in it. I was fighting for him with one hand, the other one refused to let him go. Mother might have made the cupboard, I had made the key.

Reflections

Summer, 1973

My father once told me that before mirrors were invented people used a bowl of water instead. They would find a darkly coloured bowl and fill it until their reflection looked back. He said we used reflections to prove that we were real, to prove the world was not a dream.

Chris and I looked past most other faces, let them blur. We had become reflections made of water, ebbed and flowed as one. We looked into each other's faces to soothe, to check our feelings were the same. We looked away to punish, finding that it hurt so much it never lasted long. We could say a word and tell a story, draw a picture with a glance.

Robert was the first real friend we'd had. His school agreed the weekend passes. If Chris was out of earshot Robert called them tickets out of jail. The weekends sketched him in, an extra one to find at hide and seek, a shape cut out of grey below the waves. But sketches are impressions, friendship is reflections, you are someone's mirror; they are yours. It is a water image, sometimes true as glass, sometimes a distortion blurred by what we want to see or hide.

Sunday afternoons came much too quickly. The toy train shrank him out of sight. We took his father's place to wave him off. When the friendship did not run out of steam his father bought a railcard. When

Robert dropped it I picked it up, in laughing at the photo caught by something else.

"I didn't know you had a middle name: Robert Janus Jolly, how funny!"

"No reason why you should know. If you're so stupid you don't even know what it means," he flares.

"Then tell me. I want to know."

"No you don't, you want to laugh. Well laugh then, see if I care." He turns his head pretending he is looking for the train.

"I'm sorry," I say quietly.

"So am I, sorry I forgot you were a girl."

Easy tears escape my guard.

"Quit it Robert. She said sorry." Chris's voice is cold.

The next weekend we stand upon the platform for an hour. The train is late but not as late as Robert. He isn't on it. Chris insists on waiting for the next one. I know it's pointless. You cannot miss a train you never meant to catch.

I wait until Sunday morning. Chris is still eating breakfast, piling each slice of toast with marmalade, I slip out of the door before he even notices I am gone. Undeterred by rain I trudge the mile to Robert's house. Half afraid, I knock upon the door. His father opens it and smiles.

"Well, since you're here and Robert's talking riddles maybe you're the clue. Whose is the storm and whose is the teacup?" he says playfully.

"I think I put it there," I smile. "But I can't take it back and he won't take it out."

"Then we must put milk and sugar in it and see what stirred it up. Call me a doctor as I'm guessing you haven't had breakfast?"

He's right of course. I never eat when I'm upset. It seems all wrong.

"I left Chris turning all the bread to toast," I laugh.

"Then share my porridge. It goes down well with storms."

The kitchen is warm. He hands me a towel. When my hair is only damp I comb it with my fingers, watching rain run down the window, feeling guilty to be here and Robert not. It feels strange having someone make me breakfast. Mother used to say she would but somehow never did. Chris and I learned to make our own and learned not to make a mess. Or sometimes we would rake the house for coins so somebody we hardly knew would pour us tea and smile. Intrigued to learn how oats turn water into porridge I move to help; he kindly shoos me back. He fills the teapot, puts it on the table. Two yellow roses sparkle in a vase, the petals wet with rain. They must be freshly cut. I picture him deciding which to choose: it doesn't seem the kind of thing a man would do. They make me think of egg yolks. I lean across to smell them, they smell of tea.

At home I never sit at the dining table by myself. In my ideal world I would read a book or sketch while eating meals. Mother never lets me, says it kills the conversation. Most mealtimes conversation is extinct unless you count me bickering with Chris. But here I am, in my ideal house, with the perfect chance to do whatever I want. I fetch my sketchbook from Robert's room and draw the roses. Roses are a tricky thing to draw, they must look messy but detailed too. Luckily porridge seems to take a lot of stirring. Sipping tea I sketch the leaves in. He stirs and lets me draw, the rain is soothing, the conversation sleeping. In between the stirs he pours the milk into a jug, and dribbles honey into a smaller one. Everything he places on the table matches what's already there. Our table used to do that too. Now everything is odds and ends. Like living in a jigsaw, stripes upon the cups and flowers on the saucers; patterns exchanged for anything that fits. He moves like Robert moves, as if a tree could walk, as if there is no hurry, suddenly by your side. I finish drawing as he puts the bowls down. He serves the porridge, sits upon the other chair. He waits for me to pour the milk and honey, waits for me to taste it, smiling when I smile. He lets me eat, as if there is all day. I answer no to toast, he pours more tea.

"When Robert was here all the time we argued half the time. When half became too much I made a rule. If sorry did not work we would swap seats, imagine what each other thought and felt. The argument would melt away. I sat you in Robert's chair, Grace. Does the storm still look the same?"

I always know the answer people want to hear. It rarely matches what is in my head. It would save a lot of trouble just to play the game. I'm no good at playing games, I somehow guess this man prefers the truth and that is all he wants to hear.

"I try to think like Robert, I can only think like me. I see your house and stand it next to mine. I want what Robert has, there's nothing left in mine. Except for Chris. I can't feel anything, it's all used up."

"You only see your storm Grace. You see the porridge not the bear, the bear and not the cub. Does Robert ever talk about his mother?"

"No, he only talks of you, as if you are a wizard full of spells," I smile.

"He needs it so. Perhaps I let him think so, wishing it was true. I was too scared to paint her face and painting would not bring it back. I show him photographs, he paints in black and white. Memories you cannot share are stories: more make believe than true. If anyone was full of spells it was her. I was just a doctor. I delivered babies, put them in their mothers' arms. They handed Robert to me still I looked for her. I took him home, I fed him, followed all the rules. Except there were no rules that were not broken. She was sunshine, music in a room she entered, spells she left behind. I looked after him as if he was a doll. It was June. He was asleep. I went out to the garden Nesta planned and loved. The roses had begun to bloom without her. I realised without her he would not, unless I filled the space as best I could. I went inside and found the scissors, cut a rose and put it in a glass. I did it every morning, looked each time I faltered, stumbled on. The roses faded, Robert grew and so did I."

"Does he look like her?" I ask.

"Nesta was the rose, he took the thorns, notes of sadness in the scent. The colours are different, the face the same. His laugh is mine, his smile is hers. He has my temper only time has slowed mine down. She loved to play piano, he prefers the violin. When he plays he casts a spell. I named him Robert for her father, self indulgence added on a middle name. From an end came a beginning, from the dark a passageway, a journey always glancing backwards to a future difficult to see. So I named him Janus for the god of all such things."

"Then the storm is yours," I said.

For once he looks confused. "Last week before the train arrived I saw his railcard, saw the middle name and laughed. I had no idea what it meant. He would not explain. I don't understand, Chris watched and all the time he must have known."

"It's not at all a common name, Grace."

"Chris studies Latin, reads myths as bedtime stories."

The doctor smiled. "That is what I get for playing god. I hoped before Chris went to school they would make friends. He did not go, the stage already set. I watched the balcony, saw my son more pulled to you. I guess Chris saw the same and liked the picture less. He drew the storm, let silence clear its path. The underworld is rife with jealousy and squalls the gods design. They murmur deep within us too."

"I wanted them to be friends." I said.

"They still can be. Chris isn't used to sharing you."

"Tomorrow he'll be eating humble pie not toast," I threaten.

"Don't be too hard on him, Janus oversees transitions, guards the way from childhood into adulthood. Chris stands there now, in Latin 'settles', under his protection. Robert will forgive, if Chris will give him time."

"So what do I do now? To fix it I mean. Do I tell Chris what I know, make him say sorry?"

He looks at me. With so much kindness I have to look away or cry. I find the window, the strip of grey that must be sea. So when he speaks the voice is far away.

"Is it always up to you to fix things, Grace?"

"I have to fix them. I have to try. Even if the things I fix are not for me. I have to try for him."

I look back at him, to add the words "for Chris" and though I don't know why, I know he does not need them. How wonderful to just be understood, how easily forgotten when it disappears. As if remembering will hurt too much, will only prove it's gone.

"Try to be thirteen, Grace. Leave the boys to mend their storm. Not because it's theirs, to teach them how to mend."

I want to tell him if I could stay here I could feel thirteen, the storms would all blow over, things would match again. It's far too much to say.

"May I look?" He glances at the sketchbook. Smiling I nod. He holds it, looking at the paper roses then the real ones, switching back and forth.

"You're talented, you've caught the essence of them. Robert told me you could draw but this is something special. Do you paint as well?"

"Only watercolours. Mother says my painting's an expensive waste of time." I hide the anger, knowing what is painting it: if I was Chris expensive would be worth it.

"Robert has a box of oil paints in a cupboard somewhere. Someone at his party brought them as a present. Shall I find them for you? You can use them if you'd like to. Robert never will." The way he says it tells me he knows what paints the anger too.

The following Saturday I act as if I assume Chris planned to meet the train, enjoying his discomfort, deciding that if he cannot say sorry he can worry what to say. We walk towards the station, happy to escape the heat of the empty bus. There is only one train, taking you to Norwich, as far as Chris and I have ever been, turning round to bring you back. A child's railway set, the carriages and stations neat as toys. The tracks seem put there by mistake. They float upon the marshes, slide across the fields. They zigzag round the man-made lakes or Broads, past feather beds of reeds. Around the Twelfth Century peat was warmth, wealth and fuel, Men worked with shovels to extract it, digging sharply sloping holes. Two centuries later digging stopped and the sea rose up to fill them. Time went by and people forgot, believed the lakes and rivers had always been there. We look and never guess what lies below the surface, father said. He hired a boat and told the story laughing, watching as we tried to pierce through our reflections. Water hides its ghosts.

I never know if Robert's father smoothed the waters. When Robert stepped off the train he and Chris ran off together as if nothing had happened. We spent the weekend making plans for summer. Robert would be out of school and I would be fourteen.

I remember the days seeming endless. We forgot the rain, forgot the time. I remember how it felt when grief became a wave and not a tide. Robert learned our games, he taught us new ones. The kind you play when you let people in. The kind where sandwiched in the play is something sweeter, teasing you without a name. When Robert looked straight at me I felt as if my thoughts would leak. He was as tall but stockier than Chris. I had thought him smaller when we met because he tended to look down. He could seem slow or lazy, coming second when a sprint would have brought him first. I wondered if the tricks were used to blend him in, to hide him in a horde of boys to whom an only child was prey until he was adopted, safe. When we played hide and seek his eyes could pierce the shadows, swoop and scoop you up. Yet, found, they soothed when you had not known you were lost. If he smiled at you it was impossible not to smile back. The eyes would dance with merriment, entice you in.

The villagers got used to us, reached for three ice-cream cones, three bars of chocolate. The doctor swopped my brother's marmalade for honey, served three pieces of a pie he always forgot the name of. One week the sun was sulking he asked me to answer a knock on the door. The man looked like a dwarf, as tall as me, his beard was spun of silver. He walked in without my invitation, carrying a case as if he meant to stay. The doctor stooped to greet him, smiled at me. I learned the artist's smiles were earned. He came three times a week to teach us how to make a sea from watercolours, sky from gouache. The boys soon preferred the rain to oils, the clouds to charcoal. I endured his temper, his sarcasm, his scowls, translating them to shapes and colours and textures. He arrived at ten and ate a second breakfast while he watched me paint, then I'd clear up while the doctor gave him tea and cakes. One day they sat upon the balcony as I listened hidden by the blinds.

"She sees like I do. Blood in sunsets, music in waves. I curse her and she drinks it. I smile and she feeds on it. I'd like to paint her. She reminds me of your wife. Not the face of course although the colours are alike. No, it is the chasteness shared, the waiting in the eyes. But in this child I see a sadness Nesta never had. I see it in your son. Perhaps it is what draws them."

I listen, not understanding 'draws' has more than one translation, that chasteness runs.

When he had gone I helped the doctor make the lunch, the boys were never back in time except to eat it. Saying so I waited for his laugh and saw he wasn't listening. I left the silence open, having copied this from him.

"I wonder…" he said at last.

"What do you wonder?" I asked. He had his pleased look on.

"I'll show you."

I followed him downstairs into the study, dazzled by the tardy sun. So when he stopped beside his desk it could have been the sunshine softening his face and yet the shimmer in his eyes pulled me to the painting, told me I was looking at his wife. Her face was an echo of Robert's face. Her eyes were blue green like aquamarines. Her hair had fallen to her shoulders, blonde but darker blonde than mine. Her smile was the same as Robert's, the lips that made me think of sloes when they are pricked.

"You look surprised Grace."

"In my mind I painted her dark like him. He never talks about her," I said sadly.

"He has no memory of her to talk from, like the pictures have been torn from a story, leaving only what I tell him."

"She was very beautiful," I said.

"She was my very best friend," he smiled. "When I was thirteen her family moved next door to us. I lived in Cambridge then. She was twelve: she totally ignored me."

"But you said that you were friends?" I said confused.

"We grew into friends," he grinned. "She was an only child and so was I. So even a boy was better than only! I adored her from the moment that I saw her. I waited four years for her to feel the same. Unfortunately her parents didn't."

"They didn't like you?" This seemed unthinkable.

"Oh, they liked me well enough. As a friend not a husband. Nesta's father wanted her to marry well and well meant wealthy. When he put his foot down he stamped on anybody in his way. He'd stamped his wife down long ago. He had bigger plans for his daughter than a would-be doctor. I proposed: he proposed that I forget it. I proposed again when I had finished training. He refused, assuming he had stamped me out. We let him think so, then quietly got engaged and started making plans. We'd realised love doesn't ask permission when it's fully grown. I took the job here and we were married in the village church. When he heard he cut her off without a penny, broke her mother's heart. I hoped when Nesta became pregnant he would change his mind. For her sake. All it did was set it. We had set our course against his storm, to him she would be lost at sea. We built this house so we could only look ahead not back. You build a castle thinking solid keeps you safe. It might as well be cardboard. I shouldn't be opening this box to you Grace, you can be his friend without that."

"My house is full of secrets, secrets make a trap and not a box. I want to see inside: it gets me inside him."

His face is tracing paper, see through. "Robert was still in breech when Nesta was a week before her due date. Do you know what breech means Grace?" I shook my head, afraid my voice would shake.

"A baby should come out head first, it's safer that way. We were advised she should go into hospital so she could have surgery on hand. No doctor there could turn him round, they spent too much time trying when they should have operated. They finally did and saved his life, but Nesta had lost too much blood. She died and never saw him. He cried and all I felt was anger. Anger mixed with blame. At them for not operating sooner, at me for trusting them. I trusted them and not myself. I should have argued with them. I was a doctor too."

"Robert's never told me any of this. Does he know it all?"

"He knows it how I tell it. I never hint that saving him meant losing her. It might have made no difference. All we ever write are stories, fate dictates the truth. When Nesta died I had to write a different story knowing fate could steal that too." He stopped and looked away, distracted.

"That's why I like to paint in oils. Oils can be painted over, all the storms look as if I meant them. Watercolours ask for trouble, something happens you can never cover up. It always shows. Does that make sense?" I ask to pull him back.

"More sense than I make Grace. Do you know why grown ups tell children stories? So we can pretend for just a little while they're true, that fate will sleep while you do. That houses made of gingerbread will keep you safe."

"After father died Chris would tell me stories. He'd get bored and try to change what happened: I'd make him start again. I had to know that it would happen just the same, that they would come out right. The stories had to match what I felt inside. If I was feeling brave it would be Rumpelstiltskin: I needed to be brave for the part where she has to guess his name. Even though I knew the ending off by heart in the middle I'd be her and I'd be guessing. If I was brave she would find out the answer. When I wanted safe it would be Sleeping Beauty, in my head Chris would be the prince. Because I knew he'd always wake me up."

"Nesta's story only had an end for Robert. That is why the painting stays in here. He never made it his story too. But last Sunday I found him in here after you had gone. Just staring at her, as if she suddenly might talk. I wonder if he's feeling brave enough to paint in oils and face his mother, if in you he sees a glimpse of her. Enough so he can start to make her real."

"Then I'm glad I might have helped. It's like my painting. Once I start I'm in the painting, swimming in the colours, only coming up for air. The hardest thing is that first stroke."

"I'd have thought the hardest thing was Noel. He doesn't pull his punches. But it means you're worth the fight."

"Sometimes if I didn't grit my teeth I would cry. But that would let you down and it's because of you that I have something that can make me cry or smile now. Something of my own I mean."

"You couldn't let me down Grace. If I had a daughter I would wish for one like you. And yes you have to care to cry. Or pour the feelings onto paper. Talking of pouring can you believe it's raining again?" I look out the window, guessing his next words. "Let's go make lunch, the rain will chase the boys home."

Upstairs I heat up soup and slice the bread, he clears the table. I wash up. He bangs a plate down on the worktop. I go on washing.

"Can fairy cakes fly Grace? Because I had two and you never have more than one and there were twelve this morning. Did Noel eat nine? They vanish every time he comes!" He sounds exasperated. I don't look in case I start to laugh.

"I can make more cakes," I say innocently.

"Not in time for lunch."

I decide it's best to own up now. "He did eat four. I let him take the others home. I've been bribing him with cakes. I guess the fairies aren't working. It doesn't make him any nicer." He laughed and found the biscuits.

It was one of those frustrating days when the sun was playing hide and seek among the clouds. Chris was sulking but of course he couldn't be because he'd told me only girls sulked. So I was doing my best not to laugh and Robert doing his best not to notice. I was beginning to wish I'd gone to help the doctor with the shopping. Turning to my easel I knew the painting wasn't right, my clouds had burst into balloons. I tore it off, deciding there were quite enough clouds already.

"Can you paint a face?" Robert asks.

"If I catch you." I chase him with the paintbrush.

"I'm serious, Grace. Could you paint a portrait of me for Dad? It's his birthday soon."

"I'm really not that good at people yet. It would take hours, you'd have to sit still."

"Would you try? I promise to do anything you tell me."

"That's worth painting! Okay I'll try. We'll start tomorrow though, I'd like more light. If you promise not to be disappointed if it isn't perfect," I warn him.

"I don't want perfect. Perfect isn't how a face should be."

I want to paint him on the balcony but it is bound to rain. The window is so big the effect will be the same. I soon forget my doubts, absorbed. Chris watches for a while and then gets bored and goes.

"You look so serious, Grace." my subject smiles.

"You promised to sit still. That means your mouth as well," I reprimand.

Painting someone you know well is strange. Half of you is seeing colours, shapes and lines, The other half is seeing someone new. I paint in layers Robert cannot see. The laughter pulling at the edges of his lips, the way he uses smiles as camouflage. I find out his eyes will melt like chocolate in the sun, or turn to glass when he is tired. His eyelashes are longer than my own. I don't see him painting me.

"Can I talk now?"

"If talking doesn't move your shoulders, yes."

"Do you know you only really smile when you paint? As if forgetting to be sad." For a moment I am hurt. Remembering I wanted truth I know I cannot toss it back.

"How often do you think about your mother?"

"Every day," he says.

"What do you imagine if you could paint it?"

"So many things that I'd run out of colours. Run out of paper too. What she'd look like now: all I have is photos. All the things we never had the chance to do. All the things that dad cannot fill in however much he tries. But all I do is fill in too, none of it is real."

My brush is still. His eyes are muddy puddles.

"All those things I see for real. Except they are reflections, breaking every time I look. We used up all the colour, used up all the paper. I can pull a memory out and touch it. Every time I do a little bit of it rubs off. It does not look the same when I put it back. As if I smudged it. As if sun fades it. It's easier to keep them in the dark."

"I thought it would be easier, having Chris," he says.

"It would be if we remembered the same things at the same time. But memories are different. I want to look; he wants to look away. I rain on him so often I'm a cloud. I remember things I cannot share with Chris."

"Can't you share them with your mother.?" I hear the echo... *You have one.*

"All my mother taught me how to share was hate." His eyes are raking mine.

"How can you hate your mother?"

"How many reasons would you like? We really would run out of paper."

"Pick one," he says

"She left us drowning, Robert."

"Perhaps she couldn't swim."

"Then perhaps she couldn't shop and couldn't cook, and couldn't clean. We learned to do all those things. I used to lie in bed and feel the walls were paper. I used to think the wind would blow the house right down. I used to wish I'd wake up and find out none of it was true, that he'd walk in and tell me it was just a dream. You learn to hate because she cannot even see, then I come here. I look at your house. I don't mean just the things to touch or what is pretty. I mean the smiles, the kindness. Except for Chris in mine there's nothing I would take. I can't feel happy, I don't feel sad. I remember Chris telling me when father died we had to swim to reach the other side. I keep on asking are we there yet. For if we are I should feel real. Yet if we're there it means he'll go."

He looks confused.

"Your father?"

"Chris. He's waiting for me to be strong enough to swim without him. I'm the reason he didn't take that scholarship."

"Your mother wouldn't let him."

"If he had pushed she would have given in. Because she loves him even if she doesn't let it show. Too little to make it easy for him to go, too much to make it impossible for him to leave. If he had tried. She knew he wouldn't because of me. I'm being selfish, trying not to swim too fast. Half hoping he will get another chance. Half hoping not too soon."

I have said too much. He has a way of making me forget that the talk began with him. I start to paint again.

"Can you borrow memories, Grace?"

"What do you mean?" I ask.

"Can I borrow one of yours? Will you paint me with my mother, tell it to me while I picture she is here?"

"I can paint one with my father?" I offer.

I take it out and wonder if a memory fits back in, decide if shared it is the same. I tell it as my father once told me. I light the stars for him, the path the sun will follow as he sleeps. His mother's face is shining. She tells him stars are sometimes hot and sometimes cold, that love will find the difference. Kissing him goodnight, her eyes are promises. I paint and let words fly. Set free, the words are hers.

I look at Robert, he is sleeping. In the painting he looks happy. As I tuck a blanket round him so am I.

The doctor opens up the pile of birthday presents, saving ours till last. Robert had insisted this was fair. It was hard to know which picture pleased him most, the one I painted or the one he kept on looking at: the picture of the three of us around the table as the porridge burnt.

Blowing Out Candles

July, 1973

When my fourteenth birthday came, to my amazement Mother arranged a party. A van delivered a bakery cake from town, with thirteen candles. Mother blamed the shop, found a candle in the drawer. Her gift revealed a new dress wrapped in tissue paper, white silk with scarlet polka dots. I slipped it over my head and in the mirror watched her tie the sash into a bow. The skirt was flared, the bodice cut to hint at curves. I was bewildered; I had never had a real party, never had my mother's full attention. She took a brush and did her best to give me curls, they fell to waves instead. The day obliged with sunshine, clouds were creamy swans that floated past. It was the first Saturday in July, the cake sat on a table in the garden, teacups sat on saucers, tiny sandwiches on plates. It was all so strange a dormouse could have said hello, I would have said it back. I wondered how she kept the party secret. If only for Chris I had tried to make some friends although my steps were wary, secrets heard not told. I wondered why this one had not slipped out.

    I heard the guests arrive, heard voices I didn't recognise. She had invited her friends and their husbands and daughters. There were none of my friends. My face blushing as they sang I lowered my head to the cake with its pink icing roses and blew. One candle still flickered its small flame in the breeze. A dark head was suddenly close enough to brush my hair. A stranger's laugh as he looked at my face. "Let me have this one." he said and blew out the candle.

Curious, I turned my head and looked at him. Although his voice was warm, the glitter in his eyes was shards of ice. I quickly pretended an interest in the cake. Someone handed me a knife. I pressed down hard on the fondant icing.

At least the girls at school let me fade into the background when I chose. Here I walked away from one group to hear the whispers of the last, to know as soon as I was gone my dress was ripped, my hair was pulled, my birthday marked me out. I grew bored of it and slipping through the trees I walked until the voices faded. I walked towards the bottom of the garden, seeking somewhere mother would not find me. She would not come this far, the trees a thicket, forests Chris and I would use to hide. How dare she shoo him out, insist he spent the day with Robert, make up a reason why. It seemed that fourteen was a dangerous age when girls must be protected from the animals that were boys. They had left early, Robert's father waving from the car, oblivious to their cage. I had watched the girls arrive deciding she was right: they looked as if they scared each other. They floated, coloured by numbers into cat and mouse. Here the only sound was bees. Wild roses twined through branches, grass grew tall. Careless of my dress I lay and turned the clouds to islands, sky to sea. The islands drifted, blossomed mountains, snowy peaks and valleys rose and gold.

I get lost. A shadow falls from nowhere. I look, the sun shades out a figure on the grass. I lift my hand to shield my eyes until the colours do not swim.

"You do realise you're missing your own party?"

The voice belongs to him, the stranger who likes stealing other people's candles.

"What's to miss? I can't decide who bores me most, the china dolls or the would be ballerinas."

I get up, ignore the hand he offers.

"Are you always this rude?" He sounds amused.

"No, only when I'm meant to be polite."

"Are you better at polite than I imagine?"

He smiles and makes me think how painting him would use up all my darkest colours, leave all the brighter shades untouched. His hair is Mars black, the slightest touch of brown. His eyes are dark grey brushed in silver glitter. All the whites in him are cold. The contrast makes the smile like lightning in the sky, the eyes like starry pools in snow. The darkness makes me wonder what would happen if the smile fell off.

"Why can't you imagine me polite?" I counter.

"I can't imagine you know where to start," he jumps.

"Polite means smooth or polished," I show off.

"They teach girls Latin here? *Quid magnum et caerulei oculi tibi.*"

"No, I only know a few words. My brother is teaching himself because he wants to be a doctor. Can you translate for me?"

"I said, 'what big blue eyes you have.' Where is the brother then?"

"He turned into an animal, mother sent him to the zoo." I rolled my eyes.

"Goldilocks didn't want a party?"

"How do you tell if a doll is made of plastic not china?" I ask.

"One is heavier?" he ventures.

"Good try. You drop them. So I did and came down here."

He grins. "And what are you made of, Grace?

"My mother does her best to make me sugar." I smile as proof. He sits upon the summer seat. A lazy shape I squint to see.

"I think the sugar's only on the surface." He laughs. "Tell me everything she's taught you. It may all be wrong," he warns.

"She's taught me not to talk to people I don't know. It might not count if you have a name," I tease.

"We're already talking. You might as well sit down to break the rules."

I sit as far away as the seat will let me. I like the summer seat, remember father making it when I was six. It looks like a boat cut in half from bow to stern. The wood was gold; time has bleached to silver. There's a G carved into one end and a C into the other. He said it stopped us fighting over who sat where. I can't remember any fights. The seat has shrunk as we have grown. I stop the thoughts an inch before I cry as Robert's taught me. I blink hard then look back at the stranger.

"You were miles away. I said why not forget the names? It's much more fun. You can be anyone you want to. Say anything you like. Be Goldilocks, not Grace."

"You must have someone to change back to. Or you'll get stuck."

"I may get stuck anyway. Does Sea Paalling have a petrol station? I've almost run out."

I laugh. "Sea Paalling might, Sea Palling hasn't. You pronounce it like falling or calling. It's no good asking me about petrol stations. We haven't got a car. Robert would know."

...I wonder if he's missing me.

"You've gone away again, princess. All dreamy-eyed. Is Robert your boyfriend?"

"That really would make mother mad. She won't let me have a dog never mind a boyfriend."

He laughs and tells me dogs are easier to train. It does feel easier to talk to someone with no name. Like being with Robert on the balcony, knowing no one knows what we are saying, only seeing him, forgetting to be sad or scared. Not feeling everything I say I have to listen to before I let it out. I let the thought I'd kept in go.

"You don't seem trained at all."

"There's enough labradors back there already. All the men look half asleep. With collars on."

"And the mothers only look like Siamese cats. They're worse than panthers. With polished claws."

He takes my hand and checks my nails. His hand is warm. It makes mine lonely when he gives it back. I smile to hide this.

"I'd back you against a panther, claws or not. A snow leopard with red polka dots."

He reaches for my hair and picks a lock to gently tug it. And though I mean to tell him nothing real he soon knows more about me than a single person here. Except my mother whom I savagely attack, my anger poured as if I'm watering the plants. The missing candle, the missing boys, the missing friends, Her faults are weeds among the flowerbeds, my sarcasm deadheads roses in full bloom. My feelings fountain through the air, until they empty, leave me limper than a doll. I dimly hear my mother calling me and try to find my feet and fall into his arms. He laughs.

"Not quite Grace yet?"

"I have to go ...?"

"Paul," he fills in.

"Grace, Grace, where are you?" She sounds different, the words are bees not wasps.

I sense him walk behind me. When I reach the gate I look for him, wondering how he overtook me, tell myself I'm glad he's gone.

I cannot find my mother. I decide to prove him wrong, whether he is here or not. Pretending I am a princess, I waltz from group to group, festooning compliments on girls I have ignored since they arrived. It is easy to be imitation, so much less complicated than being real. I could play this game without a single person guessing that was all it was. The porcelain dolls blush, the ballerinas favour me with smiles, the panthers purr, the labradors wake up. For once I match my name, my walk my mother's, poise that makes them marionettes. I hear her call me, spinning round. She is by the table, standing next to him. She waves me over, panic gets there first. I push it back. He must be leaving, thanking her for inviting him, saying goodbye to be polite.

"Grace, Paul tells me you two met in the garden. I thought you might remember him from Robert's party. I forgot you were too busy playing Juliet that night to even come indoors."

He flashes his teeth in amusement. I meet his eyes. Refuse to beg his silence, order it instead.

"Your daughter spoke of little else but you, Alice," he says wickedly.

"How sweet, darling," she smiles. "Now tell me both of you: how do we manage to get all these people to go home?" I puzzle at her 'both', the way her 'these' assumes he'll stay.

"Can you charm them away?" I look up, stupid, see the missing piece. This time her 'you' means him.

She spent the next few months saying you and meaning him. I learned to assume that he would stay. I could not forgive him, I hated looking foolish. I knew forgive and foolish were not words that rhymed for girls. Punish made the better rhyme.

Chris heard the edited version of the party. Ever the peacemaker he watched me punish Paul, not seeing that party games have forfeits. Paul had blinded me by not revealing how well he knew my mother, led me to reveal my secrets, played a game of Blind Man's Bluff and made me It. A stranger you expect to trick you. Once the stranger is no longer strange the trick is a betrayal. I punished him not for the betrayal but because I could not hate him. Or did I punish him for something more?

He became a frequent visitor. I waited for him to get bored as Robert had predicted: the wolf seemed tamed. I found out he came from Ely, close to Cambridge, stations rhymed on platforms, places on a map. His family had a large estate. He was thirty-three. He had no job. He joked that having fun was his natural profession and must be practised constantly in order to excel. My mother blossomed, showered with perfume and flowers. By midsummer they were engaged, the wedding set for Christmas.

Her happiness rubbed off on all but me. To me he would be nothing. She might replace my father, I could not. I was simply grateful he was the complete opposite in looks and character, for that was better than a small imitation. If she could not spot the difference she must prefer it. Since I refused to share her joy she locked me out. The key turned silently, still it turned. We blew out one another's candles seeing different faces in the flames. She had her wish, a hundred candles would not bring mine true. An invisible wall is no less real.

I proved myself polite, politeness ice, the smile on the surface smooth. I wanted him to skate and never know where or when the ice was thin. I wanted him to fall into the crack and watch the ice seal up the hole, his face beneath my ice,

Paul proved that he could skate as well as he could play. He skated on all my moods and skated off to leave me cracked in anger. He lit a fire the others bathed in as summer cooled to autumn, glitter set off sparks, and laughter licked to flames. Their faces melted in his fire. Mine became the face that watched. He smiled as if no ice was there.

The roses changed to dahlias, rows of flowers tied to stakes, their colours bled, they died but could not fall. Chris unwrapped the presents mother and I had bought. I thought it strange that Paul had bought him nothing but Paul smiled and said he had not known what to buy. He offered breakfast at the cafe near the beach. When we went outside two bicycles were propped against the wall, balloons on ribbons tied around the handlebars. Chris and I had always longed for bicycles, space rockets being just as out of reach. Chris looked as if he might take off, I looked like the balloons, unable to explode.

"Are we really going for breakfast?" Chris asked him.

"No," he grinned, "not unless you want to. I thought perhaps you'd want to show the bike to Robert."

"Grace?" Chris asks.

"I want breakfast first," I tell him. They watch him cycle off. I do not have to watch. I know that Chris will never lose his balance .

My mother always makes breakfast when Paul is here. She goes indoors. I look at him, the space electrified between us.

"I can't be bought, Paul. I'm not my mother."

"Amazing how you manage to insult two people in one sentence, Grace," he says, quietly.

"You two belong together. All you have to give is money, that is all she wants."

The words are sparks. They set the stars inside his eyes to flames.

"Your father spoilt you, Grace. Not with money, with attention. If you're not happy you make sure no one else is. When I first met you I thought you were like fireworks, sparkling, fun. Now you walk into a room and darken it by being there. Don't snuff out your brother's birthday. Use the bicycle or not. Tell everyone you're scared of falling off; I'll back you up. Hate me all you want to, I cut my teeth on hate."

I no longer need to wonder what he'd look like without his smile.

"I fall off, Paul, not break," I say. "I try not to hate. I cut my teeth upon my father's thumb. His little finger was worth thirty-two of you."

He seems to trace my shape in air. I am in the garden, waiting for Robert, late as usual. When he sits I turn to smile, Paul sits in his place.

"I didn't have to do it this way, Grace. I could have let Chris see you, watch you struggle not to cry. Credit me at least with that. Your mother and I have been talking. Money may not buy you but money buys many other things. I know Chris wanted to go to boarding school. I know your mother said no because there was no money. I can change all that. Your mother wanted to tell him on his birthday. I persuaded her to wait. I know it will be tough for you but, if he wants to go, the new term is just three weeks away."

"And if he doesn't want to go?" I stab.

"I know you, Grace, how you and Chris connect. You could make him stay. Make yourself believe he wants to. Make him believe it too. You'll always know the truth. Every day will punch a hole until he knows it too."

He looks at me with pity in his eyes but all I can do is run. I will not let him see me break.

Solitaire

August-September, 1973

If all the trees had dropped their leaves at once I would have clapped. They slowly fluttered, drawing out the game when it was lost. I tried to smile, my feelings masked. The jokes we tried to toss fell heads down, the silence cracks in pavements we fell into. If Chris was counting days I could not tell. He seemed absorbed in preparations for school and drifted off alone. I could not share this dream that drew him somewhere else, I would not draw him back. I looked up, expecting blue eyes and finding brown. For Robert knew the mask was paper, saw the storm it hid. He never tried to coax me out, he just showed up. We walked for hours on paths he knew and I did not. I wondered if the doctor's son knew the walks were pills to sleep. For sleep would bypass sadness, lead away from the graffiti of goodbye. The pathways always ended up at the upside down house. I felt at home there, my house was a waiting room for Chris to go. We ended up a threesome, Chris found his own way there. Perhaps the doctor guessed his house was now a sanctuary. He stacked the fridge with things we liked, and never minded if we made a mess. He spoke of simple things, he smiled, then left us to our own devices. He put three chairs upon the balcony, three of everything arranged as if for dwarfs who came in threes. We laughed at nothing, sharing everything except the fear of change we couldn't name.

My mother talked about Chris leaving as if she wanted me to crack. Chris must not see me cry or read it in my face. Robert wanted me to tell him what I was feeling so I told him almost nothing. Paul never asked but was the only one I talked to, feeling safe because I knew I wouldn't cry. He softened to my sadness, simply wanting smiles and laughter in the faces looking back. He tried to free the tangled strings to turn the puppet to a girl. He could guess what Chris was feeling, young enough to sketch a world of dormitories, midnight feasts, recall the sweet-sour thrill of going somewhere new, leaving someone behind. I was grateful; pictures gave me somewhere he would go. In my dreams he disappeared.

I see us run, the beach an empty playground. The sunlight turns our footprints into silver, water filling up the steps we leave behind. I look and wish my eyes would stop subtracting two from three. Three ice creams, three towels, three mugs of tea, they all remind me that three of us will melt to one. I had even started moving things apart, embarrassed by the childish game. I wished that Robert was not so good at guessing things he did not need to know, suspecting this was one.

I counted down the weeks till Chris would leave until the weeks were days. Tried not to watch as wardrobes emptied, cases filled, tried not to think about how slowly hours would crawl when days ran out. I started letting Chris and Robert spend more time alone. It was easier to watch the two of them run off without me. It was easier to blur alone, get lost in shadows than to burn in sunlight, cut out by all I could not share. If I would shrink for them I would shrink now, retreat to somewhere smallness did not matter, hide in rabbit holes, not smile as selfishness licked me even smaller.

I had wished for this, I could not ask to wish again because it had come true.

You start to let things go before they drop. So by the time the cards are shuffled you already know the rules. You can ask for more cards, not ask to turn them over first. The Kings and Queens will change their suit as easily as you change clothes. The cards you hold will smile and still you lose. You can lose every card and still play solitaire.

I could not tell Chris how I felt. Perhaps he guessed, if so his silence hurt. The summer hung in cobwebs only Robert dared to cross.

"Keep the smile for Chris, Grace, if both of you insist on being clowns. It isn't a prison, just another school. Maybe when he's gone you'll look at other people and see friends, not rows of faces to shoot down." The smile did what it was told and disappeared.

"Keep the doctor voice for patients, Robert," I bite back.

"I changed my mind, I think I'll be a vet," he smiles.

"I'm sure the animals are lining up," I taunt.

"No, but the humans have escaped," he grins.

"Doesn't anything I say make you angry?" I ask, exasperated.

"It isn't what you say, it's what you do. It's what you both do. You never talk. Not when it counts. Then other times you build a world where no one else exists. You use telepathy instead of words. It's like there's something missing, wrong unless the other one is there." He sighs.

I sit, exposed and wary. I hunt for words and prove his point.

"You know what's puzzles me most ?" He says each word as if he urges them to fit. "If neither one of you sees past the other, the rest of us get in the way, then why is he so set on leaving, why won't you talk him out of it? It scares me."

"Why?" The word so faint a candle flame would whisper.

"I've no idea," he says.

Two weeks later sun is bouncing of the windows of the car. I glance at Chris and try to read his face and watch him shut it. I only want the car to stop. I look for Robert, run to meet him and his father as they park. He asks his father something, his father nods and turns to heave the trunk out of the boot, Robert reaches for my hand, I shake my head. He checks the platform number, I follow him across the bridge and down the steps. We wait for them to catch us up.

"Are you okay?" he asks.

"Don't ask me that. As long as I don't cry I can forget its real." I turn away. He grabs my arm, a spark of anger spins me round. "Why must I cry? It won't stop either of you leaving. What do you want, an animal you can bandage?" I fire the words like plastic bullets. One must hit the centre for his head goes down.

"I'm not trying to fix it. I just wish you'd tell me when it hurts. Then I won't keep getting things so wrong." I wondered what he wanted to get right.

He looks up. Brown eyes pierce into mine. "Be what you have to be today, Grace. Do what it takes to smile and say goodbye. But mean it."

"I do mean it," I say, stung. "I wanted this for him."

"I don't mean say goodbye, do it. Don't let him go, let him shrink a little, be a star and not the moon and sun. Then ask what you want."

The train is coming, sliding through the fields and marshland, hissing as it slows.

He reaches in the pocket of his coat. A tiny box is soft inside my hand.

"Open it when you get tired of counting threes," he says and winks.

Paul puts the luggage on the train. I let my mother say goodbye first. My brother leans to kiss me on the cheek. I feel his face brush mine and reach to touch it, find his eyes and make them see me. His face is carved of stone: if stone is set with topaz - if topaz can be wet.

We wave them off, the windowpane another wall. Reflected in the glass my smile is brighter than every other smile. It is the last chance I will have to ask the cards be shuffled, change the hands that we are dealt. Instead I let him take the first step that leads where I can never follow, knowing he'll return as someone else. Yet every card I hold will show his face, except the one who looks like me. I have yet to learn the most important rule of any game there is: find out how high the stakes are if you lose. I do not know that as I smile I start to play.

Loss is shapeless. I scribble words, compare it to an iceberg, change it to a sea, the sea becomes a mine. The mine cannot contain it, loss is different every time, its shape your own. A shape we cannot yet perceive is bottomless. It has no end and no beginning. When the shape is drawn by something you will lose, it is a space, everything you feel gets stuffed inside. It is a space that is not even made yet, hollowed out by something which has not even happened yet. It is a shape that you project, a film playing in the background, constantly rewinding. You try to look away and you cannot.

When scissors cut out loss you have imagined, you feel them stab as if they stab somebody else. In that moment loss will draw the shape and you are numb, the voices actors, the scene rehearsed a thousand times before. The screen turns black, the blackness pulls you in. You fall asleep. Awake you rub your eyes and when you blink you see the shape again. Then you get up and start to fill it. It is not as you imagined: it has still to grow.

Without Chris to prop it up the house became a house of cards. It seemed so fragile anything might send the whole thing falling to the floor. My mother never even tried to offer a distraction, I had stopped wishing she would offer more. I asked Paul casually if my brother might be permitted to come home at weekends. He was not unkind, he simply pointed out that Chris needed to settle in, that boarding school was different, it was too easy for the other boys to lock him out if they imagined him so homesick he took the first train home. Refusing to be selfish I gave in. I was missing Robert almost as much as Chris but in his form weekend passes were discouraged, limited to family occasions. His father smiled and joked that in a few weeks perhaps his birthday might be brought forward. Less proud I might have spent more time at the doctor's house. After all, he was missing Robert too. Instead I took to walking near the dunes the window overlooked, gazing in where once I had gazed out.

There is a timeless kinship ties us to the sea and all her backdrops, comfort in her rhythms and her rhymes. It is comfort that asks nothing in return. The tide will make no protest as you turn to leave, the waves will not ask you to come back. She will mirror any silence, soon your moods will mirror hers. Her tears will dry, her storms will pass. She will not ask why yours do not.

There are no mountains in Norfolk, few hills a stranger would think worthy of the name. Nothing to block the sky, nothing to stop your fall towards the sea. The sea and sky will merge to one, their colours layer till you cannot pull the two apart. Look too long and everything behind you disappears. You know the land is there but do not feel it, know the sadness will be waiting for you but you do not care. It has melted into trifle.

Since memory did not flood me there, no memories chased me back. The rooms were caves his silence splashed. Here dunes were sofas, sand a cushion. I watched their shadows walk and did not run, their voices lulled me as I dug into sleep.

Castles built in sand grow cold. I would trail back, exchange solitude for solitaire, my lost king for a queen.

"This moping does not help, Grace," my mother says, watching me take off my raincoat, guessing where I've been.

I swallow hard, not to lock the words away, to seal the tears inside. For words are just umbrellas, raincoats do not stop the rain.

My almost - stepfather is an unexpected ally.

"Might as well cry in the rain, if you have to cry, Grace. Let her mope, my dear Alice, she's fourteen and good at it." My mother bites her lip and silently retreats. He smiles, unabashed by her annoyance. I almost like him.

Chris calls home once a week, it rings, our mother always manages to get there first. She keeps me glued beside her as she prattles on, ten minutes all the time he has. She never lets me talk to him alone. As time goes on it does not matter. There should be so much more to say and never is. I write to him, his letters never come. Robert's letters only rub it in. Each word I write back is shaped to cut Chris out.

The hole was not as I imagined. The shape did not pour out what I poured in. It did not scream or tear or break. It did not twist or crawl or even move. It was empty, soundless, dreamless, blind. It was not dark for there was sun. I did not shiver, neither did I burn. Looking in I looked no different. Inside there were no walls, no roof, no floor. Looking out I saw the world I saw before. I was colourblind, no face was real, no voice could stir. I waited in the hole and footsteps came and went and faces passed. But no one touched me, no one listened, no one stayed.

Two children playing hide and seek, the game no game at all. A diversion, a lesson, an adventure? You don't explore a place you know. It is the feelings you explore. To flit from nowhere, flirt with fear in being lost, to furl with joy at being found. We hide to test the rule that lost is found. Hide to prove the rule will hold. We play to dice with danger. We play because the finder makes us real. When father died I thought I could not feel that bad again but this shape was different. Then another person knew my hiding places, found me, needed me to do the same. Not a mirror of my shape, a shape that fitted mine. Chris and I had been what each was not. Without him I was lost inside a cupboard no one knew was there. You cannot hide if no one realises you are gone.

Sand Dunes For Beginners

October, 1973

You do not blame the croupier for dealing out the cards. By never asking Chris to stay I had gambled on him needing me too much to go, and I had lost. Paul had signed the cheque, not played the hand. You do not blame but neither do you tip. You hide behind the fuzz of dark and smoke; you keep your distance, he keeps his. Then one day when you meet him in the sunshine you discover he has lost far more than you. The distance melts to smoke.

At school I played the teenage game of poker. The smile pinned on fell off. Without Chris no one taught me how to play. In class a wall of faces shut me out, at playtime I drifted to the blaze of autumn trees and waited for the bell. The weeks slipped by, I gave up the game, the faces turned away. Perversely once they turned against me one day I turned and smiled. The next I could not wipe it off: I smiled at mistakes, I laughed at scolding, suddenly insolence lounged where silence sat before.

Miss Lambert kept me in till everyone had left the playground, following me out too full of words to stop. As if by magic she disappeared within a cloud of smoke. On the bench outside my soon to be stepfather casually used a flowerpot as an ashtray, tossing it the dying cigarette then stood and smiled. Before she completely melted he introduced himself and never moved his eyes from her as he pretended he was listening. I had studied the way he used this tactic on my mother when she described her day, amused to note the telltale sign of eyes that widened as if rapt when eyebrows were asleep. I longed to tell him but had decided it was much more fun to watch. Looking sternly at me he agreed to 'get to the bottom of it' and led me out of the playground. The sternness collapsed the moment she had gone.

'What's got into you, Grace? From ghost to witch in just one day!"

"I was bored," I ventured. "All of them are such babies." I risk a sidelong glance. "Are you cross?"

"No. Relieved."

"Will you tell mother?"

"I don't think my relief is that catching."

"Why relieved and why did you collect me from school?"

"Which why first, Goldilocks?" His smile catches me.

"Whichever one will make me behave tomorrow."

"That's why I'm relieved. Fourteen is too young to behave. Too fragile to have jokers playing tricks on you." He still thinks it's all about the party, doesn't know it's payback for taking Chris. Except he doesn't stop Chris writing letters or picking up the phone.

"I'm too young to play the evil stepfather. Can we make the ceasefire permanent? Your mother and I will be married soon. I won't ask you to be bridesmaid, I won't try to replace your father, couldn't if I tried."

"Why not? She has."

"No. I would never have agreed to take someone's place. Everyone needs to be special to someone. I would not simply be a substitute. Would you?"

I laugh. "I've never thought about it. I'm not ready for boys."

"You think Robert's just a friend?"

"He's special. But I only know how to be a friend. I'm not even very good at it. I don't have friends except Robert."

"He's what, sixteen?"

"And a half," I add.

"Mustn't forget the half. Then he's ready, Grace. He's just waiting for you to see him."

"What makes you the expert?" But I smile.

"I was sixteen once, and the half, and the boy. I guess that ought to count for something. I still remember how to play that game. I don't suppose they've changed the rules."

I can almost imagine him sixteen. Doing all the things that Robert doesn't. I can't imagine Robert as a boyfriend. Or can I? He seems too far away to read his face.

We have reached the car. Paul's car is racing green, the top rolls back. It only takes one passenger. The ceasefire did not include cars. Chris has been in it, though. I picture him, hand on heart, pretend relief at his survival. The roads bend sharply here, not warning you with signs, as if you ought to know. Paul did not.

"Chris says it leaves the road to fly," I say innocently.

"Good for witches then. I see no broomstick."

"I've only been a witch one day, I guess these things don't come until you pass the test?"

"Then I guess you'll have to settle for a flying car then. Are you thirsty too? How about we leave the car for now and go for tea? You must know all the shortcuts here. We'll find a cafe, lay the treaty on the table."

"You do realise I could get you lost on purpose?"

"I don't get lost." He waves me on. "Witch or no witch," he tosses.

I turn and walking fast I trace a path towards the beach. The village clusters round its one attraction, making you forget there are no more. A magician with one trick, a face with nothing beautiful except a smile. If you are born here it takes a while to notice, then you do not care. I guess that treasure can be treasured more for being small, if small is all there is. I wonder if that makes it hard to steal or worse to lose. Chris always says I look for clouds. There are no clouds today. The autumn days here are like coins in slot machines, mounting up on shuffling trays of copper, suddenly spitting out a golden one when you are left with sighs. The sun a coin I tuck inside my hand and wait for Paul.

Complacent of my speed, I jump, surprised to hear his voice. His words are smooth no dips to catch his breath. I mask my face, determined not to seem impressed.

"Which way for the tea? Or do you want ice cream?"

I always do. Except when I don't want to seem a child.

"I don't think witches eat ice cream. Anyway the shop is closed."

The shop adjoins the miniature arcade. The doors are boarded up, the toys all boxed away. They do not belong to us. They never really did. Our toys were crabs and seashells. When summer ends the village shuts up shop. I would have remembered but when Chris left it blocked out everything.

"Why are they closed?" Paul whispers.

"No tourists. Nobody here can spend enough to make it worthwhile staying open. So all the colours turn back to grey." The thought sticks clouds upon the sky. It feels like standing on a stage, the sealed up arcades and shops all cardboard, all the actors boxed inside. As if I knew the cue the boards would fall, the lights come on, and all the people would wake up and smile, return to drinking coffee, eating fish and chips as if they'd never stopped. And when I looked in the arcade he would be watching for me, tell me the machines were rigged and I would mime the words as they fell out and laugh.

"But you are colour now."

I scowl, annoyed he isn't Chris. Like Chris he isn't easy to annoy.

"What are you talking about?"

"I meant the shops have turned to grey and you've turned back to colour. Like you were before."

"Oh."

"See. You're blushing," he teases. He lifts his hand, runs it across my cheek to cup my chin. I feel the colour spread as if he's painting me, grow deeper, peach to plum. I want to lift it off but that will make it seem important. Before I can decide, it drops.

"If we run we can catch the post office shop before it closes." I clear my voice, imagine dipping it in water, watch the water turning pink. "I vote we buy some crisps and lemonade. It's warm enough to sit outside."

"Where outside?" He sounds suspicious.

"A sand-dune," I offer.

"I vote for home. I don't like sand," he sulks.

"I could ask why but asking takes up time. The shop will close."

He waits outside. The shop is empty. The boy behind the counter is a classmate, far from being a friend. He seems to takes forever serving me, forgetting I said lemonade not cola. At last I manage to escape.

"You were quick." He stamps his cigarette out and reaches for the bag. I catch the smell of smoke and something in it makes me dizzy, makes me wonder what effect the smoke would have inside. I look for a roundabout way of finding out.

"Why did mother start to smoke when she met you? She always used to call it common." I could have rhymed a list of all the things my mother said were common, from bikinis and Sugar-Puffs to playing football or eating in the street. Until this summer smoking topped the list. I guessed he would find out the rest.

"She said if the house had to smell of smoke it might as well be her smoke too." He grins as if remembering. It makes me feel left out.

"So it isn't common?" I taunt.

"Not when common leads to shared." He laughs.

"Don't laugh at me!"

"I wouldn't dare upset a witch. Bad enough the car will turn to a frog." This was true. The car could fly not carry four. I pictured the Marina now on order, thinking of a toad.

"Will you miss it?"

"A little. Being grownup means going slower, losing something, gaining something else. I get your mother, you and Chris instead."

"What age did you start smoking?"

"You're too young to know, Goldilocks."

"I hate it when grown ups say that."

"I love it when you act the ingénue."

"What does that mean?"

"To act more innocent than you are. You want to ask me something so you mix it up in something else. Now you're growling like a bear who wants her porridge. Except this little bear wants a cigarette."

My face on fire, I run and leave him standing. Up the street to where the road turns into sand and rises sharply to a hill. Behind it lies the beach. I take the path before the hill, to where the sand dunes are set like honeycomb along the cliffside. It's easier to get down sand than climb up. The cliff is crumbling to the sea. No chalk or stone to hold it, only grass. I could walk here blindfold. I pass the sand dune where I always sit with Chris, find another big enough for two. I burrow there and wait for Paul to find me, wanting to be found. I see his shadow fall before he drops the bag.

"The lemonade will fizz everywhere now." I try to look cross, can't. I make a space for him, he stays a shadow.

"What's the matter? I look up. He looks wary.

"Grace, I have never sat in a sand-dune in my life. I didn't have a childhood, I had a boarding school instead. I learned to prefer it. I like my castles made of stone." He stops as if the words slid out without permission.

"Imagine it is stone then. I imagine walls are sand. Spells work both ways."

He lowers himself down and makes me want to laugh. He looks as if he's sitting on a chair he doesn't like. I smile and when he smiles back it seems to make his body follow suit. I watch him sinking. Winds curl the grasses as they grow, sun tips them bronze. Butterflies touch down and for a moment look like flowers. In the sunshine the sea is blue as blue here ever is. I try imagining I'm Paul and all of this has folded out like popups in a book marked 'Sand-dunes for Beginners' but I can't. I glance at him, without the small talk everything too big to say. Perhaps the crisps and lemonade will change him back. I reach inside the bag and pull them out. Ivan has forgotten the plastic glasses. I try to imagine Paul drinking from a bottle labeled 'common' and wonder if he'll pull it off. The post office only sells one type of crisps. To be safe I'd bought four bags. I pass him one, he pulls it open, pops a crisp into his mouth.

"Yuck Grace, these taste like cardboard."

"They might taste better if you add the salt." I laugh. I wait and realise he has no idea what I mean. I demonstrate, ruffle in the bag, pull out the tiny blue sachet of salt. I tear it open, sprinkle some inside and hold the bag closed as I shake. I pass the bag to him. He gingerly tastes one, smiles.

"Do we have to add the sugar to the lemonade too?" he teases.

"No, silly."

He reaches for the bottle. I had made a hole as usual in the sand, entranced by digging through the layers of warm then cool, to cold and damp, had placed the bottle in and tucked the sand up to its neck. At first he cannot find it then he laughs. His laughter tugs me like the sound of waves at night. It makes me move and settle closer, closer not enough. He twists the cork and does not look or ask for glasses, giving me the bottle first then taking it and drinking, not stopping when it fizzes down his shirt.

"Okay, now I feel about twelve."

"I turned you into twelve. Best hope it wears off. I don't know how to reverse the spell," I grin.

"Grace, you're bewildering. You switch from black and white to colour, witch to fairy, storms to spells. You aren't like your mother at all. Or like Chris. Was your father more like you?"

I wonder why one tiny word can salt the lemonade, and turn the sea to grey. I wish there was a spell to change was back to is. Or blinking was enough to stop you crying. He looks at me and shakes his head.

"Does it still hurt so much to talk about your father? Sometimes Chris starts to and looks at you and stops. I understand your mother feeling awkward mentioning him in front of me. I really wouldn't mind. It's okay to miss someone."

And suddenly I want to slide right down the cliff. For words don't come in bags or write themselves in sand. They come alive and crawl inside your head, you let one out and all the rest will follow, swarm and sting you and even when you swat them off they leave the sting inside.

I try another way. I try to think in pictures, make him see. I see a wall. I see my father on one side, and us upon the other. Drifting further every day until he loses his reflection in my mind, becomes a sketch. I close my eyes and tell Paul what I see. As if it's just a picture. I do not even feel his arms go round me. Or feel my words slip out.

I lift my head and wonder how it found his shoulder, why it feels so lost without it, somehow lighter too. I stand and feel as if I stretched my arms out wide I'd fly.

"The tide is coming in," I shout against the wind.

"Grace sit back down, you're making me nervous," he orders.

"If I sit down will you tell me why you don't like sandcastles?"

He looks up at me, attempts amusement, manages exasperation.

"Can't you just take people as they are without looking inside them?"

"Not if they're asking me to trust them. Not if I like them. If I don't then I don't bother."

He seems to soften. Lost in his silence, I wait. I could be by myself. He looks as if there's no one in there. So when he speaks I jump.

"I can tell you, Grace. You might not like me afterwards though."

I want to say I will but something pulls me back. He moves the space between us, shifts by inches, goes by miles.

"I can remember when my father told me I was going, hearing words, not knowing what they meant. I didn't know that going meant away, that they'd go too, too far away to follow. I saw my father's drawing room, still see the globe he pointed to, the giant shape of India, the colours in-between. I was seven. Going when you're seven has a coming back, a going with, a going to. His going meant a leaving, leaving me behind."

I remember being six or seven. Going always had a face, a place, and meant that I was left with Chris, or he went too. "Did you cry?" I ask.

"No one cried in front of father. Tears were a sign of weakness, signs of wanting something else. I saw my sisters trying not to cry when he had punished them. He used to sit at dinner, making small talk, daring them to break down. As if to rub in salt."

"Why did he punish them?"

"For talking to boys. For talking to strangers. For talking back. For talking. We were trained to listen."

"He smacked them?" My father rarely smacked us. Somehow rarely made it rare. This hurts me more than it hurts you. Except his voice said it was true. And when he lifted me off his lap his eyes were wet. I had forgotten it, it was just what fathers did then.

Paul's eyes are black. Like tunnels they suck me in with him.

"He stripped them bare, he slapped them till his arm was tired then whipped them till the silence stopped him. He made me stay at first, until he found my cries would stop my sisters begging him to stop. He wanted them to beg. He wanted them to feel his hand so he could stroke their hair and feel them flinch."

Tears are swimming in his eyes and flooding mine. I gulp them down, he does not need mine too. Where was his mother? I pick my words like Scrabble, guessing his before he spells them out.

"She was in her room or else in bed afraid to go to them. He used to hit her too. My sisters taught each other not to cry. Anne told them tears were what he wanted most. She even tried to bargain with him, she would cry if he left them alone. He kept it for a week then made her bring them to him one by one. After that their cries came later, waking up I'd hear them."

I see his face but when I touch his hand it shakes and feels like seven.

"You think that is the worst, Grace? I did nothing. I listened to them cry, too scared to move, too scared to sleep. He knew I listened, knew I knew what happened in the drawing room. He liked the pictures that knowing drew. It saved him drawing them for me. It taught the lesson better, letting listening tell it, knowing shame would drum it in."

"You were seven, seven couldn't stop it, Paul."

"I could at least have made it real for them. Not shut it out. I left them, Grace. My parents went to India, I went to boarding school, my sisters went to relatives. I went away, not looking back."

"And boarding school? You hated it?" I half hope he'll say yes, for maybe yes means Chris will too.

"At first. Then it became a castle. Safe and sound. Made of stone. A room that rhymed with breathing, tears that stopped. Days full of noise, nights full of silence. Fights that I could win. Sand dunes won't protect you, Grace. Your skin is bare in water. I found a costume, a cloak I wove of what they preferred to see and what I wanted them to. Costumes stick till they are armour. I learned not to take it off."

I nod. "You never told anyone?"

"Soon it echoes. There is a cost to telling. Looking back can't change."

I imagine it, unable to stop the picture moving, seeing covers shaking, hearing muffled sobs. "And your sisters?"

"Grew up, got married. Happy. Never see them. Only at the funerals. They spend their inheritance, I spend mine." He smiles. "And now I really need a cigarette."

I don't know if I like him now or not. He seems more smoke than fire. I'm sure that Chris would fight anyone who hurt me, seven fiercely as fifteen.

I want the real Paul, not the smoke. To poke him out.

"Do you want to know why none of us will talk about my father?"

"Only if to tell will mend, Grace. Only if the telling's worth the cost."

"He was a boatbuilder, a toy maker, a storyteller. He left no inheritance, not in money. Perhaps my mother needed more than smiles. We children only saw the smiles and toys. When he died there was nothing left for any of us. Chris left because he could not bear to watch the house fall down. He and mother wanted more than stories, wanted happy endings that were true. Now that they have more I mean nothing to them. Now they have a story I can't share."

"What story do you want, Grace?" he asked gently.

"I used to want my father's stories back. I saw him everywhere he wasn't. I built a wall to shut him out. You think behind a wall the dead are frozen. You think the image put there stays the same. Instead they change to someone else. You know the worst part, Paul? I see him as a puppet hung behind the wall. I see it through the cracks. The wall is falling, he'll fall too."

"Why must he fall?"

"Because I put him up there. I have to let him fall so I can stand, let him sink so I can swim. He was who he was. He gave us smiles and love. I used to think those were enough to live on. Surely those ought to be enough. Now it feels like wishing on a star. Never knowing if the star is hot or cold or even real. Never asking for a story, knowing none come true."

"Now it's your turn to need a cigarette." I watch him find the box and take one out. He lights it with his own and holds it to me like a candle in the air, the red tip redder in the breeze.

"I'd better not. Mother would kill me."

"Who's to tell? I can keep a secret."

I shake my head. He stubs it out, then rakes his fingers through the sand and lifts a handful, watching as it falls like glitter in the sun then spreading it flat again, the way I do when I want to make sandcastles knowing I'm too old now. He reaches for my hand and buries it in the hole he's left, uncovering it to rub the sand off. He takes a long time like I do when something's new, which I suppose sand is to him. When he takes the other hand to do the same I know why he is taking twice as long. The first time he was stretching out the feeling of the sand and now our hands know something else is new. He stops and turns my hand over, tracing on the palm. Chris and I have played this game as long as I remember. I can read X with my eyes closed. But Chris never draws it. And I never close my eyes and see his mouth.

"Now I think you definitely need a cigarette," Paul whispers. "And want a kiss but that's more dangerous."

I watch him, dazed, as he takes one out the box and shows me how to hold it. When I get that right he lights it, shows me how to draw the smoke in, a little at a time. He takes his hand away, I draw in deeper, start to choke.

"I'll show you." He holds my other hand in his.

"Okay. Breathe in when I squeeze, out when I relax."

I concentrate, I breathe in longer, start to feel a rhythm. I had no idea smoking felt like this. Like falling and flying both at once, like time is melting. Then is gone.

I shiver. Realise the air has turned cold, the sun is orange, realise the cigarette has burnt away. He takes the end and crushes it to ash. The hand he drops feels cold.

He touches my cheek. "Goldilocks looks distinctly smudged," he laughs. The laughter breaks the spell. He stands and brushes off the sand. I trace whatever he does, lost without the feelings. It seems to take a long time to walk back to the car. I get in slowly, sink into the seat.

"Did it feel like you imagined?" His voice is wistful.

"Better. Like falling one minute, flying the next."

"I remember that. It only stays that way so long. The trouble with flying is each time you fly it feels a little more like falling. The trouble with falling is it fizzles out when you hit the ground."

"So what do you do?"

He turns the key, the engine hums.

"You find another way to fly and try not to have to land." He lets the engine go. We get home far too soon. I realise we never spoke about the treaty, wonder if we signed a pact in smoke. Or something else that makes me dizzy if I draw.

He stays for dinner, winking when my mother says he must stop smoking in the car, not cover me in smoke. Before I go to bed she always shoos him out. Tonight he stays much longer. Hiding on the landing I watch him kissing her goodnight, confused a kiss should seem so rough. I notice how his voice is milk chocolate with me yet dark with her. I think of something stupid just before I fall asleep. I can't remember if Goldilocks was eaten by the bears.

In The Mirror

December, 1973

It was December, frost a web that spun to fractals on the sand. The trees wore veils of white. Wind stung your face and drove you back indoors. The one thing colder than the wind was mother. The weeks had passed and Paul and I were close to being friends. We joked and laughed, the green car flying as he drove me home from school. He lit the fire, I made the tea and asked about the wedding plans. I thought my mother would be pleased, instead it seemed to make her ice to me, her warmth reserved for him. Nothing I could say was right and nothing I could do was good enough. She touched him with one hand and stung me with the other. Masking hurt I offered to be bridesmaid. He was delighted, showered me with smiles. To her I had only added one more chore: to find a dress. He offered to be chauffeur, left us at the dressmaker's shop. Her claws came out the moment we went in. I was too tall, no gown was the correct fit, my figure not developed yet, she said. The haughty dressmaker suggested a handmade gown. There was no time, came back the answer, the wedding only weeks away. The woman brought more styles, my mother deadheaded her dress by dress. She tossed the final dress and me aside and, cutting short the dressmaker's apologies, went off to prune the florist. Immediately the woman melted, disappearing to the stockroom for the perfect dress.

She comes back, half hidden in pink silk she places over my head. The silk is shot with every shade from raspberry to shell, like veins upon a rose. The bodice flatters, drawing subtle curves. I spin to simply watch the colours dance. She takes it off and smiles. She has it wrapped before my mother sees it, clearly having measured her as well. The doorbell rings, I turn and see Paul walk in. He should look out of place among the rows of wedding gowns, the artificial flowers. Somehow he does not. He seems to wear a coat of charm and fit wherever. He spies the box and smiles, taking out his wallet, hiding it in mock horror at the price. He pays and takes the box out to the car. I realise that soon the flying car will turn into a toad. I wonder if he minds. He must have taken mother home, come back for me.

The dressmaker's goodbye makes me laugh. I am still laughing as I get in the car. The more I look at him the more I laugh. He stops the car and folds his arms, refusing to move unless I share the joke.

"I'm not so sure you'll think it's funny."

"Try me," he said.

"She said - 'Stepmothers are always jealous, you'll always be his daughter, she'll only ever be a wife.' Shall you tell mother or should I?"

We drive home more on two wheels than on four.

Paul put her mood swings down to wedding nerves. The wedding ceremony was to take place in Norwich. There was one church in our village and my parents had stood there years before. In any case my mother preferred Norwich and it was an easier journey for Paul's friends and relatives. Since Chris was at school there we would meet him there. Paul and Mother were to fly to Paris. Chris and I would stay at Robert's home for Christmas.

My feelings were English weather. Only another fourteen year old could translate. Or better still a certain sixteen year old. Robert was invited to the wedding. Paul had promised me my mother would simply write the card and never read the name. He added on the doctor, saying anyone prepared to house two extra teenagers over Christmas deserved it. He was right about my mother, I had never seen her so flustered. She fussed about a different thing each day. She trusted no one with the task their role allotted. I was unwanted as a daughter, superfluous as a bridesmaid, excluded even as a friend.

I wished I had the kind of mother you could ask advice of. Absence did not simplify your feelings. It wrote equations, offered riddles. If no longer just a friend, the weekly letters Robert and I sent wouldn't tell me what to call him now. I had no idea how to play the opening scene. I could compose the lines for here, a stage I knew. Composure on a different stage I only hoped the costume cued. For Chris I had no script at all. His letters sketched the scenery, somebody I used to know, no clue to how the scenery had reshaped him.

A week before the wedding Paul met me with the car from school. My mother was in Norwich with my aunt, arranging seating plans, the final fitting for her dress, last minute shopping. It was Friday. Paul had been tied up with alterations to the house for weeks. The space at the side had been partly filled by a bigger kitchen, while on top a third bedroom had been added. The kitchen was a brighter lounge, a modern bathroom upstairs. Mother wanted French doors into the garden, a bigger patio. I had become a little bored. He smiled, against my will I smiled back. His eyes are sparks, excitement jumps from him to me. We drive off with the top down, my hair flying wild in the wind that stole its school ribbon. Shivering, I indulge him, stop myself from asking him to put the hood up. He skids into Beach Road scattering the pedestrians.

"I have a surprise for you," he says. "A present for the bridesmaid is, after all, traditional."

"And is it fun, or just traditional?" I tease.

"It's fun," he glints back.

He holds his hands over my eyes as we climb the stairs, a step behind me. His hands change pressure to direct me left or right. We stop but his hands stay where they were. He laughs and pushes me gently through the open door. Removing his hands he watches as I stare. My parents bedroom is transformed. A bed with gauzy drapes, a mirrored dressing table with a pink velvet stool, a china hand basin. Everything is pink or white. The lamps he left on highlight printed cushions, quilts and curtains, vases stuffed with flowers.

"Too pink?" he teases,

"Never!" I laugh.

"We thought here you'll miss Chris less. You're becoming a young lady and you should have somewhere to dream and sulk," he says, half-teasing, half-sincere.

"I do not sulk," I assert, but smile.

"Then your mother will teach you. Or you can practise. With those lips it should be easy enough."

I close my eyes in mock rebuff. At the same time, a finger finds my lips. I shiver and suddenly burn, not just my mouth but from head to toe. It is so quick and so light I tell myself I have imagined it. He stands there smiling exactly as before.

That night it feels odd to sleep in a different room. I miss the shabby wallpaper, a hundred childhood ties, from teddy bears with hardly any stuffing to corners stuffed with memories I could glimpse but never catch. I miss my brother's bed even though he is not in it. I lie and feel as if somebody tore the last few pages out a book I had not finished. I close my eyes and wrap the quilt around me. Inside the body does not feel like mine. The room my father slept in holds no trace of him. He has been papered over. That is what you do when you put up walls. However pink, it still feels like betrayal.

My mother comes home with her hair restyled into a bob. She kisses Paul. I realise he dislikes the new look and hide my smile. He almost growls when she suggests we cut mine too. The bigger car arrives the following day, expensive and grey. Paul will drive it to Norwich, Robert's father drive us back. I pack my clothes, prepare for Christmas somewhere else. The paintings I have done for both boys as presents wait at Robert's house. We are to change in the hotel where the reception will be held.

I think of Robert when he said goodbye. I remember the little box he gave me at the station, stuffed into my pocket and probably still there. I can't remember which jacket I was wearing so I check them all, relieved there so few to choose from. Found, I realise he has never asked if I have looked at it. I have never asked what is inside. I open it.

A delicate gold chain holds a locket, the type you open, close to keep a secret in. It is empty. Or too full.

The day of the wedding starts early; snow falls lightly. I sit in the back and let their voices melt away. The looping roads uncurl, begin to widen, streets lined with buildings, thinly iced in snow. Paul navigates with ease. The hotel is pretty, a mock Elizabethan-style mansion south of the city. Porters bring our luggage. Walking to the suite assigned to us I fall behind, bewildered. Mother does not notice, Paul comes to take my hand.

I am relieved that the suite is separated into three: a lounge, a master bedroom, an adjoining single room. I find my bag, unzip the plastic cover, take my dress to hang it up. I am longing to explore, be on my own. I ask, my mother says no, I have to be here for the hairdresser, who will do mine first. I wait inside my room, put on my dressing gown, sit on the bed. A woman steps in, behind her is my mother.

"I thought to put it up," my mother says.

"I can do that madam, of course. It's just that hair so beautiful seems a shame to hide."

"It will only get untidy hanging loose."

"A coronet perhaps. A single braid I pin into a crown?"

"Is there enough time?" asks mother.

"It is not as elaborate as it sounds. Ten minutes."

She relaxes when my mother leaves the room. Ten minutes later a stranger looks at me in the mirror. With a final pin the woman smiles and calls my mother to show off her work. My mother nods and leaves the room, the hairdresser obediently tailing her. I shut the door and sigh, set free with nowhere I can go. The rose gown shimmers in the winter light. It is too early to get dressed but there is nothing else to do. I slip my head and arms in and wriggling, emerge from my cocoon to tug the skirt down and use the mirror to try to reach the buttons at the back. I hear a knock and half turn to beg my mother's help. Before I take a step the door opens, pushed aside by Chris. The words I have rehearsed are gone.

"The buttons always were my job."

I want to hug him, never let him go, to run to him and make him real. Except he folds his arms and smiles. A grown up smile I try to read and read no better than all the smiles before. A language instinctively translated, the folding in a folding out. I hide my hurt and feel the effort pull my face. I wonder why he knocked and hold the question in. I look into the mirror, checking that nothing of the joy or hurt is left to see. I stand there like a statue as he fastens up my dress. Instead of buttonholes the dress has tiny loops that fit around each button. In the shop the dressmaker had quickly coupled them all and told me the design reflected the fineness of the silk. Reflected in the mirror Chris was struggling, exasperation rushing to his face. I realised the design was female, Chris's fingers simply did not fit. Instead of teasing him I wondered what was wrong with me. His fingers wrestled with the buttons, whispered on my skin, got stuck and I was lost. The statue crumbled into sand. He stood to stretch and then was Chris, stooped down and then was not. I could feel his breath upon my back, and smell his hair. His fingers reached the last few buttons, leaving me to wish I knew a spell to make them all pop out. I search his face for any sign that what just happened had not happened just to me. His reflection smiled as before.

"I'm certain they invented zips last century."

"The ones with zips were Barbie dresses!"

"Bet mother had a fit!" His voice is deeper, comes from somewhere I could knock and knock and not get in.

"She gave up after twenty." The lightness in my voice is thrown, the nonchalance is forced.

"Was this the last dress in the shop?"

"Don't you like it?"

Why must it always matter so? As if the sky is only blue if Chris agrees.

"I meant you spend an hour choosing ice cream Grace! Everything must be perfect. It used to drive me mad!."

His 'used to' tells me why he knocked. The only way you'll manage to leave is to force yourself to cross the road then run so fast that people blur behind you. You look into the distance searching for a reason you could give for turning back. You tell yourself you'll remember why you wanted this tomorrow. You run so fast and cross so many roads they cannot catch you. You build a barrier, fold your arms half to keep the 'used to's out and half to keep the sadness in. The knock was Chris's way to keep the barrier up yet be let in. I could let him back in only if I found a barrier too.

"It doesn't have to be perfect. It does have to be me."

"Then you look like strawberry mixed with raspberry ice cream." He sees me try to take away the teasing, find the truth.

"You look like a flower, Grace."

"You look tall." I want to say you grew away, you left me in the shadows. I want to tell him beauty is just a costume. Except I look in his eyes and know he had to leave or shrink. The hand that cut him free was mine.

"Is Robert downstairs?"

"Yes, and longing to see you. I never realised he saw you as a girl!"

"He told you that?" I ask and watch his face,

"He took you to a balcony, turned it into a pedestal. Be careful, Grace."

"Why?"

"You are up there, he's the one who'll fall."

"Chris, can't you stay and talk? I have so much to ask you."

"I'm under strict instructions to get back to go to the church. But you can open this when I go."

"What is it?"

""It goes with the dress." He hands me a box.

I let him go and sit on the bed. It is perfume. I spray too much on and wonder how quickly it wears off.

When it was time to leave for church the doctor took Chris and Robert in Paul's car. Paul bowed to me and gestured to a silver Lamborghini. I laughed out loud. I held my skirt to stop it falling on the ground as he helped me in the seat. A matching white one, leashed in creamy ribbon, waited for the bride.

"I decided this would be the one thing I decided on," he whispered as the engine purred, the driver let it go. The speed reduced my thoughts to pinpricks. I told myself it made no difference which car I went in, if my mother wanted Lucy with her, if she left it to the last minute to tell me. The web of country lanes became a maze of city streets. Paul pointed out the passing landmarks making me forget the reason we were there. We jolted over cobblestones so fast my head was dizzy, my body wedged to his. The car slowed down and suddenly the medieval church was grey against a greyer sky. He almost lifted me out, and held my flowers as we climbed the icy steps.

My mother had warned me that Paul's parents were dead. I had not let her know I knew. I was relieved I would not have to meet his father, curious about his sisters. Mother had decided the custom of seating the guests according to the bride or groom in church was old fashioned. I suspected the real reason was because our side would scarcely fill the first few pews. In the churchyard a throng of people tapered as they filtered into church. Paul pointed out his sisters, linking my arm in his to introduce me. The three were dark as he was. They admired my dress and wondered at my hair. I counted nine children scattered round them, one small boy hiding in his mother's skirt. Detaching him she scooped him up and gave him to her sister, leaving me unsure which of them he belonged to. Shepherding the rest they smiled as one and went inside to take their seats. Paul asked if I was nervous, nodding with approval when I shook my head. He smiled and went to check that everything was ready. I was not. My legs refused to move, my hands would not stop shaking. Finding a wooden seat I huddled there, the wood as cold as stone, nobody left to see me cry. Somebody took my flowers, laying them upon the seat. Chris sank to pull me close. That was how my mother found us.

The church is cold and dark. White lilies glow like candles. I follow mother down the aisle and leave her at the front with Paul. I sit between my aunt and Chris. When it begins I drop my eyes and wait for her to say the vows that rub my father out. Then I realise she did that long ago.

Paul had told me he rarely saw his sisters, did not care much for their choice of husbands. Still they did not act like sisters, acting all it seemed. They smiled in all the right places, saying all the right things. Yet smiles were half smiles, nothing said was real. They did not kiss my mother. Only Anne, the oldest, kissed her brother after the ceremony, a quick brush of lips upon his cheek. Rose said congratulations. The youngest, Sarah, simply smiled and let her husband wish them well. Invisible cord seemed to tie them to their husbands, pulled them back when they moved too far apart. No such ties connected them to Paul. Whenever he approached the three would make a triangle, fence him out. They came alive with their children, buttoning their coats and fitting fingers into gloves. I could not picture them ever standing as I had when Chris fastened up my dress. The children stamped their feet into the crust of snow. They threw confetti as their mothers laughed. It gathered in their footprints, landed in their hair. I watched them, drawn by a strangeness. They reminded me of Russian dolls. They seemed to slot inside each other when together, shrinking back to childhood roles, as if their grownup selves were just veneers. As oldest, Anne, was always first to speak, Rose waiting for her turn, while Sarah never spoke without a cue. At the wedding breakfast I was placed beside her, grateful that her husband sat upon my other side. He spoke of Oxford where they lived, the university, the colleges, perfectly anticipating Sarah's needs and wants. Chris and I listened politely, trying not to look at Robert. Dr Jolly's table rocked with merriment.

Paul gave the only speech. He made a comedy of his introduction to village life, of how the shop sold everything but petrol, how the road signs gave you riddles, so he followed one marked Wiveton and found a wife. Becoming serious he said to find my mother was a dream come true, to find himself a stepfather a new adventure. At last the cake was cut, my mother dancing in Paul's arms as the band played *She*. He waved to Chris and me to join them. The music changed to *I Only Have Eyes For You*. I looked at Chris and all that was familiar was the eyes, the arms that held me holding me like glass, his body ramrod straight, as if the boy I knew was lost, the man not ready to come out. The blue eyes saw the stars in mine go out and flickered something gone too fast to read. Before I could look again Paul replaced him, showed me how to waltz. His hands were warm, burned through my dress, I shivered where they touched my skin. I was relieved when Robert tapped my shoulder, cutting in. I had never danced with Robert, never been this close. I never heard the song. He held me tight, so tight I blushed, his fingers stroked my neck. His father sauntered up, his anger masked, his look a warning. Robert let me go and quickly walked away; his father steered me round the floor. I was beginning to feel like the toy in pass the parcel, going round in circles, never stopping where I wanted to, my feelings wrapped in silk.

"I apologise for Robert, Grace. He forgets you're only fourteen. Chris has every right to be angry."

I immediately look for Chris. I know my brother's anger: silent, brooding, measured now. This is not my brother. The figure in his place is stalking Robert through the room and Robert is too absorbed to sense it, too late to see him coming, to see that his hands have turned to stone, his eyes as dark as mines. He only turns when he hears his name and then the first punch flies, the second hits the air. Chris may be furious, yet at the final second his arm shifts as if it suddenly shirks its task, the contact glancing, Robert falling more surprised than hurt. Paul reaches them before the doctor, wise enough not to ask a reason he can guess, intuitively knowing punches sometimes hurt less than words, that friendship is not always better served by truth. Chris is contrite in moments, Robert quick to say that he deserved the punch. Within moments they are play fighting in the garden. Leaving me with my mother, Paul goes off to teach them how to punch. Doctor Jolly pours himself some port and settles at his table mulling over cheese and grapes.

"I'm sorry, Grace," Robert says when Chris goes in search of cake.

"Sorry you did it or sorry you got punched for it?"

"Neither. I'm sorry you're only fourteen. Chris won't always be watching."

"Is fifteen a better number?" I smile.

He reaches for my hair to take it down, bewildered by the coronet until I laugh and show him, letting waves ripple down my back. He does not tell me I am beautiful. His eyes give him away.

"You wore the locket."

"I learned to count in twos."

It was nearly midnight. I felt strange. I saw the room as if I was inside a snow globe, all the edges softened, faces nibbled, figures fuzzy. Robert noticed, slipping from my side and coming back before I felt him gone. His father sat beside me asking questions, stopping when the answers made no sense. The words did not tell who they came from.

"Not sick, just very tired...get her home...need to sleep too...drive... I'm in charge...will take at least an hour....weather..."

In the blur of goodbyes mother kisses Chris, says goodbye to me. Paul bends to kiss my cheek then shows the doctor how to work the heating in the car while Robert clears the snow. He sits in the front seat on the journey home. Chris tucks a blanket round me. I make my usual pillow in his shoulder, let the beating of his heart become a lullaby. I watch the lights go out, the buildings shrink, afraid to fall asleep in case he disappears.

Upside Down

Christmas, 1973

When we drive past the cutoff home I hold my breath but I feel nothing. It takes more than memories to make a home, more than money to put it back together. Robert took the cases in. His father showed me to a bedroom looking out upon the garden, lost in snow. The snow shone back to light the room. I whispered goodnight and shut the door. I found the covers folded back, a scent I recognised but couldn't name. I was too brimmed in sleep to look for Chris to help me with my dress. I would have to stay a bridesmaid. I climbed inside the tall brass bed, pulled the covers up then pulled them halfway down. I thought of something I told Robert on the balcony the night we met: that fear was linked to places, that somewhere else the links were weak or missing. Lying in his house I realised my somewhere else was here. I had not checked the door, or wrapped the quilt into a cocoon. I lay there knowing only footsteps separated me from Chris, that Robert's room and this one shared a wall, the doctor's sleep was glass the slightest sound would break. I did not feel protected, I felt strong, as if the fear had never been a part of me. That meant it had not always been there, something had let it in. Before I could make sense of that I fell asleep.

I woke and instantly I knew the scent was hyacinths. My father used to plant them too. It always seemed like magic. He covered up the bulbs with soil then put them in the dark to grow, to take them out to bloom in time for Christmas. I could see him smiling at the doubtful looks on our faces, promising the strange green spikes would turn to flowers. They always did. A glazed pot stood on the windowsill, the white flowers matching the perfectly white room. I sat on the bed looking in frustration at my dress: I could not go to breakfast wearing this. I found my suitcase by the door, unzipped. I pulled out trousers, jumpers, all the colours wrong and all too big. Boys' clothes. I pulled the door ajar to shout for Chris then realised they could be Robert's and shouted for him too. I waited for a minute then footsteps thundered down the stairs.

"We don't do room service, Juliet," Robert teased.

"Did you really sleep in that?" Chris asked.

"The fairy godmother didn't bring another," I answered, sarcasm dripping. "Who has my clothes?"

They looked each other up and down.

"I see a shirt, Chris. Is that a bra underneath?" Robert pointed.

"Grace doesn't wear bras."

"How would you know?" I said and slammed the door. I wandered to the window. Fairy godmothers didn't bring bras either. Mothers did. Mothers took you shopping, smiling as the woman measured you, adjusted straps with gentle fingers, took you to a shop for tea to make the bra feel special. Conspirators mirrored in each other's faces. No matter how I wished, it was too late. I heard them knock but I had melted into tears.

Tears run out and hurt will freeze inside you. Having made a tower of my room it felt too high to jump, too far to fall. My knight had turned to a jester, my king had outgrown his crown. Another knock. I would have let it go but for the paper, slipped beneath the door.

'I can't pretend to have a cure for teenage boys but I can listen.
David.
PS. I sent them out to chop more wood.'

In all this time I'd never known the doctor's name. I opened the door to find he'd left my case outside. I threw a cardigan over my dress and went upstairs.

"I'm imprisoned. I can't undo the buttons at the back," I said, shyly.

He rose up from his chair beside the fire, dropped his newspaper.

"Breakfast or buttons?" he smiled.

"I think I've been a bridesmaid long enough."

I stood as he unfastened all the buttons, longing to be me again. I went to change, returned wearing jeans, a white sweater, my hair tied back.

"Thank you." I met his eyes. "I don't know what to call you now."

"Call me whatever makes you comfortable, Grace. I don't mind."

I said yes to coffee, no to porridge, yes to toast. He sat them on the table, sat upon the other side. I tell him why I chose the sweater, why I knew the scent. He guesses I am dodging what upset me.

"I said I'd listen, Grace, but only if you want to talk. I almost made them tell me what they'd done, but something stopped me. The hurt was yours. It may not need a doctor."

"I think it needs somebody wise. I'm tangled up inside. I was used to being one of them, a tomboy. Yesterday was coronets and waltzes, the first time someone thought me beautiful whether or not they said so. I saw it in their eyes. Like stepping through a mirror. Chris and Robert shattered it, laughing at me for not having a bra. I felt just like a paper doll. I had the dress but nothing underneath. Mother never thought to buy me bras. I stole one from the changing room at school. At first it was too big and then it grew too small and it was never mine."

I looked down at the garden. "They didn't mean to upset me. It must be cold out there."

"I never meant it as a punishment, Grace. We really do need wood, the fire eats it up. You needed breathing space."

"I feel all wrong inside myself. As if I'm not myself but turning into someone else. I'm tired then too awake to sleep, I'm hungry till I start to eat, so thirsty I could drink a sea then all I taste is salt. I'm full but empty, sad but happy being sad. One minute everything is wrong then nothing matters. Nothing wonderful happens yet I could somersault with joy. I want to be alone and then I'm lonely, long for company and then feel lost. Is this what going mad feels like?'

He smiles. "I wish it were that simple. This is what becoming a woman feels like. If it helps then I can tell you Chris and Robert get befuddled too except they won't tell because becoming a man is more a silent going mad."

"Tell me."

"Oh Grace, I can't remember."

"Since doctors once were boys, I bet you do."

"Ok, you win. You do not walk if there is somewhere you can lie. You never walk when you can run. You run and don't know where you're going, get there and don't know you've arrived. You want a hug but won't admit it, want to talk but don't know how. He is your best friend but you feel like killing him. You cannot kill him so you punch instead. She is the girl you like the most but you can't show it. You cannot show it so you make her cry. You want to kiss her but you don't know where to start. You start and don't know where to stop. Your body is not yours for yours did what you told it. It feels as if you are an animal but no species that you know. She will be your best friend until one day you touch just by chance. Accidentally flying."

I hesitate, he sees the question in my eyes.

"Ask it, Grace."

"Why did you never marry again?"

"She would ask that too. She would ask because she'd want me to be happy. I would tell her this: the sun and moon have their reflections. The sun's reflection is never warm, is just a toy. I would rather spend a moment in her warmth than spend a lifetime with a reflection. I do not say the moment was enough because when you love a lifetime will not feel enough. Love bends to fate and keeps the memory, accidents don't end in flying twice."

"Are you happy?"

"Joy will shoot from nowhere, Grace, grow from nothing, die without a reason. Happiness you have to plant, and nurture like a bulb, be thankful when it blooms and in-between remember that without the darkness and cold the bulb will never make strong roots, the flowers will be short lived."

"When the woodcutters crawl back up they may not even think to ask what they did wrong. Will you tell them Grace?"

I shook my head. "Perhaps when we can laugh about it, when we're all grown up. I've missed them both too much to fuss and fight."

He smiled. "Then let's enjoy Christmas."

On Christmas morning I woke up and longed for Chris to tumble out of bed and drag me down the stairs to shake the presents, longed to unwrap my father's parcel, knowing that he had made it just for me. Last Christmas had passed unmarked by tree or presents, dinner cheese and pâté discovered in a hamper sent by Lucy, rounded off with chocolate. Robert and his father had evolved a ritual of their own for Christmas. We followed suit, unwrapping presents after breakfast, making a game of making dinner, sticking to the doctor's mandate for exercise by building a snowman. The snow became a blizzard, chasing us indoors and leaving him without a face. I offered to help with dinner, more than happy to be asked to make fairy cakes instead. The turkey was huge, the roast potatoes crisp outside and fluffy inside, the trifle drifts of cream and custard piled high on sponge and jelly. All of it a storybook Christmas marred by being treated like a doll. All day Chris and Robert skirted round me, as if no longer sure of what to do with me, so careful not to crack my feelings, instead they left me out. We sat upon the couch, the boys on either side of me, a measured space between us that they adjusted if I got too close. Escaping to the balcony I looked inside, behind the glass all three males were fast asleep. I would have swapped this Christmas there and then for last year's, if I could change us back to who and what we'd been before. Since I could not I went inside. Deciding it was time for tea I put the fairy cakes upon a plate and boiled the kettle, smiling as it whistled, scowling as they slept on. Looking at the cherries I had placed upon the icing gave me an idea. I collected what I needed from my room and went outside to where the snowman glittered in the last glints of the sun. I left her with a smile. Unable to go back upstairs I lay beneath my covers wondering if Chris and Robert felt what I felt now: this aching to be touched, to be a parcel someone opened, even if there were a thousand layers, even if you wrapped each one in sellotape.

    That night my dreams were strange, impossible to catch before they melted. Slipping on my favourite dress I went upstairs for breakfast, innocently said good morning, waited. Spreading butter on my toast I smiled as Robert called Chris to the window, watched the shock redraw my brother's face. Distracted from his magazine the doctor went to look, then turned to me and clapped. The snow-woman's lips were rose pink ribbon, blue glass beads for eyes, a button nose. She wore a hat and holly leaves for earrings, otherwise completely naked, crimson berries pointing to her snowy breasts.

Happy Families

January, 1973

Paul and mother came home bringing Paris with them. Perfume and jewellery, chocolates and champagne. Paul had bought Chris a camera. We took a hundred photographs. None captured the difference in my mother. Suddenly her smile was real, included me, no longer stolen, always meant for someone else. It made me think about the music box, the woman father carved from wood Paul had brought to life. A little part of me felt sad, a bigger part knew boxes must have lids. The photos cannot catch the feelings that cling to them. Paul brought fun back, a different kind of fun, exciting and expensive. In between the fun his face could switch to boredom in a flash. I began to dream of sleep, to snatch it in the car, for Paul only went home when fun ran out. He laughed and made you want to find him. He could smile and mother would eat ice-cream for dinner, make me forget hot chocolate was for children. Chris was easily drawn in. Paul offered to teach him how to drive, he followed Paul around the house, unconsciously echoing his sarcasm, wasting it on me. My mother took me shopping, teasing me from jeans to dresses, blue to red. We went to Norwich to see the Russian ballet dance The Nutcracker, came home to find our bedrooms full of sweets. The fights were snowball fights, the arguments were pantomime. I discovered that money bought much more than I'd imagined. Then Chris left, reminding me that it stole as well.

I looked at the window, wanting it to crack and let me out. I was tired of reading, tired of playing records spinning songs with needles of their own. I had heard Paul drive off to see a friend. Chris would be at school surrounded by them. I hear a tap and opening the door know it must be mother. She tucks her hair behind one ear the way she does when she is nervous.

"If you're busy I can go away?"

"It's no good being busy by yourself," I smile ruefully.

"May I come in, then?"

"Of course."

"I thought you might be bored. I wondered if you'd like a makeup lesson? We have all the makeup I bought in Paris." She smiles, not the smile she keeps for Chris, as if he brings the sunshine out, or the one she saves for Paul that hints at secrets. This smile is completely new, a bit is shy, a bit is scared, a bit is me.

"I think Chris would say I need a lesson!"

"Every girl needs to learn. And friends are usually no help because they make the same mistakes."

I bypass this. "What are my mistakes then?"

"Nothing we can't fix. I'll fetch the makeup. Tie your hair back. We need another stool. I'll bring mine." Animated by something to organise she dashes off.

She puts the stool down by the mirror, moves mine from the window, fully opening the curtains. Luckily the bedroom caught what sun there was till noon. I realised I never thought of it as mine. A shadow slept here; I'd never left the room I'd shared with Chris. She does not look out of the window. I wonder if her shadow does. I try but can't remember what this room was like before. I only knew it had my father in it, then did not.

She puts the makeup case upon the bed and asks if I can clear the dressing table. She peels the cellophane off the boxes brought from Paris, boxes made of cardboard shining like silk. They smell of perfume, excitement, somewhere else.

"I went a little mad," she says. "I have all these things already. Paul said that didn't matter."

She looks at me then pulls my hair loose and finds a hairband, sweeping it off my face. Immediately I feel too bare.

"The first thing to remember is even when you think it's clean your face is not. Think of it as starting over."

She takes a pad of cotton wool, pouring something from a bottle on it. The scent is sweet but out of place, like smelling June in January.

"Rosewater," she smiles. "It cleans and softens. Now you're a blank canvas Grace. What would you paint?"

"Someone people notice. Someone new."

"Will you let me try?" I nod.

"I'm not going to use foundation. You have no blemishes. A sweep of powder gives an even surface. Brush it on the lips and eyelids too. A base of taupe over the whole space from brow to lash. In the deepest part bronze for definition. Purple on the eyelid then iridescent purple on the middle. Dark brown eyeliner and last of all mascara. On the lips pearl pink you coat with gloss. Use blusher last, don't overdo it, a petal not the rose."

"Take a look. There's a stranger in your mirror." Leaning in she makes it two. She's been a stranger my whole life.

"Don't you like it?"

"You're the artist with this kind of paint. I see now why Chris laughed when I tried." My tone is light, self mocking.

"Must you take everything so seriously Grace?"

"You have Paul for jokes."

"You're missing Chris. Shall I tell you a secret?" She moves to sit upon the bed and pats the space beside her. Sitting I feel wary. Secrets are like gobstoppers, choke the one you tell.

"Paul and I have been talking about moving to Norwich. This house is much too small for him, Sea Palling too much sea for me."

I guess the makeup doesn't cover shock because she tries to backtrack.

"Nothing is decided Grace. But can't you picture it as an adventure? I know you grew up here but why not finish growing somewhere else?"

I feel my face freeze, although my head is racing. Norwich gives me Chris back, takes everything I've ever known away. Like offering the sun and moon and taking all the stars. A whole new story leaving all the others once upon a time. I try to think of leaving as a sheet of paper, nothing drawn yet.

"Does Chris know?"

"No, I shouldn't really have told you. I know you don't have any secrets from each other. Will you keep this one for me., Grace? You know how unhappy I am here. You were listening the day I argued with your father over moving. You're wondering how I knew? Your door was open when I went downstairs, shut when I came up. I heard you crying, Chris talking. So I guess you heard the part about the baby too. I've often wondered how much you told Chris."

I look at her and words float up a staircase as if to eavesdrop once has glued me there.

"Back then I told him anything he asked. He asked for nothing, nothing was exactly what I told. But I remember all of it. You said you wanted somewhere sunshine coloured in. You said you could be different somewhere else." I want to say 'you said you never wanted me' but nothing she says now can rub that out.

"We have to find a house first. We'll tell Chris soon." She puts her finger on my lips. "Secret, Grace?" I nod. She takes the finger off and laughs. Still sealed I look at her, confused. She holds her finger up to show me. She has turned it pink with lipstick. All I can do is smile. I cannot make it match the smile she painted. Secrets can't be pink.

"I better go make lunch. Paul said he'd be back by twelve. Which means one. Or when he's hungry!" I can tell my time is up, don't have to wait for her to move, she isn't with me any more: I am dismissed. The bed is lighter when she stands and I'm too heavy to try to. I watch her go and when the door is shut I shut the somewhere else somewhere I can keep it blank. The only thing I want to colour in is Chris and moving will not bring him back, just give me someone who looks the same but different until I cannot spot it because I'll be different too.

The greys mixed into March, the sky lustrous as the inside of a seashell. From my bedroom window trees were skeletons, paper buds unfurling to skin of silver green. I stood beneath them, punishing Chris for not telling me he was coming home this weekend. leaving him to find me when he worked out I had gone. I shiver, anger ice the footsteps do not melt. The steps are Paul's.

"Blame me Grace. I wanted to surprise you, Chris just played along. We tried to phone you from the station, couldn't find a phone box." I turn, the anger running down my cheeks, too late to stop it melting. Taking a step he wraps me in his arms.

"The tears are freezing on your eyelashes." he whispers. I can't talk, can't move, not from the cold, because he feels so warm I want to go on melting. Touching my face he smiles and sets me free.

"That's better, you're defrosted. Come inside. You know it's you he wants to see."

I follow him into the house. Chris is sitting on the couch with mother in the living room. He dodges when I try to catch his eyes. If it is me he wants to see it doesn't show. I hide the hurt. Paul puts more wood upon the fire and asks me to play Scrabble, Words are jokes that only we two get. He grins as I spell dummy, adding male. I blunt the hurt with blocks. I lay down bighead, he strikes with chop. I laugh and glance at Chris, it glances off. I look at Paul, he tips the board and all the words slide off. I stand and know he'll follow, reach my room and leave the door ajar. I hear him shut it, let him hold me, keep the tears at bay.

"She must have told him. I wanted this to wait until tomorrow," he says.

"What to wait?"

"Let's sit down." He steers me to the bed and when I sit he sits beside me.

"There's no easy way to tell you this. She's pregnant Grace. About four months. She's worried sick she'll lose it, I don't know why she seems so sure."

I could tell him why except my mind is whirring, pieces slotting into place. I saw her take the stairs more slowly, hug her tummy when she sank into the armchair, fill his cup with coffee hers with tea and wondered how I'd been so blind. I feel Paul's hand in mine not sure who joined them. I search for words confused when suddenly he points towards the door. He reaches it just as I hear the running on the stairs. He whispers, "Act for me."

I smile at Chris and tell him that Paul has fixed my record player with a fuse. I sit beside him at dinner while Paul pours champagne and tells us why tonight we're allowed a glass. I sip it and look across the table seeing everything I'd missed.

My fourteen years had never counted hers as thirty-five. My mother never celebrated birthdays, never seemed to alter in appearance. Now I looked and saw the worry loud and clear. Instead of glowing she was grey, instead of being fatter she was thinner. Eating was no more than pushing food around her plate. I fetched the pudding, she had disappeared. When Paul went to check on her she was fast asleep and fully dressed in bed. I looked at him and hoped for his sake the baby was a girl.

The makeup lesson was designed to win me over, tell me a secret, making sure I hadn't told the darker one. The move to Norwich was not for Chris and me at all, but only feathering a nest. The pieces fitted, leaving no one I could show or tell. Paul said goodnight then I waited for Chris to say something and when nothing came I said goodnight and went to hide inside my room. Paul was sitting on the stool, too big and yet too small.

"I'm sorry, Grace. I didn't mean to frighten you."

"I'm not that easily frightened," I said softly. "The stool might be."

He tries to smile. I sit down on the bed. Like this we are suddenly at eye level. His are wet.

"She's right, she is going to lose it. Don't pretend, you see it too."

"Paul, I know nothing about babies. What does the doctor say?"

"What doctor? She won't let one near her."

"Then how did you find out?"

"That she was pregnant? She wouldn't let me near her either."

I can feel my blush.

"Damn me! I shouldn't be involving you. I forget you're younger than you seem. She only wanted Chris to know. I said that wasn't fair."

So Chris would have known and never told me. I drop my head in case I cry. He strokes my hair.

"I'm making this worse not better. Talk to me. Do you mind about the baby? ...Stupid question. Of course you do."

"I'll learn not to mind. The important thing is looking after her. She ought to see a doctor. Robert's father?"

"I suggested that. She said he was too close. Anyone is too close. I thought a sister... Lucy would have dropped everything to come. Your mother wouldn't speak to her. Or me for calling her."

"Chris will manage to persuade her to see a doctor. Let me talk to him," I reassure him.

"I'm grateful. And, Grace..."

He holds my eyes.

"A baby would have its own place, you know, not take yours."

I believed he meant it, knowing all it really meant was now.

I could talk to Chris tomorrow, forget about the baby. Closing my eyes only drew a picture of Chris asleep in the room we used to share. If he couldn't tell when to share a secret then I wouldn't let him sleep. A baby could not take his place when he was never here. He knew how little room it would leave me.

I crossed the landing and gently pushed the door, closing it as quietly behind me, breathing in the cold. Against the sea wind the window was only cellophane. Below the wind I searched for breathing hearing only mine. I traced the darkness seeing what he'd done. I used to do it too. When I was cold I'd pull the covers over me to make a tent. The anger collapsed. I remembered when the wind would howl and Chris would feel me sliding in beside him too full of sleep to send me back. I bent across the bed and said his name to check how deep his sleep was, heard his breathing keep its tune. The sculpture of his body shaped the tent. I reached for the edge of the covers realising he had tucked it in. A hand came out and lifted them.

"I heard you all the time." His voice overspills with laughter. "Get in for now, you must be freezing."

I slide inside expecting pyjamas, finding skin. I try pretending not to notice and find it impossible; heat melts my nightdress, glues me to him.

"Don't, Grace."

"Don't what?" I whisper.

"I don't know. You don't feel like my sister in the dark."

"What do I feel like?"

"Like a witch. Go to sleep."

I guess the wind has stirred me, see the room is muddy grey, not yet dawn, no longer night. His arms are wrapped around me, leaving me too close to sleep and him too far away to wake. Untangling myself I slide out of the bed and feel the cold air follow me as I slip out the door. I cut across the shadows to quickly step inside my room.

Chris tried to talk her round but mother was determined not to see a doctor. He left looking worried. He was right to be. The first week in May one evening she began to moan in pain. By bedtime she was doubled up, unable to catch her breath. I watched by the window for the doctor's car. Robert's father told us she was in too much pain to risk the time examining her and called an ambulance to take her into hospital. Chris caught the early train, arriving in the corridor to hear her scream. She gave birth to a boy, a dead boy. Paul said he had looked perfect then he said no more. I never saw him cry. He brought my mother home from hospital she went upstairs. He said she needed rest. Rest turned to space and space to time. He took her meals, the trays came down as they'd gone up. It took a week for her to find the stairs. Chris wanted to stay, I heard Paul tell him to go back to school, that sometimes getting on with things was easier. Time went by and seemed to make things harder. When I told her I was sorry she said nothing. Finding me Paul hugged me, said what might have been was best forgot. Then he did not speak of it again. His face was taut, the glitter in his eyes was gone. My mother rarely spoke and when she did talked as if the baby never was. Chris phoned and asked me how she was and echoed Paul: some things were easier blocked out. The house was cheerless, figures drifting making no connection when they met.

If Paul reached to hold her hand she pulled away. He left the room and only her eyes would follow. May turned warm. The air was cold in any room they shared. Her smile was neither real nor imitation. She would go nowhere and no one could get in. My stepfather answered the telephone, relayed invitations she refused. I cooked her meals that went untouched. I watched her dresses fade as flowers bloomed outside. I started wearing makeup hoping if she copied me it would be a start at least. Paul teased me, made the blusher real. He laughed and joked, but jokes crashed without a landing path and laughter circled far above her head. They touched by accident and looked as if the touching hurt. He bought her presents, each no sooner opened than put down. I wondered how this could be easier, when rubbing out the pain only rubbed it in.

He was not a man who saw resolution in talking, preferring treats and diversions. When neither worked he turned away, she did not seem to care. He started drinking whisky in the evenings, moved to Chris's room to sleep, she started taking sleeping pills and sleeping till midday. She refused to speak to Robert's father as a doctor or a friend. When Chris came home in May she barely noticed he was there. It was a holiday weekend, children played outside the window. I remember wishing I could be there too.

My mother had gone to have a nap. A nap could last all day if no one found a way to get her out of her room. I had gone in one day and found her staring in the mirror as if to find the face she used to wear.

"I think she has depression," Chris told Paul.

"Does it matter if we pin a name on it?" Paul said impatiently. "Whatever we call it she has to decide to fight it, want to. That was my son too, Chris."

Chris looked at Paul. The look that meant I shouldn't be listening. Paul nodded. Furious, I looked hard at both of them.

"So I have to live with it, but pretend I don't see it?"

"See what, Grace?" He sounds irritated with me, like I'm a child interrupting a grownup conversation.

"How she's stopped caring so he stops trying. She's not eating, smoking far too much, she used to dress for dinner, now she sometimes isn't dressed for lunch. She wouldn't open the door without makeup, now she won't go through it. With or without."

'Well you're doing your best to make up for her. You look like a doll," Chris said. It was quiet, barbed, a sting when cutting roses.

"Enough, Chris. Don't take it out on Grace." I glance at Paul. Then back at Chris.

"All the makeup in the world won't make you see me. I am a doll. A doll you used to dress and treat like china. Now the doll can dress herself and still she's china, only now the chips don't matter. Neither does the doll."

Paul looks at me as if Goldilocks has turned into a bear. I turn on him. "You told me once I turned the light off just by walking in a room. Now it's your turn to do that."

"There isn't a magic wand for sadness, Grace. Or spells to make it disappear."

"You all have other ways of disappearing. Chris goes back to school. You shrink yourself inside a bottle. Mother's playing Sleeping Beauty. I'm going out. Maybe then you'll see me."

It got better after that, at least with Paul. He was trying. Trying did not turn a stepfather to a father, or a brother back into a friend. I wanted a mother back, however little she wanted me. I pictured her with Paul when they returned from honeymoon and wanted her to look like that when he came in a room. All my wants were moonshine. When Chris rang he rang to speak to Paul, to ask if there was any change in mother. When Paul passed the phone to me all I did was fill the silence, all Chris did was dig another, nothing real was safe to say. I shopped and cooked and cleaned and went to school, invisible no matter where or what. Robert's letters went unanswered. He rang, I brushed him off. Instead of running to the phone I would not pick it up. My mother's eyes were wells. Words were stones that never hit the bottom. Wanting turned to anger, silence into blame. I found a way to make them see me.

The end of May was hot and sunny. In the evenings Paul would go out for a drive and sometimes take me with him. I never knew if he would ask me to or not. He never made it sound as if it mattered if I came. I played along, not sulking if he went without me, never saying yes too fast. He always stopped somewhere to smoke. He'd open the box, take out two cigarettes and find his lighter. It was silver, gold on top, I liked to watch the flame jump out. He would light the first then catch my eyes before he lit the second, giving in before he burnt his fingers, passing one to me. He said that one was not enough to make a habit, laughing when I told him they added up.

We'd roll the windows down to let the breeze float through. I never asked him for another, knowing it would feel like begging. That night I decided I would beg if I needed to. Lightheaded it was easier to let the words slip out than think about the fire they would start.

"It's Friday. Isn't that the one night habits never count?" I opened.

He laughs. He's in a good mood, sunshine did the same to me.

"I only have this habit left. You made me give up whisky. Just when I was almost Scottish."

"I only said I didn't like the smell." A smile escapes.

"I couldn't do the accent anyway. 'Hiv anither lassie then.'"

He lights it with his own. I take it knowing I must do this now or not at all. I breathe the smoke in hard.

"When mother's better, Chris said that he and I prove there's a chance she'll have another baby."

"Babies take a little more than chance, Grace," he says drily.

"A girl would be easier."

"I don't know if you're proof of that."

It's nearly over. In the plan the last words just slid out. These feel like bullets.

"Chris doesn't always know as much as I do."

He locks his eyes to mine "What do you know?"

"Once I..."

"This isn't story-time Grace." His voice is cold, the car too small.

"Chris wasn't mother's firstborn son."

"All of it." He grips my shoulders hard.

"The first baby died. He wasn't father's. That's all I know."

He reads my fear, believes me. He asks who else knows, believes me when I answer no one. He starts the car and we are hurtling fast enough to skid on every bend and junction, flying over dips and bumps.

He brakes so fast as we approach the house my stomach rolls. We stop and I breathe out, look at him and gasp it back.

"Get out Grace. Stay out. I don't care where. Come back when it gets dark."

I am too weak to stay for her. I run. As trapped at fourteen as he had been when he was seven.

I hang around the amusement arcade until it shuts at ten o'clock then run all the way home. The windows look like his eyes. All the lights are off. I open the door as quietly as I can, the house is silent. I climb the stairs more frightened by the silence than by screams. I crawl into bed and tuck the covers tight around me. When I stir the room is dark still. All I hear is wind, the seagulls crying.

I wake up to the smell of bacon. I walk into the kitchen, see my mother at the cooker, Paul smiles from the table, pats the chair beside him.

"Your mother is feeling so much better. Aren't you my dear?"

She slowly turned to face me. Her smile made up is bright. Her eyes are pools of tears.

Tennis

June, 1974

I have a hundred versions of the story in my mind, some edited by someone else, a person I can never be again. In others I am the author and I am powerful, I cut bits out to change it, starting with the parts where I was happy, where I felt special. I cannot look into that girl's eyes and know what I let happen. Other days I write it in my head as if he never entered my world. In sunshine I remember that summer and it burns somewhere deep and sad. I change the weather, characters are written in who were never there, who somehow make the ending different. People who even shout to me what to do or say, or who to tell. In wilder hours and moods I will invent versions where I stopped him, where I run away just before I am drawn in. I change the tense sometimes to make it feel more faraway, to make it feel like looking in a window, listening on a stair. I see it looking down, it was not me. On braver days I write as if it's happening, let the cries be mine. For if I don't I'll always be there. So many different stories: why can't another one be real?

    The house felt like a prison. Even if nobody punished me I knew what I had done could not be undone. I locked myself up in my room and spoke when I was spoken to. When Paul decided I should learn to play tennis I was simply grateful, sensing sunshine bailed me out. He drove into town to buy the balls and racquets, laughing as he told me I'd spend more time in the beginning chasing balls than hitting them. The village tennis court was usually empty. There was a tall yew hedge all around. The court itself was a pitted grey concrete, grass being too expensive to maintain. The hedge provided warm shelter from the sea breeze. At some point someone had built a small summerhouse, wooden with blue paint long faded and cracked, so it looked like eggshell. Pink and vanilla roses, petals like raspberry ripple ice-cream grew half wild. Nobody else ever came so we brought two ancient garden chairs together with a folding table. He taught me how to hold the racquet, hitting easy balls across the net until they were more steadfast in coming back. He was a patient teacher, easy company. We played at weekends and after school was finished. I'd run home knowing he'd be waiting for me to change and go. Between sets and before going home, we would drink lemonade in long glasses, tall bottles bought from the village shop. As I grew more proficient, the matches lasted longer and when the last ball rolled away he seemed content to relax and let the shadows tell the time. I remember thinking of my mother waiting at home but the guilt was left behind the hedge. We floated the ball in rainbow arcs across the net. Eyes shut, its path imprinted on my retina, tattooed by sun. On cooler days, the air would buzz in razor blade rallies, racquets cut the air, to send the ball across the court and carve a fast sharp line you could almost see. I would be breathing fast and prepared to lose, but only after exhausting myself, the winning shot a cue prompting my race to the chairs. He talked of nothing important. He noticed a new tennis dress, only smiled when I started plaiting my hair, and before we drove home he would watch lazily as I undid the plaits to brush it into waves. It is now impossible to fix a line across that summer marking anywhere I could have changed what started.

It was the hottest summer I could remember. Even in the village shops nobody talked about the weather any more. The ice-cream shop showed off their new soft ice cream machine by giving free chocolate flake bars with each one. Paul bought me one he ate himself as he queued up for another so I could have the flake not dipped in ice cream. I disliked my flavours mixed up.

"Does this mean you'll turn into the flake girl melting in a field of poppies?" he grinned, referring to the television advert.

"No it means we melt on the wall outside to eat before these both melt in my hands!" I returned. "Anyway the flake girl's hair is far too short." I tossed mine back and saw him start to laugh,

"You've dipped it in the ice-cream."

"Can't you just hold these while I get this off my hair?" I snap.

He looks thoughtfully at me as he twists off the lemonade cap then pours the bottle over my head. He is still laughing when we reach the tennis court, I am still sulking.

"For goodness sake, Grace, snap out of it. There's nobody else here and nothing to see."

"It's sticky," I complain.

"It's raining," he answers. I look at him stupidly as if he's joking, then I hear the thunder, lift my head and feel the rain fall on my face. The uneven tennis court is swimming in minutes, puddles spreading into lakes.

"The summer house? " he suggests wryly.

"When I've finished rinsing my hair!" I laugh.

He smiles indulgently and picks up the bag and racquets. I follow on, my hair like seaweed but clean. The summerhouse is dark and smells faintly musty together with a note of cedar that by now I recognise as Paul's aftershave. I can't see him until I reach the bench along the back. He has poured the rest of the lemonade into glasses and is stretched out upon the wood. He looks completely comfortable. He gets up and passes me a glass, our arms brushing as I take it. His is warm.

"Hot chocolate might be better - you're freezing. Want my sweater?"

He becomes a shadow. As I shake my head I realise he can't see me. He must be trying to find the bag. When he gives it to me I quickly put it on and sink into it, pulling out my hair to dry. My eyes adjusting to the dark I see him pat the bench and sit beside him.

"Sorry if it smells smoky. Sorry about the lemonade too. Childish. Most people grow out of pranks in boarding school. In my case not. They passed the time."

"What did you do?" I asked, trying to sound bored.

"Anything to embarrass my father. They got worse until he had to deal with it. Skipping classes, getting drunk, playing poker, disappearing without permission, taking a dog into the dormitory..."

The last demanded interruption "Why?"

"I like dogs. It liked school food, I didn't. It liked me, I preferred its company to most of the alternatives." His face is poker straight.

"How do you hide a dog?"

"The maids liked me. One of them would let the grapevine know if a teacher was about to come anywhere near the dorm and one took Joker to the kitchen. If Joker hadn't found his way to class..."

"Weren't you scared of what they'd do to punish you?"

"Expel me? Father had to beg them not to. I didn't give a damn. I missed the dog though."

"What happened to it?"

"The school had a young doctor. Knew someone just finishing his training. Moving to Norfolk. He took Joker. I could go visit him there."

"Robert's dad?!"

"Yes." He grinned at me.

"What's funny?" I demanded.

"I'm trying to imagine sending you to boarding school. Sleeping in a dormitory, eating in a dining hall. And hockey would be a blood sport!"

"Nobody sends me anywhere. What's hockey?"

"A good question. Like football for girls but the ball is small and you pass it with a stick. Or in your case pass on hockey and get lost in the gardens looking at the clouds!"

"Till you disturbed me," I reminded him. I couldn't help wondering how long he'd watched me for that day before I saw his shadow.

"And blood sport?" I ask.

"Almost invariably the match ends with someone being clouted by a stick. Usually with no intention of hitting the ball!" he says drily. I laugh. He reaches out and touches my hair.

"Your hair's almost dry. It's so warm in here."

"It's too long. And messy. The brush is in the car."

"No it's not. It's in the bag with the lemonade. You were trying to brush the ice cream out. May I?"

At first I'm not sure what he's asking. Then it seems silly to say no. I nod. He gets the brush and sits behind me, separating the hair into sections then moving each to one side as he brushes, till I don't want him to stop. There's a faint drum of rain upon the roof still, I have no idea what time it is, why he isn't talking, why any word I try to say gets stuck. He stops and lifts my hair to let it fall again. When he says nothing silence seems too deep.

"Did the dog like the beach?" I ask. My voice is wrong, like words won't join up.

"Do you know the strange thing, Grace? I loved that dog but I never did go to see him. It would have hurt too much to see him run to someone else."

It was the end of June and school was over, summer stretched ahead. Chris would soon be home. The beach was lost beneath the swarm of tourists dressed so bright they stung your eyes. They wrestled with deckchairs, sat and couldn't settle, flying to and fro between the shops, the cafes, and the toy arcade, replaced by villagers escaping those same places when they could, aware the sunshine would not last. We stocked up on lemonade and cigarettes and then escaped. The tennis court muffled distant shouts and laughter. By now I was more opponent than pupil. He seemed pleased with me and how keen I was to learn. His smiles felt like points. My serves were strong, my volleys well-placed and fast. Today the concentration on his face was new. I was three points away from winning the match. He was firing shots hard and low across the net, which I raced to reach and slam back. It felt like it was meant to be my day, my win. I hit a ball I would have missed a week before, sent flying in a long arrow shaped backhand.

It cut the line, no bounce at all, dead on the ground a second before he could reach it. The next point he won, the rally left me empty, felt more fight than play, to leave me nothing if I had to fight again. My ace was more desperation than design. I stood at match point feeling I was on a cliff and served not looking down. The shot was so weak it took him by surprise, he hit too hard and sent it out. The end has somehow sharpened the memory of everything which came before to images now branded in my mind. In slow motion I feel my body pushing through the warm, heavy air, I smell the dry scorched grass, the scent of hot concrete mixed with roses, hear me shouting 'out' as his shot flies too far, delighting in the win, the sun, the joy of knowing fourteen will soon be fifteen. My face and hair are wet, I taste the salt upon my lips and feel them stinging where the sun had burned them. I run to him expecting him to laugh or joke as usual; he doesn't smile or say a word. It feels as if I have done something wrong but since this makes no sense I go into the summerhouse and leave the thought outside. It feels like going underwater, dark and cool, the sound cut off. I walk slowly to the bench, too tired to even want the lemonade. I hear him come in, hear the sound of pouring, see him come towards me with a glass and wonder vaguely why there's only one. Relieved to see him smile I reach for it, confused when he brings the glass up to my mouth. He presses the cold glass to my lips, the rim parting them, so they seem to open automatically, letting me drink. It feels odd, stupidly childish, but mixed with a new feeling I only half sense. He takes the glass away and I wait for him to refill it. Instead he fills the gap between us and brings his lips to mine. I pull away, he pulls my hair to pull me back, keeps the pull to hold me while he kisses me. I hold my breath. I have no idea what I did to make this happen, how to stop it happening or what will happen next. My legs refuse to move. His lips move softly over mine then firmly, fast then slow. My feelings swirl: I have no names for them, he fills me with them, empties me. I shut my eyes to find some part of me that feels like me and instantly his lips are hard on mine, the pressure forcing mine open, letting him go deep inside. He whispers into my mouth,

"I always win, princess."

We drove back home as if it never happened. He asked if I was hungry, said how well I'd played. The days turned over, normal words and pictures blotting out those flashing in my mind. I looked at him, he smiled, the stranger's smile was gone. He was my stepfather, kind, indulgent, teasing, nothing more. It was easy to believe it never happened, or when reason disagreed decide he had not wanted it to happen. I traced his lips and felt them tracing mine. Retraced it had the feeling of a dream. I could have let it be if memory could be flat and smooth. But memory painted taste, and texture, using watercolours one day, oil the next. The oil was shame. The kiss had painted whole new colours. Some had frightened me, some had painted feelings I had never felt, like burning in ice cream. It had tasted wrong, but mixed with shame was something with no name. I did not realise the painting had been his design; the artist chose his subject well.

One night I woke to glimpse a shadow moving in the room. I let my eyes adapt to darkness, willing every muscle silent. Eyes used to swimming underwater swam in and out the shapes and shadows that belonged there, finding one did not. Near the door a mosaic of greys became a figure, melted as soon as it was real. I woke up late and pulled on clothes for breakfast, automatically reached to open the door. It was ajar. I always shut the door. Chris always teased me for checking it another time each birthday, used to say he hoped the world grew safer faster than I grew. That night I checked the handle fourteen times, feeling silly as I placed the paper on the floor. We used to use the trick to find out if our mother had been in our room. I almost heard Chris laugh. Just like the sea was almost blue.

Eventually I fell asleep. In the morning, paper pinned me to the bed, afraid to look. I inched towards the door and picked it up. The paper was slightly dirty, creased. I didn't even see the stairs. The tiles in the kitchen cracked beneath my feet. I reached the chair, relieved to feel it holding me. My smile was camouflage. He smiled at me across the table. His face was smooth, his black eyes pebbles polished by the sea.

The nights belonged to him, the darkness games. The echo of cigarette smoke when I woke, the dampness of my pillow, hair sticking when I tried to move my head, my hairbrush on the floor, a lemonade cap in the sink. The tricks a grown up child plays. One morning I sat to brush my hair and in the mirror saw a face above my own, the features drawn in lipstick. I asked my mother if I could have a lock put on my door, pretending I was having nightmares. She told me I was being childish, to try warm milk instead. That night I went to bed and found a mug of cocoa on the bedside table, marshmallows melting on the top. It didn't stop the nightmare coming, being real. The night the nightmare came the games stopped.

Robert

July–August, 1974

Two weeks later Chris came home. The letters he had never written I could rub out. The trains he always missed I could let go. I couldn't tell him Paul had kissed me. I only wanted things to be the same. Instead I listened as he talked of school and Norwich, telling me and never needing words how much he missed it, telling me without them how little he missed me. Hurt had prodded at a distance, close to him it stabbed. We had always had our own telepathy, I could smile and he would know the smile was wrong. It seemed he'd lost the signal. When we argued our apology was food. We left chocolate under the bedclothes, we would throw a bag of crisps, if caught it meant 'are we friends?' if dropped we knew to wait. Now I threw a bag to hit him, stung to realise the bag was all he caught, my fury soared across his head. He ate the crisps and waited for the next bag. Since Paul had bought the colour television all of us were black and white to Chris. He didn't notice mother's painted smile, or catch me blush when I heard the voice on the phone. I left a bowl beside him, full of cheese and onion crisps he hated, wishing we had a dog so I could use that bowl instead. Then I brushed my hair and left.

    The cafe is crammed with tourists talking over children they forgot to teach to queue. They wear expensive uniforms that match the colours of the ice cream, swirls and stripes that match the candy on the shelves. They jostle with the local teenagers wearing sports clothes brighter than the lights in the arcade. I cannot see him then someone scoops me off my feet and swings me round.

"Robert! People are looking!"

"Let them." He puts me down, not letting me go. I look at him and cannot match the body to the face.

"When did you turn into a bear?"

"It's been six months, Grace." The words are light, yet make me look into his eyes and wish that I could rub the darkness out.

"I wish I could tell you why. Can we start again?"

"I don't need to know. Or want to start again."

"You asked me here to tell me that?"

"No, to find out if you really cared."

"And?"

"I still don't know. You have all summer to convince me."

We join the queue. I grab the coffees, Robert follows with the hotdogs, three for him and one for me. He smothers his with ketchup. The tourists have taken all the tables.

"Why must they ask their children to eat?" I whisper as Robert smiles at a group about to leave.

"I can't wait till you have children." He grins as we sit down.

"I won't say shall we try it, darling? or would you like to, sweetheart?"

"Eat, Grace."

"Why didn't you come back with Chris?" He seems to play words over in his head as if this must come out right.

"I could lie, say something you'd believe, like dad had things to do in Norwich. I used to be good at it."

"I can't imagine that."

"I'll tell you sometime. I hate lies now."

"I hadn't seen Dad for two months. School wouldn't let us go home. Not in exam term. I wanted things simple, just him and me. That's one part but it was more. Chris changes things. You make a joke and then you wait as if you must have his permission first to laugh. Or leave a gap and he will fill it, or leave a space and know he'll puncture it. He's good fun Grace, he's hard work too."

"I thought you two were friends."

"Because of you. At times because of you we're not."

He looks at my abandoned hotdog.

"Shall we go home? Dad has been reminded what a fridge is for. I dare say we'll find something else that you'll forget to eat."

He stands up, moves too fast. The other Robert would have waited for me first. The easy way he says go home conjures up a hundred days like this, yet going feels like being given something back that I don't deserve. I trace his figure through the scrum, shot down by half of the girls left behind. Outside, the cloudless blue sky could have fallen out of the TV screen. Our footsteps tap then melt away. He slows his pace to mine the way Chris never does. The silence fills with sounds I never hear alone, the songs of bees and hidden birds my thoughts chase off. We reach the house before it comes towards me.

"Dad's out." The drive is empty. Tourists steal the doctor's summer. Raspberries into poison, bluebottles into wasps.

Relieved I watch him search his pockets, glad to find that one thing hasn't changed: the key has jumped all by itself.

He quietly opens the door as if the house is sleeping. In the hall the air is cool. We climb the stairs to find the door has been left closed, the living room is baking hot. We are flies shut in a jam-jar, the window pouring sun like syrup.

"Shall we sit on the balcony, sweetheart?" He grins.

"Please!" I gasp.

The chair still feels like mine. The iron swirled into roses, painted green, the cushions patterned with leaves. The table fits the space no more, the balcony is as long as Robert, only leaning out as far as me. The view is endless. You do not look, you soar; you do not turn around, you tear yourself away. I feel it lure me, pull me up to claim me back. I half hear Robert say he'll fetch us drinks and jump when he returns with the tray. I sit, he passes me a glass.

"Taste it."

Whatever it is it looks suspicious, it froths like beer, the colour of blood oranges when they are cut. I sip expecting sour and tasting sweet.

"Do you like it?"

"I can't decide. What is it?"

"Dad bought a Sodastream. It uses water, mixes in the syrup, shooting it with bubbles. It keeps on making drinks until you run out of syrup."

"We'd best get Chris one then."

His eyes swoop down, the sigh I hushed he caught.

"What's wrong, Grace?"

"I haven't got a brother just a boarder. He's like a tourist, Robert. Everything here too dull, too small. He never leaves the television. We have to take him food and drinks. Like an animal. When he looks at me I feel small and dull as well, he looks like someone I don't know. I swear if I could take the television back I would, if it brought him back." The feeling of betrayal I started with has gone. I tell him about the crisps, the imaginary dog bowl.

"There's no television at school. I guess it's just a new toy to a six-foot kid. Boarding school is kind of like a cage. You don't know what to do when you're let out. He'll get bored with it, Grace. Cartoon friends are easier than school friends. They smile all the time, they don't make you feel small."

"Chris is good at making friends."

"Making isn't keeping." He looks uncomfortable, as if my guilt has passed to him.

"He's my brother. Tell me what you meant."

"If I say something, will you think before you throw the crisps?"

I can't help smiling.

"If you take away the screen he's nowhere near as confident as he appears. He thinks he is because when he was growing up you made him the centre of your world, he knew you needed him, there was nothing he couldn't put right and nothing he could do wrong. That's a good feeling, Grace, hard to lose. I never had it so I'm guessing."

"Why not?"

"Why I never felt it?"

I nod.

"Do you remember when you mother wouldn't let Chris go to boarding school? When I was angry you wouldn't ask him not to go?"

"Should I have told him? I did what was best for him, she didn't."

"I used to fight with dad when I came home. I thought it was my way to punish him for sending me away. I really wanted someone to love me so much they couldn't let me go. You did the right thing, so did dad. Doesn't mean I knew that then. Chris will settle down. He has nobody to draw a line for him, nobody to say he's crossed it. A stepfather can't step in."

"Huh! Paul thinks it's funny, says I'm to stop feeding him, that animals change their behaviour when they're hungry," I fume.

"It's funny if you let it be, Grace." The echo rubs at me. I know it is one, cannot trace it. Somehow soothed, I smile. I reach to kiss him on the cheek.

"What was that for?" But he looks pleased.

"For being wise. When do I get to be wise?"

"It's overrated," he grinned. "Is that what you want for your birthday?"

"Would you get it for me?"

"I'll think of something better. Is it to be a family only day?"

"So far it's just a day."

"Have you still got the bicycle?"

"I think so. Why?"

"Just find the bike. I'll do the rest."

I paused before we said goodbye to see if he would kiss me. He said goodbye.

I found the bicycles underneath a sheet in the shed. I wondered who had covered them. Chris had been over the moon about the Chopper at the time but Chris's toys lost their shine more quickly than the kind you won in the arcade. If Paul's name had not been stamped all over the bike I would have treasured it. I would have to find my balance quickly, Robert had no idea I'd never even sat on it and now the thought of riding it within a week felt more impossible than flying.

"Chris is looking for you," Paul's voice said.

I pulled the sheet back.

"Why? Has he worked out the TV people aren't real?"

"Where were you?" He smiles and I get the feeling he has guessed.

"With Robert. Don't worry. I fed the dog first."

Chris laughed the next morning when I asked him to teach me how to ride the bike.

"It's not a horse, Grace. You sit on it and pedal."

After two hours of getting nowhere and being laughed at I sacked the teacher, telling him I'd sooner fall all by myself than pratfall for his entertainment. I went indoors to get a drink and smooth my pride. I was still trying to think how I'd explain to them I didn't want a family birthday, knowing it was just a day while Paul was planning it, knowing Chris was just pretending to forget. I knew Paul liked surprises, never having had them as a child. His birthday was Guy Fawkes Day, a boarding school birthday, bonfires and fireworks he always had to share while teachers told him all of it was just for him. He'd told me making it sound funny. Funny didn't turn your voice to sandpaper.

My mother went out the kitchen when I went in. Paul smiled as if to soften it.

"Still polishing the road, Goldilocks?"

"Learning to fall gracefully," I corrected.

I drank the lemonade, too bruised inside to go back out.

The next morning after breakfast Chris took out his bicycle. Thinking he was going to try to teach by showing me instead of telling, I watched him sailing down the street and fetched my own. I stood upon the pavement waiting till he turned back. I gave him fifteen minutes needing only five to realise he had just been showing off, the ten to kill the hope he'd prove me wrong. I looked down at the bike and wished that I could follow him. Not to catch him up, to knock him down.

He came back around lunchtime. Hidden beneath the jaunty walk and casual grin I saw the Chris who'd performed heart surgery on my teddy bear, who'd sacrificed my favourite doll to the sea-god, the Chris who'd do something wrong and multiply the wrong by hiding it and letting you find out. I'd learned to skip the first step.

"Tell me what you've done. It's written all over you."

"Having lunch with Robert?" He lifts an eyebrow. "We ate sandwiches and talked about nothing. He sends his love."

"He wouldn't do that."

"He's not in love? You're slipping, Grace. He's usually eating out of your hand by now."

"You're the one with the bowl, Chris. You know what? I'll ask him."

I am halfway out of the door when truth smacks me in the face. When I go back I look at him and realise this isn't hurting anymore.

"The birthday party you're pretending you've forgotten?"

He looks up and sees I know.

"Don't plan on being there," I throw.

I run the mile to Robert's house. His father opens the door and seems to read the urgency, sending me straight up. I know where he will be. Just not what I will feel. I see him standing looking at the view and want him to turn round to wrap me in his arms.

He says he knew about the bike before Chris told him.

"I knew when you never phoned me in the morning. You always want to meet for breakfast when I'm home or come over here and plan the day out. I remembered I had never seen you on the bicycle, only ever Chris. I wanted you to tell me. Not to rub it in, to rub it out. Because it doesn't matter. You ride a bike when you are ready to."

"So what did you two talk about over lunch?"

He looks confused. "What lunch? I knew exactly what he came for and it wasn't lunch. Chris never just pops in, he schedules you. He asked if he could try the Sodastream, I showed him to the tap. I told him if I had a sister I'd be the one protecting her not hurting her. For some reason, after that he left."

He looks at me and grins when I do. We laugh until it hurts, until we have to stop looking at each other to make it stop. We go indoors to make some lunch. His father has tactfully vanished. Like the wizard Robert used to paint in words that made me jealous.

"I can't imagine you afraid of falling off a bike, though. I didn't think there was anything that scared you. Not dark, not spiders, nothing other girls are scared of."

I wish that could be true. That I could go back in time till only simple things could scare me. Not pictures in my head I can't get out. Not coming home afraid of what I'll find. There are no words that paint those.

"It wasn't the falling off, it was the laughing. Why do people have to watch you fall so they can laugh? As if they grow the more you shrink."

He steers me to the sofa, sitting down and putting me upon his lap, his arms around me so I can't fall off. It feels so safe I want to lean into his shirt and cry.

"It's human nature. Think about it. We invented clowns so they could fall and keep on falling to keep us laughing. So we can go home believing nobody got hurt. The adults laugh, the children cry. The children know that falling ought to hurt. The clown becomes a monster for them when he keeps on smiling. Chris didn't want to hurt you, he wanted to feel bigger."

I want to keep him talking so he'll keep on holding me.

"There is one thing that scares me that you don't know." To think the word is to feel it, to lift my hand to smooth my hair.

"You don't have to tell me."

"I want to. I'm terrified of worms."

His arms move, I wobble slightly, then he tightens them.

"I know. I knew you'd believe I'd dropped it in your hair." His voice is scared. I want to move but can't trust my legs to stand. I stare at him. The eyes are just the same if I adjust the size.

"That was you?" I picture it, the bush, their faces willing me to cry, the worm dangling. The fury carved on Chris's face.

"For a while I was. I grew out of him, remembered you each time I saw you in the street. I'd cross the road to leave him there. By the time I could have told you it mattered too much to be your friend. Dad didn't want me to go to boarding school. He wanted me to grow up here. I was bigger on the outside than the inside, too different to fit. I was slow and clumsy, stupid too. They hurt me. You don't hurt them, you pick someone who won't fight back. That day it was you."

"Why did Chris never tell me?"

"Because it hurt you if he did. I understand feeling different. When I started school I had a mother I'd brought back to life. They soon found out the truth. It took me longer to learn not to lie. Chris has good sides. It's easier to see the cartoon than the person. Especially when you're used to coming second whenever he's around. He gives you second chances, tries to see the best. Dad told me boarding school was a second chance. They would see me all the time, who they saw was up to me." He finds my eyes. "Who do you see, Grace?"

"Still the worm," I smile.

I told him I would try to halve my birthday, spend the day with them, leave the evening ours. I told them over dinner, knowing neither Paul nor Chris was pleased when the pudding spoons went down.

"What we had planned would take all day." Paul said. Chris nodded.

"At fifteen don't I get a say in planning? You're not being fair. You're blowing out the candles seeing half a cake. Making it vanilla knowing I want chocolate." They look as if I'm talking nonsense.

My mother stood up quietly. "Let Grace have what she wants. Or choose the cake and swallow her." She cleared the table as we sat in silence then left the room.

They took me to the carnival. Giant robots with eyes that flashed in time with pop music pulled me in, shot me to the sky then let me drop. The candy-floss was bittersweet. I was trying to forgive Chris, he was trying too hard. Forced laughter made me sad. I shut my eyes and longed for peace and quiet. At home I opened up my present, the biggest bar of chocolate I had ever seen.

I take time dressing, seeing Paul look at Chris when I walk downstairs in a mini skirt and fitted blouse, my hair left loose, a silver headband turning it to gold. I wear no makeup but gold lipstick. The black tights and the wedges were my mother's present, left upon the bed when I went to have a bath. Chris is silent as I get in the car with Paul.

"I'd tell you not to play with fire if I couldn't see the sparks already. Just make sure you only burn your fingers, Goldilocks," he warns.

"How will you know?"

"I'll know," he promises.

Robert's father kisses me on the cheek. He says he's under strict instructions to eat quickly and go. Robert is cooking dinner. In the kitchen it is chaos, the host is wearing jeans, a faded T shirt. He comes to greet me missing out the kiss. I open his father's card and burst out laughing. He has managed to find a card with a huge badge that says fifteen. Robert whispers something to him while I pin it on. He goes downstairs, I hear the car grumble off.

"I thought he was staying?"

"I forgot something. He's gone to help. You look fantastic. I should change."

"That means leaving me all by myself," I pout.

"Come and watch, then!" he dares.

I slip out to the balcony just so he can find me, heartbeat so loud it must betray me, turning away so when it does he'll have to say my name. I hear the door slide, his steps come through. His hand finds mine and pulls me in. The tablecloth is linen, the glasses crystal, the lemonade is pink. The plates are white as seashells, piled with fish and chips.

"Ketchup?" his father teases.

"I'm sorry Grace. I put the meat in the oven, forgot to turn it on."

"This is better." I say.

He says the present is from both of them. I open the envelope, sliding out two tickets. To Romeo and Juliet.

His father says he'll be home when we least expect it.

"What does that mean?" I ask when he has gone.

"To not do anything we can't hide quickly."

I sit down on the couch. He reads my glance and sits beside me, looking in my eyes. His finger finds my lips as if to check the way, the kiss that followed soft and slow, unsure. The second kiss was firmer, learning from the first. His arms enclosed me, his body warm, his lips a spell until my mouth was his.

"What happens next?" he says.

"You tell me you're convinced I care, then I convince you more."

Truth or Dare

September, 1974

Out of the blue Chris came home one Friday afternoon when he was meant to be in school. I had been sitting in a classroom all afternoon, bewildered by the point of doing geography when no one ever really left here, so in spite of how we'd said goodbye (or hadn't) I could understand. It seemed the school's Headmaster when he tracked Chris down had not. Neither had my stepfather when the Head reminded him that missing class and leaving school grounds without a reason justified expulsion unless the reason satisfied the Head. It seemed Chris had no reason, or none that would not compound the crime. He simply said he had to leave before he punched someone.

"Might I suggest you find a better reason, Chris," Paul glinted. "Or invent one. Beg your sister's help. She's usually good at that kind of skullduggery."

I couldn't decide if I was being flattered or insulted. I decided it didn't matter if I could make Chris beg.

The head had given Chris till Sunday to explain why he had run away, leaving me to teach the runaway to beg. It was like trying to train a lion to walk a tightrope. The lion had made himself a cage. Chris had fought a storm for me, chased the clouds for me, the one thing he would never do was beg.

"You don't really need to beg. Just say please," I smile.

"Please get lost, then."

"So you have a plan?"

"I don't need tricks. I'm the clever one, remember."

"No, Chris. You're just the one they pay to send to school." I wonder if I even know him. "I can't decide what I want the most, to get rid of you or see your face when they do."

I had to speak to Robert. He was bound to have some idea of what had happened. I asked his father to pass a message on to him to call me, well versed in the peculiar rules of communication at boarding school. Other boys might be able to pretend a girl caller was a sister; other boys had sisters.

"Mr Frost said my sister was charmingly persuasive if not convincing! I disown you, Grace." For once he sounded angry.

"You didn't phone," I accused.

"I didn't phone because you only want to get Chris off the hook. Make him talk." He hung up on me. Chris had not mastered talking yet. I suddenly thought of something Robert's father once told me. If they met him in the street the villagers would talk like trains, forgetting how to stop. In the surgery they would stop at every sentence, their words were platform signs in rain, their silences stretching into tunnels they got lost in. I had asked him how he made them talk, expecting him to say what Robert said with pride, how well his father had been trained. Instead he smiled and said at first he tried to get them out of the tunnels, getting stuck there too. He said no training taught you how to push a train, you had to learn to follow through the tunnels, to shunt them to a different track. You let the train unload what it was carrying inside.

I realised Chris needed me to lead him out of his cage. When he started talking words would just fall out. I knocked upon the door and when he ignored it barged in anyway.

"It's too hot to fight. Let's go swimming," I lure him.

"On one condition," he smiles.

"Name it."

"We make it a race. If I win you have to find a way to help me get out of trouble."

"And if I win?"

"The probability is so low I hadn't thought that far ahead."

"If I win you have to tell me why you ran away."

It was no fun swimming when the beach was crowded. We agreed to wait until evening when we'd have it to ourselves. It was six o'clock, Paul said he and mother were going out for dinner if she narrowed down the twenty dresses on the bed to one. Chris grinned, we were wearing beach clothes, swimsuits underneath.

"Robert telephoned, Grace. He said it was important," Paul said.

I smiled. "Then he'd best keep trying."

The beach was empty. A few men walking dogs as old in dog years as the grey haired men, some children flying kites the falling sun turns into jewels. The sand is ruffled, the sandcastles abandoned. I look at Chris, not wondering why he ran away from school but how he ever tore himself from here. It seems that every time he goes a piece of him does not come back. Whatever roots me so deeply to this strip of sand is tumbleweed for him.

This time I will not let him win. I must be faster now; he swims in a tub of water, my pool is the sea. Undressing quickly, I find a stone to pin my clothes down and wait for him to pin his next to mine. Instead he finds his own stone. I watch him as he walks towards me, hurt to think of how he used to run. The stone is now a rock his steps push deep inside my throat. Each step is proof how well he grew without me. It would take a sister to notice all the changes in him: the longer legs, the firmer pillow of his chest, the spreading back and shoulders, tapering to his waist, the muscles dancing as he moves, the head held high as if to be is to belong. Her eyes explore each place she used to know. Yet take away the sister and it feels like falling into sand and hitting stone. All of him is hard where I am soft. I want a spell to change him back to when we used to fit like twins, yet long to trace each change in him by touch. I hear him laugh, relieved my face no longer tells him all my thoughts.

"Since when did you wear bikinis?"

"Since when did you notice how I dress?"

"I'm not sure that counts as dressing."

"The wind agrees. Can we please get in the water?"

We have a point we always race from. The floor is sand for thirty strokes then falls away so suddenly the water turns cold and if you dive below you see the cliff you swam across. Keep swimming out past the reefs, you reach a warning flag. From there we race to push our bodies back to shore, the winner is the first to stand. We always swim out friends and swim in foes. Today we are contestants, silence colder than the water, stinging more than salt. I stop beside the flag and he is waiting, meaning he will get to shout go. I stare ahead but not too far, to focus on the shore will slow you down. I hear him yell go and pour the hurt into the water, sensing he is close but not even glancing to see how close he is.

I slice underwater, feel the current try to grab me, cut myself free. When I break the surface I swim with all my breath. I can see the grey sand, can hear his gasps behind me, can tell he's running out of strength. I keep on swimming till my belly rubs the sand. Triumphantly I try to stand and slip. I have lost my line and landed on a shallow slope. I try again and fall. I hear him laugh and know his legs will push him up no matter what and start to cry. I read the indecision on his face, the brother wants to comfort me, the racer wants to win. He passes me and stands and in that moment all I feel is hate. I never knew that you could lose so much so fast.

"Grace?"

I pull my dress on, knowing if I meet his eyes I am naked.

"Just go home, Chris. Wherever that means now."

"I'm not leaving you here."

"Why not? You already have. You know what really hurts? I would have helped you, win or lose."

The car is not outside. I open the door relieved I need not pretend and slip upstairs longing to hide in sleep. By breakfast time only we are up. Chris is in the garden. Taking tea out I sit the tray upon the table, feel the sun spill through the apple tree above. I still remember father planting it, a twiggy sapling that he staked into the ground. The moment he had finished it had rained. We went indoors and though the rivers running down the glass it looked forlorn. My father had thrown us each an apple from the bowl and smiled. "It only needs the stake for now. It needs a prop until the roots are strong. Leave the stake in and it will always need one. Take it out when you think it's strong enough and hope you are not wrong. Still you have to dare and watch it bending in the wind. It is the same as you, it needs rain as much as sun."

I pour Chris tea. I can be a prop, will not be a stake.

"You have to tell me what made you come home. The truth is what you tell him, whether or not it may get you thrown out."

"I can't."

"Yes you can."

"You won't understand." I hear the boy.

"I don't understand now. So explain."

"I wanted to punch Robert."

"For what?"

"It began with truth or dare. Robert took truth. Then when he heard the question asked for a different one. The others would have let him off. I said that was cheating."

"What was the question?" He drops his eyes. "You asked for it, Chris. I'm guessing he told you. Robert never lies."

"Who was the first girl he ever kissed. I'm guessing you will know."

"I guessed."

"That wasn't all he said. He said you were the only girl he would ever want to kiss. Do you feel the same Grace?"

"I'm not playing truth or dare. I don't have to answer that. I will, though. I don't have a clue. I wish I could be as sure about things as he is. Not because I want to feel the same, because it would be nice to have something that I felt that sure about or something that nobody could take away.

Your headmaster is how old?" I ask.

"Acts a hundred. Maybe thirty-five? He has two daughters."

I smile. "Then you are home and dry."

I listened to Paul telephone the headmaster. Saying Chris was due more praise than punishment. He said it was a matter of family honour, one the Head would surely understand. The Head said he would expect Chris back on the morning train.

I swim beyond the flag, careful of the currents. Here they writhe below the calmest sea, the bluest grey. I swim back in and rest upon the sand and watch the clouds dissolve to skeins of burnt orange, shut my eyes and feel the last licks of the sun become the fingers of the breeze. Tomorrow morning he will leave and all we've done is hurt each other more. If I lie still enough it feels like blending with the sand. I must have dozed for suddenly the sun has gone and taken back the warmth of the day. The breeze is autumn's. Sitting up, I rub the sand off and hug my arms around my knees to watch the darkness settle, torn between the urge to find him and knowing finding will not keep. I forget his eyes are sharper in the dark than mine. I shiver when I see him, too cold to talk, my dress too thin, my hair still wet. He tuts then taking off his jacket bends over putting it on me instead and pulling up the zip. His fingers brush my neck and when I shiver this time it can't be from the cold, my heart is beating much too fast. I smell the leather then the smell melts back to him. I'd thought I had run out of things to miss and now he's here I know there are too many, know there always will be more. He combs my hair with his fingers, plaiting it, pushing it deep inside the jacket.

"You'll ruin the leather."

"Don't care. It looks better on you anyway. Brothers aren't supposed to notice."

"Notice what?"

"Forget I ever told you this when I go back to school. The way you sit completely still when you try to hide from me. The way you dovetail to me when I plait your hair, the way I want to keep on plaiting when you do. The rush I feel when I find you in the dark. The shape of you that changes every time I see you. It's pitch black and still I see it. I see it every time I shut my eyes. I open them and see my sister. Then I think of Robert kissing you and want it to be me."

"I want it to be you. Forget I'm me."

"I can't. Once I start forgetting I won't know how to stop. Will you stop me?"

I was an expert at forgetting then. I reached for him to stop him talking, stop him thinking, stop him doing anything but kiss me, kissing me till I feel him pull the zip down, feel his hands move in the leather, feel them turn my dress to paper, discovering that skin decides by touch not name who is let in, everywhere he touches leads to somewhere else that comes alive, no borders tell me where to stop but one. Tomorrow.

I pull away. He tries to pull me back. "No. I can forget for tonight. Tomorrow I'll be me and you will leave. Let me go first. Just once." I put the jacket round his shoulders, smile.

"Stay," he begs.

"If I say that to you tomorrow, will it make a difference?" I let the silence speak.

Are You Ready?

Autumn 1974

The end of September was more moody than I was, blue skies pulled apart by winds and rain. I was trying to get used to Chris and Robert being gone again. I was happy half the time and half the time too confused to know. I counted down the days at school until the weekends. I had left it too late to make real friends. I knew that friendship was a language, school a foreign country, I had learned enough words to cross the border, hang around the outskirts, smile my way in. Certain words were passwords, words like boyfriend. It didn't matter if they'd never seen him, never met him, he could be a story, still it told. At school a boyfriend didn't even have to be a friend. He was someone you could say had asked you to the disco, everyone knew it was for show, that he would give his friends your name and they would nod or wish that they had asked you first. It never mattered when you got there, girls danced with girls and boys expected that. They hung in edges of the room and watched and laughed. The only dance boys danced would be the last, except they never really danced. They moved like robots, clumsy with the need to pinch and grab. If you stopped them touching you they called you names you didn't understand. If you let them you were whispers in the playground, echoes from the toilets, scribbles on the walls. I was happy being a spectator. A boyfriend locked in boarding school was perfect. He was a reason not to bother with the disco, only curiosity had got me there at all, I had described it all to Robert at the weekend, wishing curiosity didn't kill so slowly, didn't have to stop at kisses. When Robert kissed me I could feel him holding back, the doctor's son knew all the reasons why. By Sunday reason was starting to get lost. The weekends were only long enough to confuse it, only frequent enough to change holding back to hold. On Sunday he would hold me tightly, melting through my clothes on empty platforms, leaving me with hurried goodbyes. Those Sunday evenings I was moody, disappearing after dinner to my room to vanish in a coat of paint. On weekdays evenings were abstracts, meals were still-lifes. As painting blotted out the weekends too the colours turned from blue to black. My mother had never knocked on my door again, we were polite as strangers. Paul was the only person who felt real. No matter how moody I was he always said goodnight when I could not make good from black. One night I went upstairs and realised the night had been left black. I lay and read a book, too tired to bring the characters to life, too upset Robert had not phoned to fall asleep. I went downstairs, deciding this deserved hot chocolate, and stood beside the window as the milk warmed, rehearsing what I'd say when Robert deigned to phone.

"Shouldn't you be sleeping, Grace?" I jumped and turned surprised to see him in a jacket, bristled at Grace not Goldilocks.

"I can't sleep. Where were you?"

He smiled. "You'll make a good wife one day. Just the right amount of concern, not too much accusation. I went for a drive that's all. Not an option moody teenagers have ... What's boiling over on the stove?"

I rushed to rescue it, glaring at him for just standing watching.

"It was to be hot chocolate. You took my mind off it." I fetched a cloth.

"Your mind should be asleep. Leave the mess till morning."

The smell of burnt milk, the darkened kitchen, caught inside me, blurring black to blue.

"Grace? Are you crying?" He bent down to meet my eyes.

I'd ask you what was wrong but at fifteen nothing's right. Will a cuddle do?"

He throws the cloth into the sink and pulls me to him, strokes my hair.

I noticed that after dinner Paul would drive off and I was usually in bed by the time I heard him come upstairs. I was not conscious of listening for him although I never fell asleep until he got home. One evening I watched him after dinner, saw him leave without his jacket. Grabbing it from the hook I followed him. He was already in the car, he rolled the window down and smiled.

"Coming, Goldilocks?"

I nodded, jumping in. Paul never ever locked the car. He had said once he was hoping someone stole it. It had not sounded like a joke. He leaned across to do my seatbelt up.

"Clunk click, princess." I smiled. The television adverts had made no impression on Sea Palling. As if the people secretly agreed this was as close to living dangerously as they would get.

Driving with Paul was as close to flying as it came. My mother sat with her eyes shut. The villagers ran for the pavement on sight. Stop signs were suggestions, speed signs invitations. The traffic lights were lollipops, the highway code graffiti. Luckily the roads were mostly empty, letting him swap lanes at need. His pet hate was single track roads, passing places ending up showdowns. Level crossings were Russian roulette.

At first I floated in the silence, occasionally glancing up at him, caught by notes of sandalwood and leather playing in the air. Paul always bought the same cologne, it came all the way from Norwich, stayed when he left a room. His white shirt was linen, short-sleeved. I watched his hands as he was driving, moving on the wheel. I started to feel cross. We seemed in the middle of nowhere, silence had tarnished. Even the trees were different shapes, the fields dotted with sheep. I was running out of patience, tempted to ask why he'd asked me at all.

"Where are we going?"

"You mean 'Are we there yet?' You followed me, Princess."

"You're usually more fun."

"Then try amusing me," he drawls.

Completely lost for words I turn to glare at the window, suddenly breaking into giggles, catching it he starts to laugh. He suddenly pulls over, braking hard to stop before we run into a field. I sit back in relief, then watch him reach for me and know exactly what he means to do. He finds out where I'm ticklish, tickling till I'm breathless. Ruthlessly the hands come back and turn me to jelly till I beg for him to stop.

"I think I heard beg somewhere? I'm not sure..."

He grins and in the twilight suddenly reminds me of Robert's wolf. I laugh.

"You made me think of something Robert said. You know he used to nickname you The Wolf?"

"No, but I can guess why. What did he tell you?"

"Something along the lines that you ate blondes for breakfast. And liked fast cars."

"Lucky Robert doesn't know you're here, then. Most of them were supper. Blonde or not, back then they were like candy-floss, too sweet and sticky to rub off. All boys talk about at boarding school is girls. When the girls are real you don't know what to say. The candy-floss girls don't want talk. The trouble is they don't want kisses either. The easier they were to catch the less they justified the chase. You hunt and still feel empty when you catch them so you keep on hunting. I learned to be content with porridge. I'm still stuck on fast cars though."

He proves it as we drive back. If you drive in the middle of the road it's harder to talk. I was too busy wondering if Chris and Robert would get stuck on candy-floss girls to tell him left was right.

Sunday it rained all afternoon. I ran out of things to do to stop me looking for him. Sunday was the one day mother bothered if we didn't dress for dinner. I decided to wear a blouse I liked because the buttons looked like butterflies, with a lavender blue skirt. Paul's idea of dressing for dinner was wearing a tie. My mother soon ran out of small talk. Neither of us doing more than silently rearranging what was on our plates, she ate her own and went upstairs. Leaving the room he glanced at me then at the window. Two minutes later I was waiting in the car. The rain had washed the sky to match my skirt. I smiled when Paul got in and drove away and pulled his tie off as we left the village, undoing the top two buttons of his shirt with one hand as the other held the wheel. I knew my heartbeat was too fast to blame his driving. Rain began to scatter on the windscreen, poured to leave no clues of where he stopped. By the time his cigarette was finished, it was getting dark and damp air filled the car. We quickly rolled the windows up. He told me jokes I only half understood, the other half too spellbound by his laugh to care. The jokes ran out. He wanted to smoke again. I wanted my hair to smell like mine.

"What does your hair smell like then?"

"Either coconut or chocolate." I laughed. I was trying two bottles of shampoo, not sure which I preferred.

I saw him move expecting him to smell my hair. Instead he combed his fingers through it, lifting it to sweep it from my back to drop around my shoulders, moving it to cover up the butterflies upon my blouse. I could smell the chocolate every time he moved my hair, surprised it was taking him so long. I waited, half tempted to tell him. He didn't stop, I couldn't tell him. He was playing hide and seek with the butterflies, separating the waves of hair to strands until he found them, stroking it back to make them disappear. I closed my eyes, not sure if he knew that each time he hid the buttons his fingers brushed my breasts, the hiding turning into seeking, finding something deep inside me, tugging it until I swore the sigh to silence, pulling till I heard it. He stopped and smoothed my hair back.

"Look at me, Grace," he whispered.

He held my face between his hands and grinned.

"I think the chocolate melted."

From that day on he never asked if I would go with him, he never had to. It didn't matter if it rained. It could have snowed; he only had to touch my hair and I was blinded. I never knew what he would do from one night to the next. Some evenings as he drove he'd talk and joke and others anything I said fell into silence When he stopped he'd light a cigarette and make me wait until he finished it then turn me to face the window. He'd open the glove compartment, take out the tie he kept there, gather up my hair and make the tie a ribbon, pull it tight then slowly inch it down. Some nights he'd pull until my hair fell loose then start again but others he would stop halfway and I would hold my breath knowing what came next. He'd say that I was shivering, brush his fingers on my arm until the shivering was real then quickly free the tie and turn me round to stroke his finger on my lips until they burned. He touched me nowhere else. Before we left he'd do my seatbelt up and put his jacket round my shoulders. There were nights he'd drive for miles then reach across to tug my hair. I never knew if tugging meant he'd stop the car or turn and drive us back.

In the beginning he told me jokes, I told him anything inside my head. He listened making anything important. I could tell him how it hurt that Chris hardly ever phoned, how I missed him although it felt like he was missing when he did, because no matter what I said it didn't matter in his world. Paul never criticised Chris, just said boarding school was a different world, you had to change to fit or show the other boys you didn't care enough to try, and then they'd act as if the world revolved around you. He'd laugh and I'd feel safe, the darkness shut from place and time. As the days shortened we stayed out longer, buying time with lies that fell on top of lies like leaves. He never told me where he was going anymore, I never asked him when we'd get there, it would make no difference as long as it was somewhere else. Soon all he had to do was stroke my hair and anything was everything, my secrets his. No secret was so big the keeping mattered when he made me feel so safe.

His hands know their way now, the slightest touch can leave me helpless. When he tickles me I beg for him to stop, surprised when he lets me catch my breath. He smiles. I feel it charge the air.

"If I keep on doing that I'll end up kissing you. The first kiss might be accidental, the second gets more dangerous. I was never sure you liked it first time." He doesn't say it like a question. I answer anyway.

"I was scared. It was a year ago. A lot can happen in a year."

I mean Robert but guess from his silence that for him the year will always mean the baby, something that should have happened, might not happen this year or any other.

"A lot of kisses princess? And does Robert stop at kissing?"

"Yes, of course," I said.

"That sounds as if he's stopping when the lights are green!"

"He's stopping where he thinks he should," I say defensively.

"When I touch you all the lights say go. If you let me kiss you I promise to stop if they change to amber."

"I just have to say stop?"

"Cross my heart."

I nod. And then his lips are barely touching me. The rain streams down the windows, drumming on the roof. When I shut my eyes he moves his mouth on mine until there's nothing else to feel. He puts his finger on my lips and traces them till they open. Then he lets them close.

"I'm guessing this time you liked it." His smile is too certain.

"Does it stop hurting after the first few kisses?" He stops smiling.

"Hurting where?"

"I don't know. Inside me. Like something empty, achy." He smiles again.

"You're smiling when I'm telling you I'm hurting?" I attack.

"I'm smiling because you're telling me how much you liked it. Princess, they don't tell you this in fairy tales. In real life if Sleeping Beauty woke up to a kiss and no more she'd have gone back to sleep! Some kind of spell makes two people want to fit together so much it aches not to. If the spell doesn't break it will keep on hurting till their bodies fit. Like a lock and key. It feels empty when you don't have the key. It feels like being lost when you don't have the lock. But the two must fit precisely. When the fit is wrong it might feel good at first but it won't last. When they truly fit it feels like magic."

"What sets the spell?"

"Who knows? You can spend a lifetime waiting, think it's real and find it's not, discover it has happened when you least expect it. When the spell is set it's like you're half without them. Like nothing else matters."

"How do bodies fit?"

"Do you ever stop asking questions?"

"I will if you kiss me."

"I think you've had enough kissing for tonight."

There were too many nights. He knew too many ways to kiss. He drove in first gear until I begged for second, swapping gears so many times the aching turned to pain. He'd soothe with long slow kisses, speeding up until I gasped. Driving back we never called it home.

It was surprisingly easy to turn a car into a den. A den where I was younger he was older, numbers didn't count. A place without any rules except the one he never needed: I would do anything he told me. When I said that I was cold he said the back seat was warmer. After that I always moved there when he stopped. The darkness fell and took the world outside away. Occasionally headlamps flickered past the car to leave us shadows moving closer, shadows hearing other voices echo, quickly learning echoes vanished if they had no names. This was easy when they felt more imaginary all the time. My brother was a ten-minute phone call – when he remembered he had a sister. I hated him and missed him too. When he phoned he laughed about things that happened at school and when I went quiet he said you had to be there. Robert phoned and when he did he only seemed further away. He said he had important exams soon and if he had to study most of the weekend he couldn't see the point of coming home. If he couldn't see one I felt too unimportant to try to be one. I never told Paul any of this.

He never told me where he told my mother he was going, I never told him where I told her I was supposed to be. I never told him when we got back I lay in bed imagining him kissing her as he had me, or wondered where the kisses led to if he did. I didn't want him calling me a child. And most of all I never told him I was child enough to wonder if by blowing out a candle he had set a spell on me. It felt like being pulled inside a story-book. As if we had stepped back to meeting in the garden, skipping all the pages in-between, to end up here.

But where was here? No fairy story ended in a car. He was still the shadow he had been that day, I was still pretending I was someone else. We were driving with the lights off. I pushed it to the back of my mind and told myself that was what the boot was for.

Paul never really parked; he stopped when he was bored with driving. That night he drove along the coast road faster than the wind, indulging me by stopping near the pier and buying candy-floss. When he pulled over by the seafront I was too surprised by this to catch the wolf behind his smile.

"You're on your territory. Show me you're not candy-floss."

I saw the dare and took it, finding as he held my eyes that it felt like drowning, reaching for his mouth, discovering if I closed my eyes my mouth knew more than I did, moved instinctively with his until I let it open, telling him all my secrets, letting him go deeper reaching somewhere only wanting mattered, wanting him and only caring that he wanted me. I felt the feelings surge until the waves were much too high, the current pulled me under, feeling him take over, take his mouth away to pull me back, pull on my hair to pull me out. He held me close and searched my face.

"You do know what road this is? It only goes one way."

I can't find any answer. Only questions I'm too afraid to ask and only half the words to ask them with. He reads enough to let it go.

"I think we forgot something." He smiles and reaches for the candy-floss. He feeds it to me between kisses, laughing when I say I don't want any more. The question in my mouth is all I taste, comes out all by itself.

"Do you love me?" It is so small I wonder if he heard it, so big it fills the car.

Then arms grab me, pull me from the dark, the kiss so hard it stubs the tears and turns my lips to paper, setting it alight and leaving me on fire.

"I don't know what love means. How could I? Nobody stayed long enough. Or made me care if they did."

"What if I told you I think I love you?"

"I'd tell you to rethink it."

I hear the engine growl. Ten seconds later we are hurtling through the night. I glance at the speedometer as it hits seventy miles an hour.

It was a few days later. The missed out meals had passed the limit. When I saw the sign for Blakeney I asked if we could turn back and stop there, find a cafe. Paul said no. It wasn't the kind of no he'd said before, the kind I'd wheedle into yes. He kept on driving, duelling with the Z bends, carving each to S. He found a lay-by, stopped and let me move into the back. I waited as he spun a silence out of smoke. When he moved beside me I let him kiss me, not kissing back.

"Stop sulking, Grace."

"I was hungry that's all. That's why I asked to stop."

"Do you really want to sit inside a cafe knowing I'll make you my stepdaughter if I have to? The world outside this car is much too small. There's no such thing as strangers here."

"You are. I can't even see you."

He pulls me to him. He draws around my body with his hands and fills the space with touch.

"Tell me you can't see me now, Grace."

"I can't see anything when you do that. This is like a game I don't know the rules of. Like being taken somewhere not knowing where I'm going."

He smiles. "That's exactly why you want it. Or if you don't, why are you here?"

He kisses me until it's dark inside my head, his hands going where they want to. When Chris had found me on the beach the touching felt like being found. Paul touched me and it felt like getting lost. When he stops kissing me I open my eyes to find his. He smiles, his fingers playing with the buttons on my blouse.

"Can I take this off?"

"Why?" I play for time.

"To see you properly."

"It doesn't sound very proper."

"Don't you trust me? If I'd wanted to without asking a few minutes ago you'd have let me."

I give in. He undoes the buttons so matter-of-factly. I relax then shiver as the blouse falls on the car seat, the bra dropping too. The moonlight seems to burn me as he looks.

"You're perfect, Grace. Half dressed. Half undressed. Which is it?"

"It's cold," I remind him.

"It shows," he grins.

I follow his eyes then dodge them, feeling his amusement as I reach for my clothes, not understanding it until I do. He's holding them.

"Let's drive back with you like that."

It's not a let at all. I will not beg. He smiles as he opens the door to get back in the front, the night air rushing in the car. I know if I stay here then he's won. I tell myself I'm dressed and let the cold block out the hurt, the shame is almost hate when I sit down. Without a word I put my seatbelt on, ashamed because I half want him to do it like he always does so I can make believe this is no different from all the other nights. He drives in silence, glancing at me. I look away. He stops outside the village, giving me my clothes back. I get dressed and when he looks at me I know I never can. His eyes will see the other picture any time he looks. He kisses me until my mouth is sore.

"You're mine, Grace. Or nobody's."

I shiver, dressed or not.

It is a week before Paul's birthday. He drives so long I lose all track of where we are; he seems too far away to ask him where he's going. By the time he stops the car the night is black, each song the radio plays is blue.

"Can I have one?" I ask as the cigarette smoke makes me feel left out.

"What would Robert say?" he laughs.

"If he finds a phone I'll tell him," I fire back.

"I wouldn't recommend it." He puts his finger on my mouth as if to hush me, stroking till my lips are burning, pushing gently till they open, putting his own cigarette inside and lighting up another. I smile as the car begins to close us in, the dreaminess holding in my mouth like toffee the moment when he touches me,

"What do you want for your birthday? No fireworks I guess?"

"Better than fireworks I hope. To make you mine."

I throw the cigarette end out of the window, breathing in to borrow time I cannot buy.

"I'm yours already. As much as I can be."

I touch his hand. He wraps mine inside it.

"No you're not, princess. Not even half."

He kisses me then stops so suddenly I look at him to find out why.

"We can't be together like this on my birthday Grace. Or if we can it rushes something that shouldn't be rushed. I want your first time to be perfect, hurt only as much as it has to: not happen in a car. I brought you here because a friend lives up this road. I have the keys to his house while he's away. If we go there we can take it slowly. But it's only fair to warn you that tonight I won't stop unless you ask me to and I don't think you will."

He smiles. "We'll fit too well."

"You don't love me." I don't say it as a question.

"You're as close as I get to love."

"Then prove it. I'll ask you three questions. If you get two right you're close enough."

He gets the ice-cream right. He doesn't know the thing I'm scared of most is worms. I make the last one easy.

"What happens at the end of Goldilocks and The Bears?"

"They eat her."

"No, she runs away."

"Is that what you're going to do?"

"No, I couldn't if I wanted to. Not because I'm your stepdaughter, I can't go back to that. I can be a friend. If you let me."

I could tell a different story. Say the echoes got too loud to silence, say the boot got too full of lies. I'd only add another. You can do almost anything when you're fifteen: you can make the dark a den, you can tangle right and wrong, want what you can't even see, take what isn't even yours. The one thing you cannot do is go nowhere. Sooner or later you come out. To live the fairytale, not live in it.

I'd have to paint his face to capture how he looked at me. Words can only tell a story.

"Is this because I mentioned Robert? I touch you and you forget his name. Like he will yours."

"I'll take my chances. It isn't Robert. I'm fifteen years old. I want that back."

I hear the pleading in my voice and know he has too when he smiles.

"I can teach you the rest, Grace. I've let you set the pace, made sure I didn't scare you. So you'd be ready. Fifteen's just a number. There's always been something between us. You're so ready you light up in my hands." His voice is urgent, raw. Not taunting me. Not begging either.

"Suppose all that is true. You said when it's right nothing else matters. Can't you see? Too much else will always matter."

"Suppose I don't let go. I warned you. No U turns."

"Then you'll have to be a wolf again. Because I run fast."

He turns the key, lets the engine idle.

"One question, Grace: if I'm a wolf what does that make you?"

Changing Shape

November-December, 1974

When we are small the seas in picture books are always blue. If you need to hide, a blue sea is transparent. You are a fish inside a bowl. Grey will swallow you. Close itself around you. Blend you in and paint you out. To swim here is to watch your body disappear. Your feet may touch the bottom yet you cannot see them. New bathing suits look old. Storms here stir the greyness into darker grey. Sun will burnish it to silver. Stay and every other sea will seem too blue. The tourists do not swim; they wade, too scared to see their body swallowed up. They ask for blue skies to make up for the sea. We never saw the sky for long enough to care. We swam underwater, vied to see who gave in first and rose to breathe. We always knew that Chris would win, we played for fun. We swam until it grew too cold, too dangerous to swim. We swam when we ran out of other things to do. My father made one rule: we never swam alone. Found out, he punished us by banning swimming for a week and punished both for one. Not because he wanted to be mean but because he knew what hurt two meant the most. He never pictured a day when there would be no choice, that someday one would go away and leave the other swimming to survive. Not because we meant to hurt, because to hurt one hurt the least.

I could swim in the sea when I was three years old. Here, where the sea surrounds you, you can lick the salt upon your lips and your brain can tell one cove from another by its taste. Here, children are taught to respect the sea but taught to swim as toddlers. 'Taught' is too formal a word for what I remember. We watched the older children swim; our siblings carried us to shallow blood-warm pools between sand and sea. There we stretched out our arms for crabs and shells, the swimming instinct. I swim nearly every day. I will laugh it off or change the subject if you ask me why. For I know why, the water whispers to me every night, from somewhere out there in the dark. You won't see me, I am completely covered by quilt. I won't hear you, I am waiting. For him.

I began to wake at night, my dreams of swimming, Chris and me kicking, never finding any surface. Or when we did it was a lid of ice. I woke up crying, sweating, chilled, my heartbeat racing. I lay and tried to stay awake.

The new dream came two nights later. Chris was beside me, stroking my hair. He touched my shoulders, burning fingers through my nightdress. I shivered. Fingers slid to loosen the buttons, hunting something…stopped. The fingers found my breasts and traced a spiral until I gasped. Their touch was hot and cold, the swirl of sea on sunburned skin. I float upon my back. The fingers pinch and then I know. Chris would never hurt me. The hands are Paul's. Fear steals my cry and pins me to the bed. He is smiling but his eyes are blacker than the dark.

"I don't want to hurt you. I want you to want this. It's easier if you do."

His hand moves faster than the scream inside my throat and keeps it there, as hard as stone. I freeze until the hand is lighter, more a warning, gather strength as his mouth comes down to taste me, breathing on me, breathing me in. When I try to break free he laughs, the glitter dancing in his eyes.

"Fight all you want to, Grace. But I'll win. Because you have nowhere to run and I have all night every night."

His hands are in my hair. They tug and tangle in it, tangle me inside until I do not want the hands to stop. But what do I want? He seemed to sense the moment that thought was there, his voice changing, warmer, softer too. It takes me back inside the car, my body giving in, remembering him, betraying me. He strokes my hair until I cling to him, until the hand inside my nightdress is no longer strange, the stranger is me, pleasure him, the patterns and colours new, his fingers drawing on my breasts, the heat of his mouth, the aching when he stops. I wake and he is lying next to me, his arms around me. Mine are tighter.

He came to my room every night then. I began to wait for him, to burn for his hands. At first the hands were silk, the kisses moths. He left and left my skin on fire. The hands would move and trace a path, then stop. The path goes a little further every time. Each time I fight he waits, then lulls me in. The colours swim. Each time I cry he steps back, then jumps and overtakes. The path slopes sharply down. I cannot climb back up. The ground is suddenly sand. I slip and fall. The kisses turn to snakes. The hands begin to dig, to hurt. I try to move; they hold me down. They are cold as steel. I beg for him to stop; he stops then circles back. His hands take more of me each time.

The dark feels different now. He is in my dark. The colours are all his. He does not care how much I hate them. He paints yet does not see me. I am an outline he fills, then empties. I have no shape he cannot change.

By day there are no footprints anyone can see. No path, no signs, just normal backdrops. He smiles, the hands that tore me pouring orange juice. By night there are no exits, only changes of direction. The shell I make, his hands can prise apart, the flesh inside now his to mould and stab. The sky is red. The sand is dry then wet. He leaves me then. I lie there cold, the black sky a relief. The pictures will not fade. They turn into a film with all the feelings felt anew. It does not matter if it's day or night or if the dark is mine again. He is inside me every time I see the film. I cannot turn it off.

Weeks passed like scenery, everyday roads that led to night. I wondered where he went to in the daytime, where one person ended and the other one began. There had to be a join. Some nights he was almost what he'd been before. His hands were gentle, turning letting into longing, finding ways to make me want him, showing me the path could lead to pleasure, opening me to fit me to him, moving till it felt like falling off a cliff and flying. If he had stayed like that I could have forgiven him the first path and let the film fade. I could have said the words he'd told me to rethink, not caring if he was close enough to love to say them back. Without any warning he would change and pull me out of sleep to make the path go deeper, longer, leaving me to lie and cry as everything he'd done my mind retraced until I had no feelings left. The nights rewound the path until I learned to let him do exactly what he wanted, act as if I wanted it because when it was over he would hold me till it didn't matter where the path had gone, it only mattered that he held me. In his arms I'd fall asleep, then sleep would blur the memory. In the morning he would be as if it never happened, whatever had happened felt unreal.

Chris telephoned and someone else would talk, not me. Like gasps for air the words would rise from deep inside, as if the truth was climbing to get out. So many times I almost told him, so many times I screamed and willed him by a spell to hear. There are only so many times you scream before you learn the rules. You scream and it will hurt the most. You scream and you are screaming underwater, it will not make him stop. You will run out of things to try, and screams are dead ends.

You find the exits when you realise there is no way out. Or no way out you choose to take. I knew that telling Chris would draw him in, destroy his dreams. For dreams had price tags, the hand that changed my dreams to nightmares paid so his came true. I lay and thought of telling Robert, slept with it inside my hand. In the morning I would let it drop, the thought a picture oiled with shame. I saw the picture Paul would show him, painting every colour I had worn. He would take my screams and turn them into sighs. I would hear the echo, know at first that one had run into the other, could not lie. A picture does not tell a story, does not tell you which story to believe. I had never wanted names for Robert's feelings, found a name for mine. Without a name

I did not know if what he felt was strong enough to hold the picture that he had of me, believe the face that telling showed. In the end the telling all led back to Chris. I made the choice. I would tread water, stay an outline so that Chris could fill instead. I gave up looking for a way out and found a place to go.

I spent the days upon the beach. When winds were breathing ice it was still warmer than my room, the sky no darker than his eyes. One day I saw a grey head in the water, disappearing to roam a safer world below. That night when he has gone I lie upon the sand and know my shell is useless, beached he finds me helpless. I think about the one place I can hide, remembering the seal. There are many here, velvet heads that bob beside you as you swim, their swim like dancers pulled by tunes I cannot hear. Their home is made upon a sand and shingle spit, a fringe of crescents almost islands where the land runs out. To reach it you must walk for miles or find a boat to take you there. You look, they stare at you with giant eyes that barely see. Their vision has evolved to swim in darkness, live in grey. They blend and vanish, need no sun.

They say an old man watches over them, son of the sea god. They say his kingdom lies below the sea, a treeless land of mountains, cliffs and chasms. He knows each cave, each hiding place. He can assume the form of any creature, tell the future if you catch him. He must be caught asleep and held or he will change to something else. I realise Paul has no power over me in water. Pain is what I take, not what he gives. I close my eyes and when I reach that kingdom trace its landscapes, swim until I disappear. He touches water, pierces a reflection. I make his face the sky, the glitter stars. I learn to look as if I am still there yet swim away. I time the moment I will dive to when he will not see me leave.

He punished me for hiding if he caught me. Sensing I had kicked away he dragged me back. His punishments were words. Words will never show yet hurt the most, will echo till they stay.

I call out for my father, rend the silence.

He smiles.

"Do that again, Grace, and I will be your father. Doing everything I'm doing now. I'll make you call for him yet call for me. I'll tell you each place he will touch you next. Or shall we make it Chris?"

"My brother would kill you if I called for him!"

"Then see if he will hear you when you're begging him to stop."

I lay there silent, staying silent while he turned the pain up. I would not use the first name I had learned to turn it down.

He dries my tears with corners of the sheets. He says it would hurt less if I admit I wanted it. I nod and like a child he kisses me and tucks me in.

"Say goodnight, Grace."

I learn fast. I say the words, I use my mother's voice.

He hunts me in the dark but cannot see the shape he hunts. I can be a seal, a jellyfish, a crab. I can survive this. Chris need never know.

I run to reach the phone. It is Saturday morning, two weeks till Christmas, a week till Chris comes home. I pick it up and listen, slam it down. He is not coming, he is going. Going with Robert and his father to Vienna, hoping I don't mind. I don't mind, I hate him, hate all of them. Robert calls straight back. I let him say he's sorry, then hang up. I let my mother tell Paul and mask my face. I wait for him to smile, for sparks to burn, for the join to show.

"I'm sorry, Grace. I know you'll miss him. But boys are boys and need adventures. I'll buy you anything you want for Christmas, do anything to make you smile. We'll buy the biggest tree that we can find, the biggest star to put on top."

I look at him, the kindness in his voice is real. Perhaps it's me who's not.

I lie as stone, the quilt tucked tight around me. I pull it over my head and breathe my breath back in, the taste of fear and swallowed tears. I stay like that a long, long time. He does not come. I realise I wanted pain to numb me, cover up the ache I cannot numb, the truth the silence breathes: I do not love Chris as a sister loves a brother, cannot make him into something else. I turn into a mouse, creep down the stairs and watch the lights that glow like fireflies in the tree. There is a cost to changing shape. A piece of you does not change back. You end up with a hundred places you can go but none a home. You can be anything you want except be real. You will swim and be weightless, walk and carry twice your weight in secrets, tuck them in beside you when you sleep. This price tag Chris must never see. I promised long ago to let him go. Whatever way I love him, loving someone leaves no other way.

I often see the seals. I envy them the kingdom I can only borrow, a simpler world. I never see the old man. I wish that he'd been real. So that I could pin him down and learn the future. To take a different path.

Drawing Circles

March, 1975

It is March. I watch the bustle on the platform when a train arrives, the people getting off and on. I play no part except to wait. I watch for trains I never catch. I used to long to buy a ticket, to just get on and not get off, to see the scenery rush past, to know what going felt like, see all the places they would see. I'd pretend I travelled all the time and tut and check my watch. I'd paint the passing pictures in my head, blend in by looking bored. I'd watch the others getting off at Norwich, let the train retrace its tracks.

 I never went. Only children run away without a place to go. A ticket is just a token. A token buys a train ride or a carousel ride. I am standing here because I chose the carousel, knowing that even if the weekend flies his face will make Paul's blur, that when it's over Paul will make me pay, the faces will swap round.

 I'm far too early for his train. I told Paul three not four. I told Robert train platforms were only romantic in films, that love you put in letters shrank to fit. He felt the stones between the lines. He said his father told school something he called being economical with the truth to get him home. He said it meant as little as you got away with telling. In which case I have coppers left. Once upon a time I would have waited in the cafe, fitting stories to the faces. Now it hurts too much. They have stories, I have hiding places. Even when pretending I am careful now. I'm never anything I used to be: all the selkies are now seals, all the mermaids are just fish. I don't go very far when I escape him. I am swimming in a sea with cages, living in a house with cliffs.

The platform fills with faces, Robert's none of them. Then hands are covering my eyes, my body swept up in his arms. His smile chases off my sadness. In that smile I know how it would feel to stay with him. Like never asking are we there yet for there is always where he'd be.

"I don't want to let you go but Dad's waiting in the car park." He tucks my hand in his, picks up his bag.

I should have expected this. Robert gets more homesick than he admits and knows his father misses him. I don't mind; I like to watch them fit like jigsaw.

His father is scraping ice off the windscreen. He waves and opens the door for me.

From the backseat I watch us cut a tunnel through the fog, Behind us fog fills up the hole. His father needs no backdrop. He knows his way at night. A doctor's map is drawn from nights torn out of sleep, from racing death along these roads. He drives and only talks when close to home, the streetlights of the village fuzzy snowballs in the dark.

I hear him asking Robert what still gnaws at me.

"Why did Chris not come with you?"

"He says he's miles behind in Maths prep," Robert laughs.

I could not have said it better. I count the weekends since Chris came home. The total says I do not count.

It is snowing lightly when we reach the house. Upstairs his father feeds the fire more wood. I smile as Robert says it's time for dinner knowing he will ask for fish and chips. He laughs and says the fish at school come out of the pond. They argue over who will fetch them, Robert wins as usual. He says it's much too cold to walk. I listen to them as I stand beside the window, watching snow fill up the sky. I feel left out, not sure how to get back in. I look around the room to check if anything has changed. The walls are plain to best display the paintings. Most of mine are here, my mother says the sea should stay out of the house. The painting of the beach I did for Chris is here. He said it got left behind by accident. This hurts less now that I know how easily accidents happen. There is a new painting, the Prater Ferris Wheel at night. I look away.

"I should go home," I say reluctantly. My mother is in Cambridge for the weekend, staying with Lucy. I dare not anger Paul.

"Hey, I promised Chris I'd look after you," he jokes.

"Well if he's your reason I should stay I'll go." I get up.

"You're angry with Chris?"

"I'm angry with both of you. Was Vienna fun?"

"So that's it. No it wasn't. Not without you."

"I wasn't invited," I say angrily.

"Grace, Dad spoke to Paul himself. He said you wanted a family Christmas. He said the same to Chris."

I add it up, remembering my storm of tears, the tree, the star, how he never came that night, his pathway inched the next. He watched me cry. Then let the salt sink in. I let him comfort me. I broke the rules. He punished me. The perfect join: a circle.

"I told Chris it seemed odd. He said perhaps things were better with your mother," Robert puzzles.

I quickly backtrack, know I must not draw him into this.

"Maybe he thought my being there would help? He's like a child who never had a childhood. Playing happy families." I shrug.

"I wish Dad would hurry up." Robert is always hungry.

"I really should go home, it's late."

"Stay for supper first. I can't eat for two. Dad will drive you home."

"I'll come for breakfast early," I bargain.

I hear his father push the door open, it always sticks. His footsteps tap in circles up the spiral staircase. Taking off his coat he throws the fish and chips to Robert, parcelled up inside brown paper. Shops in town use newspaper but nothing happens here to print. I watch them eat, too scared to join them, part of me feels hungry, part of me feels sick. Escaping to the balcony I breathe the frozen air in gulps. I know why I feel sick. I know he'll smile at the door when Robert's father drives me home. I know the smile taunts me. I know they'll never tell. I'm sick of secrets, knowing I can never tell.

I look inside the glass. Like a child watching a film she's seen so often she knows exactly what will happen next, has memorised every line. It is a scene I make believe I'm part of. I touch it, taste it, smell it, steal it. It isn't mine. Longing will not make it so.

I freeze-frame the other scenes behind my eyes, the games he makes me play. On nights I've been with Robert he makes me choose the game. I can have him touch me everywhere that Robert did or everywhere he didn't. When he laid this out I knew Robert would stop at kisses so I chose the first. Laughing as he claimed my mouth he'd whispered he looked forward to kisses moving somewhere else. He had tricked me into telling him the truth. The strange thing was I knew he'd keep the deal. He couldn't understand why I always picked the second. The second would never mirror what was real or mock it. Tonight I will pretend I'm here upon the balcony, seeing only darkness, feeling only wind. I slide the door open, steel myself to smile and feel it pull the muscles in my face.

"Would you mind if we walked back, Robert?" I never call it home.

"It's really cold out there, Grace, and you don't have a scarf or hat."

Predictably his father does not argue. Robert fetches me a scarf. I say goodnight, almost falling down the stairs.

We walk in silence, Robert slowing to my pace. It is a mile from his house to mine but quicker being flat. Tonight I do not care how quick we are or care if we get there at all. There is a drone of voices from the pub, no passers by but shadows walking dogs. The fog has shrunk to ghosts. I start to walk more slowly, knowing that when we get there I can never ask him in. I have to keep him on a balcony where Paul will never reach him. When we near the house I hide inside his arms then run before he kisses me.

Next morning the doctor meets me at the door, about to leave. The postmaster said his son has been awake all night and wonders if he's sick with tummy worms. The villagers ills are rhymes without an end, their tragedies ends without a rhyme. I know he'll listen, hearing both. The house is cold. I find the poker, rouse the fire. It is dark inside and out, the morning star a tell of dawn. The sky is just beginning to separate from the sea. It is no more than colour rearranging in your eyes when you have blinked, so subtle you must learn it long before you know the word for sea.

I find him in the kitchen. Used to fending for ourselves we have a ritual at weekends. I set the table, Robert pours the coffee. I make toast. He stirs the porridge, carries in the bowls and plates. We eat and bet on how long the sun will last.

"You look as if you need a prince to wake you up! Bad dreams?"

I could tell him dreams this bad are nightmares. I will wake and will not know which parts were real. I cannot tell him I stand upon his balcony as they happen, hidden in his dark. I cannot tell him why I know the sun will never stay.

By the time the doctor returns the room is bathed in sun. I go to make him toast and coffee, I give him my seat beside the fire and he smiles.

"What took so long Dad? Ivan can't have tummy worms. They're parasites you get abroad."

The doctor looks at me. "Not over breakfast, Robert. Can you check the car, I think I left my bag in there."

Robert makes a face but goes.

"Grace, your face is almost white. Is something wrong at home?"

I shake my head.

"I won't tell Robert. Doctors must keep secrets."

So must sisters. Even when the secrets squirm like worms.

"A weekend always ends too fast." I dodge his gaze.

"Then come when Robert goes. You don't need appointments."

"I'll remember. Robert's taking ages. Boys are bad at finding things, they only see what's put in front of them."

"Don't underestimate him, Grace. He looks at you and I don't see a boy."

He glances down. His bag is by his feet.

The doctor pours Robert coffee, adding extra sugar to dissolve his son's exasperation when the bag is 'found'. When Robert drains the cup

I judge it safe to talk. His anger is like peat. Although slow to light it smoulders underground when you believe it's gone. Then something else will reignite it. I rarely see it, never tease it.

"Can we walk along the beach?"

His face says no then changes it to yes. He knows the waves can make me talk, as if I talk to them, forget he'll hear. I raise my guard. Outside the ground is slippery, the grass is blades of ice. The breeze shakes the snow from the trees. The beach is dazzling, sugar-coated in snow. I shade my eyes. This kind of day the sky is sunrise frozen into place. The sea is cobalt blue, the waves are blown from glass. They shatter into a million tiny mirrors as they hit the shore and catch the sun. The sea wall sparkles thirty strokes away, a curving row of stones like teeth. Our footprints crack the sand.

I walk carefully. He reaches for my hand; I let it stay. We walk in silence, joined yet apart. It scares me, as though if we keep on walking there will be nothing to turn back for.

He suddenly stops and drops my hand.

"You put it back, Grace. Not to stop you slipping, not to keep yours warm. Because you want to."

"Why are you doing this?"

"I have to. I need you to know that I love you. So you know this isn't a game."

He waits, about to turn around when I reach for him. Not for his hand, for his mouth. Not knowing that my kiss is wild. At once his arms imprison me. Kissing me he tries to read my eyes. He stops and pulls away.

"What's wrong, Grace? Other than the fact that I'm not Chris."

I stare at him. "Chris is my brother."

"Not just a brother. Like you're not just a sister for him. Don't lie please."

His eyes are wet. I owe him the truth or as much of it as I dare.

"Can we go somewhere? Your dad's surgery?"

I know he has a spare key. His dad had said it was somewhere to go if the weather turned. I see him breathe in hard to stop anger coming out. He nods. He walks as if I'm not there, too fast. The surgery is by the church. The building is tiny, two rooms. Robert unlocks the office. There is only space for two chairs and a table, shelves crammed with books fill up the walls. They could tell me how we breathe, what makes a heart keep beating, how we grow, not why a sister grows to love a brother in two different ways. I sit down first, my legs are shaking. When Robert sits I force myself to meet his eyes, not finding him there when I do.

"Well, Grace? What's so bad the wind can't hear? I know how economical the truth can be. I can read your thoughts right now. You're wondering how much I already know, remembering how good I am at guessing, working out how much to tell. Shall I help you? Let's start with Chris, I'm used to that. I've shared a room with him at school. I know things you don't. He keeps a photograph of you in his bedside drawer. Brothers might do that. They don't look at it before they go to sleep or touch it when they can't."

I long to know which photograph Chris has and see him read this too.

"Ask him which one and when you do why not tell him what's underneath your pillow? Or does he know you keep his sweater there? I wasn't snooping, Grace. I'd gone in to hide some chocolate to surprise you, lifted up the pillow, finding the surprise myself. I tried to tell myself it was just a kind of comfort blanket. Things kept on piling up. Not big things, little things. You start to look for them they'd fill a book. You always phone him first when anything is wrong. Or any time we play chess it's in your eyes you're willing him to win. If you're wondering, it's the same for him. He says your name as if he's tasting it, invents excuses to touch you, I see them move your face. I don't think either of you know you're doing it. That only makes it worse."

"I don't want to love him like I do. Or want to want him in that way. I don't know why it's like that. Maybe when a brother is all you have for far too long, the only one who loves you, you love them far too much. He doesn't know I love him."

"How far has it gone?"

I am being dissected. What more is left to lose by telling?

"When he ran away from school we found each other on the beach. We kissed once, touched each other. The confessional is next door, Robert."

"You don't think it's too much of a coincidence that he ran home just after finding out how I felt about you?" I hear the felt and feel the difference.

"You know the weird thing, Robert? I wanted to tell you. You're not just my boyfriend you're my best friend. I used to tell you everything, you'd help me understand."

"Maybe I do. That doesn't mean I'm willing to take second place forever. I think I've always known. I know you both so well. Do you want to know how I knew he'd kissed you? He came back to school and walked like he was flying, looked like he was in a dream. It felt like seeing my reflection."

I knew what stopped him coming home at weekends, why he hadn't found the time to phone. Why I'd felt so small. Because I was small.

"Can I ask you two more questions, Grace? Which one of us did you just kiss? Him or me? I won't stand in for him."

"I kissed you. I know you won't believe me. I pretend a thousand things are true. I can turn tears to paint, sea to sky. I could never turn you to Chris or want to."

"Which one do you dream about?"

I want to tell him I don't have dreams any more. Do nightmares count? If what happens in the nightmare matters maybe they count more. By revealing who you cannot bear to lose? I see him read the answer, add it to the one before, see the shock eat up his eyes.

"You can't mean you love both of us!"

"What good are questions if you don't believe the answer?"

"I need some time to think, Grace." I know him well enough to know he means no more than this, too well to beg or borrow time right now.

He turns and runs. I cannot follow him. I put the key through the letterbox.

The letter comes two weeks later.

"Dear Grace

I won't ask you to choose. I won't ask you for promises. You're all I want. The dark's too dark without you. Dad will give you this. He knows we have to sort this out. I think we can. And so I'll wait.

Robert"

His father handed it to me. "He's all I have, Grace. I think you'll hurt him, whether or not you want to. I'm here if you want to talk. All I ask is please don't settle for him, make him second best. Because he's not."

The Only Way Out

Easter 1975

I shiver in his arms. The cold goes deep inside. I cannot find a reason to fight this that is mine. He does not come every night now, circles when I ask him why. It was the fear he fed on. He has labelled everything I feared, stolen everything I loved. Now I do not fight he does not hurt. I am not whole enough to tear. He comes to fill his hunger then he leaves me with my stars. There is not one I dare to wish upon, nor any wishes left.

    I only know I'm fifteen while at school. The uniform is just a costume, will make me look the same not be the same. There are no feelings I can show, no secrets I can tell. I watch them from a balcony. I do not know the play and when I have to speak the speech is lines. I smile to stop them drawing questions, I begin to fall asleep in class, to drug myself to stay awake with coffee in the morning, slugging cola down to get me through the afternoon. The nights he cuts in half at least will stitch to let me sleep. The nights without him break to pieces, dozing in and out of nightmares, treading water till the morning. When I wake to find him there I turn towards him, When he takes me he makes me want him first. It feels like wanting whisky when you only wanted ginger beer. I don't ask him if he loves me or know if I love him. I long for him to be the friend he was before and know no path will take us back. I have forgotten paths in sand get washed away while you sleep.

I wake one night and feel his mouth on mine,. Some nights he waits for me to take the nightdress off; he's taught me how to do it slowly, touching every place he'll touch. It isn't even mine. He bought two nightdresses, red and black. They make me feel more naked with them on. Tonight he turns me over facing him. This means he wants to take it off himself. He pulls it from the bottom up, his hands invading as he pulls, I move to make it easier. Suddenly the silk is cool upon my face, it blindfolds me. I hear him laugh and know he wants to hide from what he'll do. I wait, his hands are firm on my breasts, not stroking, pressing in, not moulding, cupping. Lifting off the silk his eyes hold mine.

"When did you last bleed?"

His hands take back my breasts, his fingers push as if to get inside. It hurts.

I tried to think and couldn't remember. All I knew was he did not come to my room then. When did that last happen?

"Why does it matter now? I'm sleepy. Maybe before Christmas?"

"Three months ago," he says quietly.

"Okay, you're better at Maths." I pull the covers over my breasts.

"You're pregnant, Grace."

"Don't you want a baby?" I laugh. I don't believe him.

"Don't you be a baby. This can't happen, Grace."

"Oops. Maybe you should have thought of that before."

He slowly pulls the covers down. I shut my eyes. If I am not here what happens in-between need not be real.

The hand across my mouth is real. My eyes snap open. In time to see his right hand swing to slap my breasts. The pain is blinding. Raising his arm he waits to slap again.

"Oops, Grace. Did that hurt? Of course you'll never tell me. So I'll have to make sure."

I don't remember when it stopped. I wake up alone and throw up in the sink he so thoughtfully provided. In the mirror above, his handprints fall on top of one another, scarlet on my breasts. He brings me breakfast on a tray and sits upon the bed.

"I'm sorry I had to hurt you. You made me angry. We have to stop this, Grace."

I thought he meant what we were doing. Then I saw him looking at my tummy. He meant stop 'it'.

"How?"

"There are people, doctors, who take care of it. As if nothing happened. Just a train-ride to London. We have to fix this. For you, but most of all your mother. She can't have another child. Think what yours would do to her."

"We should tell Dr Jolly. He won't tell anyone. He can help us find a doctor. I have to tell Chris the truth. I want my brother," I begged.

His reaction was terrifying. He smiled.

"I know you do. Only you don't want him as a brother, do you, Grace? I've been there when you dream. You say his name."

"Not like that. You're lying."

"Bodies don't lie Grace. When I first touched you, you saw his face. Whispered his name. Greedy little Grace. She wants Chris, she wants Robert. She wants them both. She can't decide. I'll make it easier, Grace. If you tell anyone I'll say this baby could belong to either. God knows they'll believe me. Chris spends half his time watching you; Robert's with you every minute he comes home. There, Grace, now you don't have to choose. Just be silent. Let me sort this out."

There was no choice. The weeks turned over. The silence was easy. I was never sick again. I didn't get fat, or even change much at first. But my body was different. Heavier, tired. Outside my skin was rosy, my hair thick and shiny. No one spotted the difference.

When I wake up I see the moon and he is gone. He leaves no footprints in the sand, the waves will backfill any cries I make. I feel the pain lap deep inside as I haul myself upon my knees, refuse to think of what it means. I bend and fill my hand with sand and rub the grains across my face, and know the sea itself can only clean the shell, not me inside.

When the water swirls around my feet it numbs the pain. I wade out slowly, disappearing into grey, immune to cold. I do not have to see the bottom, know exactly where the sea will take my steps away.

I reach my hand and splay my fingers out to break the surface. Below it lies another world where this one is not real. I dive and, swimming, push my body deeper, opening my eyes, familiar with a land where grey is grey at first and then becomes a paintbox. Moonlight filters down, silver slants like scissors slicing pools of cloudy lemonade, bursting chains of bubbles into foam. Below me arches made of chalk are ruined castles, moats of teal.

When my lungs feel moments from exploding I rise for air. One gulp and then I see her. Her head bobs up and down a mere few strokes away, the same shape as a dog's, a flatter nose, Impossibly huge eyes scoop up the light. She disappears to break the waves again to stare as if surprised I am still here. She plays as if they are a roller-coaster ride. She dives, I follow. Underwater she is home. Her world is upside down for when she swims she flies, the sea her sky. The pools of lemonade to her are clouds. She is a seal, her dance perfection made to look like nothing. Out of water she is clumsy. She cannot run, can barely see. She is too slow to move, too quick to trust. Tonight I'd swap her world for mine. By morning this will be a room, the sand a bed. The walls are pink, the covers white, the colours lie. I still see black and red. The sun will rise and only tell the time.

I wake, my head beneath the quilt. I slowly pull the covers back. I move my hand down to the swelling of my belly, feel it swim inside. I don't know if I feel relieved or not.

When Chris came home for Easter I was different:?tense, jumpy, bad-tempered. I knew he thought me angry knowing he would leave again. As this was partly true I let him think it whole. The weather was cold for late in April. The star magnolia opened its flowers only for frost to brown them by morning. Paul was sarcastic and distant. I knew he was afraid that Chris would guess something was wrong.

"Want to go swimming?" my brother said. It was very early, only us two up.

I nearly said no. But I wanted to. I thought hard: the sea was warm enough if we swam fast enough. If I put on my costume now, wrapped a towel round me while undressing, dropped it at the last minute, nothing need show. Paul would not be suspicious: Chris and I swam with the weather not the calendar. I found my swimsuit, kept out of sight of my reflection as I peeled it on.

On the walk I was almost happy. It was 7 am, the sky still grey, the shots of silver might go either way. Wind swirled along the beach road, sudden gusts that took us with it, blew us to the hill. I wrapped the towel round me as I pulled my clothes off, turning round to hide the bulge. While Chris found some rocks to pin the clothes and towels down, I ran into the water, gasping as the cold went through me. In the sea I turned to Grace again, my body buoyant, swimming easily, a brand new kind of seal. The sunrise on the water scalloped it to orange fish-scales. Blinded we pierced underwater, swimming deeper to the cliff then disappearing, resurfacing to smile as if to say that here we were still twins.

After half an hour the cold forced us out. The sun would have to work much harder to do more than scratch the surface. The wind had calmed, the sky was pink and gold. Ahead of him, in running for my towel I forgot my point of balance had shifted, stumbling on the sand ripples, fighting to correct it, standing up to topple over. Laughing as I picked myself up I rubbed the sand off, the towel forgotten. But there was no mirrored laugh from my brother: he was staring at the roundness of my belly.

"Whose, Grace?" he rasps. His face is white as if the sun has gone.

I grasp for answers, as if gasping for air. But the lies would never hold together. So I told him, thought I knew this scene from keeping it inside my head to stop me telling this, imagined anger, questions, blame. He simply held me tightly, shaking, as if for the first time he could not find his balance.

"When did he start this?" he whispered.

I cannot explain to him that nothing marks where it begins. At first there are no lines, only ripples. Imprints left in sand the waves will wash away. Then holes the water fills. Then wounds it doesn't. I cannot tell him all the colours are not black and white.

"It blurs, Chris. He meant it to. The first time he came to my room you had just gone back to school. I think he used to watch me when

I was asleep. Your paper trick?" I smile. He does not smile back. His eyes are whirlpools.

"I let this happen. I left you here. I didn't come home often enough. I was too scared if I did I wouldn't want to leave. At first it felt as if a part of me was missing, nothing felt right without you. Each time the train arrived and made the leaving real I'd only just manage to get on. I'd wake up at night at school and wonder where I was. I'd go to sleep and wish that in the morning I'd be home. I'd go home and nothing made it home but you. I thought that if I stayed too long I'd find the train would vanish. Soon it started to feel more like home at school. I liked the routines, patterns the days made, the lights that never quite went off at night, the tidiness I felt inside. And you would smile and I would know the smile hurt. Each time you said goodbye mine got harder to say. If I didn't see you I didn't need goodbye. I scarcely read your letters, I hardly ever wrote. The words would hurt to write, hurt more to read."

Suddenly he is telling me everything I longed to know. All the answers to the questions I could never ask.

"I think I understand, Chris. I used to read your letters looking inbetween the lines and finding nothing telling me what mattered. Places sketched and faces outlined, nowhere I could picture you, no space left for me. It got easier to stop myself from looking, look forward to you coming home instead. But you didn't. Robert did, I wrote to him, I wrote as if you read them."

He smiles. "He wouldn't let me, He said I was being selfish. He said if I was big enough to leave, I was big enough to write. He loves you, Grace. In many ways he knows you better than I do. He looks at you like something he will never have and never lets that matter, never lets you down. I looked at you and knew the cost you paid to let me go and let you pay it anyway. I hid from you, believed I'd lost you. Once I found you I was too late to notice you were lost. I was greedy, Grace. I wanted school, I wanted to be a doctor. I made you want my wants. So did Paul. He got inside your skin then turned you inside out. If I'd been here he never would have dared."

Listening, I am torn between wanting to hear more and knowing it's too late, that words are only paper, only cover cracks. What matters is what we do, not what we say. I look at him and suddenly I am older than he is.

"We were only children, only pawns. He used one of us to trap the other, mother made that easy. We didn't need words until you went away, Chris. Children don't need words. Especially not us. We were too close to use them, too close to learn them. Words are for guessing, for telling secrets. We never thought we'd have secrets to guess. But he never truly got inside me. It was never me; I found ways to disappear."

He is calmer, eyes no longer wild. He is holding me now, seeing me. He wrapped the towel round me, gently patted me dry. We dressed and found a sand dune, with curving sides, as if dug by a spoon.

"Surely mother will believe the baby's his?" he says.

"Are you sure, Chris? Has she ever been there when we needed her? Will she believe you over him? He'll make the baby Robert's." He glances at me. "See. Even you've been thinking that. The answer's no. Unless kisses make babies." I laugh bitterly.

"Mother's as much under his spell as I was, Chris."

I think back to the night I told Paul about mother's baby, how next morning she was standing where he put her. What he'd told me when I asked one night how he could go straight from me back to her.

"How can you pretend like that?" I asked him, truly curious.

"Grace, your mother is happy. She has the things she wanted, it was always pretence she wanted me," he said.

"Then what did you want?" I asked him, bewildered.

"Does it matter now? I guess I wanted somewhere I felt needed. You were lonely, sad. I wanted you to smile, feel loved again.

"You promised you would love my mother when you married her."

"You are so naïve, Grace. Your mother loves herself more than she ever loved me, more than you and Chris. All she wanted was what I could buy her. She locked herself inside each time I touched her. You looked like her but you were different. Love was all you wanted."

"So why hurt me?"

"You were beautiful, so alive. You were crying out for somebody to touch you. But you didn't need me, or truly see me. You never wanted me the way you wanted Chris. You let me taste you then you ran. It made me want you more."

"And now?" I taunted, looking at my belly.

"You're mine now. I'll teach you how to love me. When this is over, you'll be beautiful again, all mine again, I made very discreet enquiries. I've found a doctor. Three weeks today we'll take the train to London. It will be like you're asleep, nothing to feel. Nothing to remember. You know how scared your mother is of doctors. All we have to tell her is you're having blood tests, you're so sleepy all the time it will make sense."

"Chris will want to come. He'll be worried." I knew Chris would insist.

"I won't stop him. Either he becomes the father or comes with us. He'll know exactly how the doctor gets that baby out. He'll feel everything you can't."

I knew him then. I hated him. I had believed he had not been able to stop himself. To know how well he planned each step mapped out my path. He would do what he wanted to me. He would destroy each person in his way, use the ones I loved the most to silence me. Nobody would see through his disguise. All he needed was to time it right. All he had to do was pay.

"You persuaded mother to let Chris go to boarding school, didn't you? You knew without him I'd be lost. You wanted me to turn to you."

He laughs. "I'm not that clever! She asked me to help. She didn't want Chris stuck here. But you turned so easily, didn't you? I would have let you go. Except by then I wanted you too much to let Chris have you. You wanted a lot more than kisses from him."

"Chris didn't want that."

"Oh, I think he did. I've watched you going in his room. I've watched you coming out. In-between I don't think you were sharing childhood stories."

I shiver in the sand dune, remembering the blackness of Paul's eyes, moving close to make Chris real. I tell him what I have to. "I won't let him hurt you any more. What do you want to happen, Grace? Tell me. I'll make it happen."

"I want him far away. Then I'll think about the baby. I want to make choices, even if they're wrong, as long as they're mine. You know what Chris? Sometimes when he did it he used to light a candle and I would watch the flame and wish that he would stop. It used up all my wishes. But if I had one left I'd wish him dead, not the baby." I say bitterly.

"Then I'll kill him," he says.

The sun is high now, the sand-dune warm. I see Paul's face and realise he's wrong. A sand-dune can be a castle if you need it to. I feel Chris playing chess, picking up the pieces, moving them, anticipating how each move plays out. He doesn't know Paul. I do. I start to move the pieces too. It's almost abstract. When it's over only two pieces will remain.

"We haven't much time, Grace. There's no other way but to kill him. He's been too clever, no-one will believe you, not even Mother. Robert's in too deep. His father will protect him first. We could poison him, or hit him over the head. Those may not kill him. And there can't be a body. But there is one way," Chris said, looking towards the sea.

"You mean drown him," I said.

"It's all that I can think of. But it presents problems. He doesn't swim and you know how cold that water is. He never comes here. Our one advantage, our affinity with the sea, is outweighed by the problem of getting him in it."

I know he's right. I sit thinking, picturing moves, counter moves, jumping, trying to win.

"I can think of one, maybe two ways. The first will only work if he believes me. I act more and more depressed and write a note saying I'm going to solve all the problems my way, by drowning myself. I leave it for you. You leave him guessing about what you know, you beg his help to stop me, and we hope he bites. I'll be there already when you get there, in the water, stay this side of the cliff. You tell him he doesn't need to swim, it isn't deep, I'm being dragged down by my clothes, that all he has to do is help you pull me in to safety."

"Then what?"

"You know where the cliff is, Chris, he doesn't. He's tall as you, his feet will feel the bottom, then they won't. You never know the cliff is there until you're falling," I say bitterly. "All you'll have to do is push him over."

"And the second?" my brother demands.

"I tell him I've told you everything, that you want to talk, now, here. You take a knife, surprise him, Or I arrive, distract him, give you long enough to stab him and when he falls we drag him in the water. Even if he's not dead straight away, he will be."

I say this, know if killing is the only way out the first must work, that I can ask the sea to help us kill him, not help Chris murder him. We choose the first. It got him closer to the sea. It left no murder, if the sea swallowed hard no body either. We pull our clothes on, something new between us, something lost. The new is how he looks at me, as if he's scared to read my eyes, as if he's wondering why I can plan a murder better than he can. When all it takes is hate. The lost is how we look at one another now, I look at him no longer looking up, he looks at me no longer seeing all my thoughts, as if the difference grew while we were sleeping. When all it took was time.

We put off going back by eating breakfast in the café. The doughnuts come and leave me full of holes. I am always hungry now, too sick with fear to eat. Fear nibbles me in daytime, swallows me at night. It never did before. What is there to fear in darkness? Ghosts are drifters, lost and blind. The shapes we need to fear are shaped like us. Our nightmares are mosaics of what we see each day. The eyes that scan you in the dark can tell your secrets, fingers test each string that moves you. They know your treasures, know exactly what you'll do to keep them, which you cannot bear to lose. But surely seals could outwit wolves and set a snare in water?

Undercurrents

May 1975

The village I grew up in could be sketched in ten lines or so. A road curved towards the sea, a side shoot from the green edged road that curved along the coast, villages sprouting from each side shoot, putting down their own roots as they spread, like spider plants. The roads would often be white with mist, in the mornings and afternoons, hanging white blossom only the sun or wind dispersed. The road reaches almost to the sea then splits into two, veering off at right angles. One runs past a playground, and a car park to split into three streets, ours the last one. The other grew some shops and houses, the Church and post office, ending with the pub, the amusement arcade and the café. It narrows then, becoming sandier, climbing steeply to a hill to fall upon the beach at the other side. If you cut off before the hill a path worn by time takes you to the sand dunes.

The beach has two sides, one allowing dogs, the other welcoming the tourists; in the summer there's a beach chair hut. The beach is almost perfect sand. The sea has two sides as well: the one the tourists see and the one the villagers watch. The sea here is higher than the land and land is either half liquid or just borrowed; man has drained it for his own purposes but the sea will take it back. A few feet nibbled away each year, but the sea can afford to take its time. We fight it back with walls of stones. We turn the waves to ripples, sieve the sand to grains of gold. We filter out the cold and tame the currents. Seas are never tamed. The history of the village could be punctuated by the very stones protecting it. The rocks grow bigger every time the sea storms back. The sand-dunes melt and are replaced by concrete. Inside the café the people eat their ice-cream, drink their coffee, never noticing the pictures on the walls. The newspaper cut-outs are framed just like the photographs and just like them they disappear; real stories are easier to forget. The pictures tell the story of the village, words contain the nightmares left behind each time the sea fights back.

I can never excuse or forget what I did. All I can do is tell it.

Chris and I run from the house and trace a path we know by heart. We time how long it takes to reach the hill, how long to cross the sand. Put together they add up to fifteen minutes, twenty if Paul's slower. None of it seems real until we touch each other's hand. We touch as if to glue us back together. We need to stick like glue or one of us will wonder if there is another way. We pull each other back.

"Why can't we just run away?" I ask him.

"Go where Grace? How far do we go? How much money do we have? I have none that counts. Paul sends me cheques each month. He always buys us what we want. I bet he does the same with mother. That means there's nothing we can even steal. And you're pregnant, Grace. What happens if you need a doctor?"

He doesn't say what I know he's thinking: what if I lose babies too? I want to talk to him about the baby. I want to know what he's thinking, what will happen after we kill Paul. I want to ask him what we'll tell people when we have to, how we'll look after it. He never lets me. It's as if the baby isn't stuck in me. As if he can forget it if he never talks about it. I'm running out of baggy clothes and feeling scared each time I feel it move. When Paul and mother go out we end up in his room. Nowhere else feels safe. It's too safe. We talk as if the words are Scrabble, careful when we make them in our heads, they even sound like plastic. If I try to talk about the baby I might as well be plastic too.

I'm only real if I don't have a middle, only Grace as long as it is dark. The nights Paul goes out to dinner with mother are the only nights I know he'll stay away from me because he'll drink. I found this out a while ago pretending I was hurt he'd stayed with her. He said she'd order wine and think it odd unless he drank some too. I lie in bed with Chris and know the risk we're taking and don't care. I don't care if all we ever can be now is brother and sister because the dark has different rules, will turn us into who we want. He holds me tightly till I long to turn round but if I do he'll turn back because he'll feel the baby. I know it's safe to fall asleep, he'll wake me up at dawn and Paul will come downstairs to find us eating breakfast. When I'm scared I want him to hold me and know the only way to make him do that is to cry. If I cry he'll worry I'm not strong enough to do this. I want to tell him tears can make you strong as well. I feel like shaking him until the Chris I know comes out. I'm too afraid of what might fall out of me to start a fight.

Thoughts split like roads into what is safe to say and what is not and what we have to say to make this work. The roads end up dead ends or feel as if he's blocking me. The 'have to says' are worst. When Chris came, Paul must have waited to see if I would talk. Now he thinks it's safe he smiles and tells me I am not. This is the only thing that makes Chris cry. He can't do anything he hasn't done already. But none of that Chris had to have a picture of or see it in my eyes.

I think back now and know that it was worse for Chris.

I was water, anything he did reflections. Water does not fight, it waits. All I had to do was wait and he would sink. No ripples told upon my face before he kissed me. My body was a spit of sand he stood on, waves would sweep him off. I never cried. My tears would drown him later.

"I could kill him now. I lie there knowing what he's doing. I could run in with a knife." He cries but I know he means every word.

"Remember at the wedding when he taught you and Robert how to punch? That was play-fighting; this isn't. He's strong, Chris. What if you get hurt instead? Suppose you kill him – what do we tell the police? Suppose you don't – what will he tell them? And there's a baby. They'll know it wasn't the first time. You have to close your eyes."

"How?"

"Like I did." I knew this wasn't fair. I had shut it out to keep Chris where he'd never know what Paul was doing, knowing he was listening in our room had made the shutting out both easier and harder, easier because I didn't feel alone, hard because I knew Chris knew I wasn't.

My mother was the only one I knew might guess. I fell asleep too easily, I rarely wanted food except at night. I felt the tiny flutterings, my fingers drawn to trace them, tracing them already if I wasn't careful. I was careful to go out of rooms that she was in. When Chris followed she was used to that. I never told Chris I could feel it flutter when he sat beside me.

I let the phone ring knowing Robert must be home, knowing only he would know to ring at fifteen minutes past the hour. I heard him trying every hour, shrinking smaller every time. "What if I just answer it and tell him nothing's wrong?"

"Your voice will tell him for you if words do not. How will you explain you don't want to see him? Especially when I know you do."

When all the whats and ifs ran out the plan took shape. We tried to remember how mother had been after the baby died. I would grow more distant, spend more time alone, stop going out. Chris would tell Paul he was worried, plant the seeds. The trouble was there wasn't time for them to grow, the baby growing all the time. The plan was like the baby, only half was formed. Half must be enough. When Paul became more gentle I knew the roots were there. The stalks would be a letter two would write, the letter that must coil around him, pull him to the beach. The words that Chris would use pretending he had found it must convince Paul I would drown myself, persuading him to go with Chris to save me. We had to hope he'd follow Chris into the water thinking I was drowning, let Chris lead him to a cliff he would not know was there. Then Chris would pull him over, force him down. I must pretend that I was drowning well enough until the sea agreed to take Paul's body in exchange.

'My darling brother,

Please remember two things when you read this. One, that to let me go is all that you can do now to give me peace. It is what I want. Two, that what I allowed him to do was so wrong I do not deserve to live nor deserve your love. I was unhappy and easily drawn into his hands but I should have been strong enough to run away, brave enough to fight him. Don't ever think you could have stopped me, I want to die, there is no other way out. There is nothing left. Tell mother the truth and, if she needs proof, to go to his sisters: it began with them. It wasn't all his fault, he meant to love me, part of me loved him. Remember me as a star, our father's sort. ~ Grace'

I show it to Chris. I know he thinks the part about the love a clever lie. I think back to the nights I cried Paul's name and didn't scream for Chris.

I wake confused, the smell of chocolate floating in the room. I lift my head to find his shape. He sits a mug upon the bedside table, sits upon the stool. I know he'll break the silence first. When silence fills the hours it haunts you till your own voice scares you most. You learn to time a minute by your heartbeat. I get to ten and hear him sigh.

"Why didn't you tell me about you and Robert? You've gone out at weekends saying you were seeing him, you even let me play that stupid game and punish you for wanting to see him."

"What's to tell? You weren't to blame. He knows about Chris. He's known for months and guessed for years."

"If you'd told me...."

"You'd what, Paul? Say sorry for changing lollipops to blow-jobs, candy-floss to striptease? See how well I know the words now? I kissed Robert and it was you I tasted. Not Chris. I might not have known tickling gives you butterflies, it didn't stop me chasing them, did it?"

"I'd have left you alone. Perhaps not to fly away, to see if you'd fly back. So now I will. You don't have to drink it. Go to sleep again."

I pull the quilt down to free myself enough to reach the mug and hold it out of habit. Nothing I eat or drink now makes me want to taste it. Since it's there I sip it, sip again, then drink it slowly till it empties.

Even if he goes it's cost too much already. It brings back the car, the sweetness of the dark, the want I drank until the wanting curdled.

All I want is why. Since there's nothing left to lose I ask him.

"Does it change anything? You were sad and I was too. I only meant to comfort you. I tried to comfort Sarah after father hurt her. She used to crawl into my bed when she couldn't sleep. I only cuddled her to stop her crying and waking him and she ran. To him. He didn't beat me. He locked me in the cellar for a week. I had to promise to not let Sarah in again before he'd let me out. Then Anne told me he had beaten Sarah black and blue for getting in my bed. She told me what he'd done to her when the beatings started, what he'd said would happen to Rose if Anne ever told. He had raped Anne when she fell unconscious. I knew then why he hit them, to punish them for what they made him want to do. A month after that he took the post in India, sent me away. I knew too much. So I'm far worse than him. Because I never told, because I knew you trusted me. It started off a game. The more I played the more I wished that it was real. Once I made it real it was too real for you. I knew you, Grace. Knew exactly what you'd do to pay for Chris's dream. I guess it's just as well your mother lost the baby. Who knows what you pass down? My father's part of me no matter how I hated him."

For a month he gave me back my dark. It was so black I rubbed my eyes until they bled with colour, longed for pain to shut the darkness out. It didn't matter that he'd made the holes, without him I was empty.

I can still see him in the firelight. I had stayed awake until I heard one set of footsteps climb the stairs. I could hear a movie play downstairs. He isn't watching it. I wait until he feels me in the room. His smile is quizzical, a question answered by my kiss. We take the fire with us. He had taught me how to burn, that night he taught me how to glow.

I filled the dark with him. When he hurt me I'd see it coming, know what it would feel like, find a place to hide. I would not give him me to see him run before I got to ten.

I sealed the letter. Hoped it was enough. We picked a Sunday evening, people getting ready for work, an empty beach. We agreed how far I'd go into the sea. I'd stop before the cliff.

I am truly withdrawn that day. I wait until twilight to slip out of Chris's room, a shadow tracing a path down the staircase to the door. The clock chimes six. He has no more than an hour left to breathe air. Then water will swallow him.

It is the beginning of my nightmare, in my dreams a broken jigsaw, the pieces I have never found before. I am fighting to find the sandy bottom, my feet touch nothing. I slip under. There is no floor here; I am too far out. And my body is bloated and heavy. The undercurrent is too strong, pulling me deeper, hungry.

I kick hard and fight to reach the surface. Punch holes in the grey shell. Tearing holes for my arms, another hole for my head. My eyes stinging, pieces of sky blurring, then clearing. My brother and stepfather are pushing the water aside to reach me. There is terror on Paul's face and I know he has remembered the time I told him of how seas have hidden mountains, secret cliffs. I look at Chris but he is watching Paul. He thinks I'm pretending. If I shout out the truth, Paul will know our plan. There is nothing to do but keep fighting the water, buy Chris time. For my brother is steering him towards the edge of the shelf: then he is ours, then it is over.

The last images I have of Paul is Chris pushing him under, Paul struggling to break free, his arms flailing, his feet desperate to find something to push against, finding nothing. Then I see nothing but grey water, then nothing at all.

Chris is holding me and pulling me upwards. I begin to help him. His face is white in the grey water; there is no sky. I am numb with cold. All I can see is the colour changing as we push towards the surface, moving through a spectrum of greys.

I am lying on the sand, and gulping air as if I have forgotten the sweetness, sea-salt mingling with relief. I cannot get enough. I look for Chris. A few feet away. He is still.

I tried to bring him back. Breathe air into him, force his heart to beat. Pump water out. It was too late. I lay upon the sand and tried to burrow into it, because if I looked anywhere else all I saw was stars. Cold stars.

It was Robert who found us joined on the sand, who knew enough to spot the difference between alive and dead when both were cold, who gave me warmth until I felt enough to know that the difference was too big for Chris. His father's urgency moved us out of the way. He threw Robert a blanket, knelt by Chris as Robert wrapped it round us. I watched him turn into a doctor, trying everything I'd tried and more. He had to shout to make me hear him when he asked where Paul was. Robert held me tighter, shouting back.

"Not now Dad!"

"It must be now. For her sake more than his. Trust me, Grace, silence won't help Chris. Tell me what happened. I won't stop. I could do this half asleep." I grimace as he rolls Chris over, trying to get water out.

"I need facts, Grace. Facts I can reset if I have to. Where is he?"

"The sea has him. We drowned him. He was meant to think I was trying to drown myself. To get him in the water." I touched my belly. "He had to be dead to save the baby he wanted me to kill," I spat. I felt the words hit Robert, saw them freeze his father's hands.

"Don't stop! Just bring my brother back. Because he might have pushed Paul under but it was me who made him hate enough to do it. I don't know who I hate more, him or me. Because I let it go too far to tell."

I see his hands stop trying, turn from a doctor's to a father's, lost like Chris's hands when there is something they can't fix, and stop him with my eyes before he says the word that makes it real.

I sat too numb to feel, too blank to see my mother till her cry was part of mine. I found out later she had found our letter in the hall and called the only person she could trust before she ran to meet the sea she knew too well to trust. She reached Chris first and curled beside him as he once did in her. I ran from Robert and shut her out to lie upon the other side, as divided by his body now as we had been when it had been full of life. I met her eyes by accident, suddenly wondering if she had forgotten Paul or couldn't make it real by asking. Doctors cannot cure the truth. I have a hazy memory of him somehow getting her to follow him and when she sank back down she seemed the small. I looked at her and she looked back then stared down at my belly, in the moment when we looked at each other saying all there was to say. I wasn't him, she wasn't him, looking only rubbed that in. The doctor gently told me the police must be told, I must let them take my brother's body, tell myself that I'd keep all that mattered. In the end Robert had to put his body in Chris's place before I'd let it go. He told me later that his father told them that when the police got there I must be gone, told Robert to take me back to their house while he went to the surgery to phone them. Robert talked me from the beach. I can remember sitting in the car and laughing when I took in that he was driving it, giggling as if the sound rewound the reel. I remember him half carrying me upstairs, him lying down beside me on the couch, me asking where they'd take Chris, then kissing him to stop him crying. I must have fell asleep, because the next piece I have is of being jolted back by anger, Robert arguing with his father who was saying something making little sense about avoiding questions dressed in uniforms, answers locked in tape recorders. I didn't want to listen, couldn't stand to hear them fight.

"Stop it! Chris is dead because of me. I'll tell the police that."

Robert looked at his father as if lost for words,

"Make some tea and toast, Robert." I nearly said no then realised what he was doing. Getting Robert out to talk to me alone. I sat up, not wanting to be lying down for what was in his face. When he sat down the space he left between us told me it would be the doctor who would speak.

"You didn't kill Chris, Grace. Neither did the sea."

"He drowned to save me. Drowned Paul because I wanted him dead."

"I think Chris had a heart attack. There was so little water in him to come out. Unless you..."

"No, but I just assumed I wasn't doing it properly."

"Nobody knew Chris better than you did but I know one thing for sure: he hated killing anything. So killing Paul was his choice too, Grace. Did he know you were pregnant?"

"Yes. Not because I told him though. Because I forgot to hide it well enough. When we went swimming." I started to cry.

"You keep something hidden too long it comes out because it gets too big to keep inside. I should have noticed something wrong. You were so pale, so quiet. I thought you were missing Chris."

"I was missing both of them. And wanting to tell them and never knowing how or when. Just knowing what Paul would do if I did." I told him how Paul had kept me silent, neither of us noticing Robert there.

"I would have killed him too. I can't believe I thought I knew him." He looked at his father. "You can't let her tell them. Will the police care more about a baby or a murder? Grace? What if you tell the truth and they don't care about your side of it?"

"He's right. It's up to you, Grace. I can't tell you to lie but if you say nothing I can stop them asking, stop them pushing you to tell. Protect you. But you need to decide tonight because they'll be here tomorrow morning. Go to bed, son. I'll look after her." Robert went reluctantly. His father made fresh tea and toast and told me just to swallow. Then he sat beside me while I told him everything I didn't want in Robert's head. I told it from the beginning, letting him sew up the gaps with questions, for Chris's sake deciding all the police would get would be the threads. He smiled and took my hand.

"She or he will be as big as this soon."

"That isn't big enough to love it. I'm doing this for Chris."

"You don't have to love it yet. Just let it grow. The love will too. Stay here as long as you want."

"That isn't fair on Robert. I only care about Chris not being here, not who is."

"It's what he wants. Chris was his friend too. Shall I put you in your room to try to sleep?"

"I won't sleep. I can't feel the baby moving."

He asks me to lie back on the sofa. Hands press gently on my belly,

"Grace, I need to examine you properly but not tonight. Are you sure about the dates?"

I shake my head. I ask him to do it now. I tell him why. It doesn't hurt. I keep telling myself where I am. When he tells me, I am lost.

My mother never told anyone about the letter. She simply said she called the doctor's house to ask if Chris and I were there. It was easier for her if people thought Paul died to save me than imagine her asleep while he abused me. It was the only version I could choose, not because it was the easiest, it was the safest. By taking me home Robert and his father had become a part of what I'd done. I had loved this house since I first looked out of the window. We could only keep it safe if no one looked inside. The truth would blow it down.

The more the doctor shielded me, the more I saw we'd planned like children. In the morning he phoned to check how mother was. When the police car came up the drive he told me to stay in bed. I listened as he kept the two men where he wanted them. It had to be a family thing, for Robert did it too. Remembering the balcony he'd glued me to, I smiled. I knew the men would leave and each would blame the other for not getting past the hall. I heard one ask why I was here and not at home and him reply a woman should not be asked to comfort a daughter when her son and husband had just drowned. The words were cut by scalpel, you barely felt them going in. I could imagine them arguing already over who had asked the stupid question, could hear Chris warning me they would not all be stupid. In that moment it stabbed me that it would always be like this. Nobody but Chris would thrust the knife and only I would see the wound. I would know exactly what he'd say and never hear him say it. I would laugh at jokes that no one else would get, begin a sentence that hurt too much to finish. If this was how it felt to lose someone you loved too much, a little was too much.

You pick a point to reach and tell yourself tomorrow doesn't matter. You feel the pain run through you. You bargain, promise if it gets too bad you'll stop. I was always running after him but I could always see him, know he would be smiling when I got there, know the smile would cancel out the pain. He wasn't meant to stop and I don't want to overtake him. I can't pretend this isn't real. You swing from wanting nothing back to finding something you can cling to. Robert's always there. Tomorrow and the next day. Any further I don't look. I know at some point momentum will take over. That is how you run when tears run out. On sand.

I watched the church fill up with black. There were no flowers but bluebells I had picked. My mother sat beside me too far away to touch. Robert held my hand when his father gave the reading she had wanted. When the villagers threw sand upon my brother's coffin I did too. Then I looked up to the sky remembering the bird he tried to save, imagining the two of them dodging in and out the clouds.

The doctor had arranged with mother he would offer tea at his house, partly knowing mother didn't have the strength to arrange anything and partly knowing an upside down house was better when people felt upside down. It also meant he could contain the gossip. He refused to call the tea a wake. I only noticed Lucy when she touched my shoulder. Wearing black she looked like mother, mother for today had glued herself to Lucy's side. I was trying to avoid my mother's look, if looks could kill the tea would be for me. A part of me was grateful black was slimming while the other part was sick of slimming down the truth. In my black dress I was just puppy fat when only Robert's look was stopping me shout pregnant. Knowing I wouldn't want to upset Lucy he released me.

"I keep thinking Chris would never have wanted people wearing black for him." Lucy whispered.

"Chris would have wanted people looking like themselves. It didn't matter what he would have wanted, what I asked for. Mother wanted black. Where is she?" I heard myself and wondered what my aunt must hear. Not a sympathetic daughter but a stony sister but the stones were caught from her.

"She's taking pills to calm her down. It must be time to take one. Yesterday she asked me to drive her into town. Does she have a different doctor?"

"I wouldn't know. She'd never tell me. I do know Paul did. He told me doctors were better staying doctors than becoming friends." I almost smiled, could catch his voice, followed it.

"Well your boyfriend's father seems to be a doctor and a friend. And very good at keeping them apart when one is better I suspect! He wanted me to know what happened, what is happening. Would you stay with us in Cambridge if it gets too hard here?"

"It feels like leaving Chris behind."

"I think he'd understand. I always saw Chris without you, never you without Chris. Occasionally we'd meet in Norwich. Edward says boarding school is good for teaching boys not feeding them. We'd take Chris out for lunch."

I realise all over again Chris had a world I wasn't part of. Different people in it. All the differences I couldn't bear to spot were now full stops. I wasn't clumsy now just in a rush. I wasn't slow just scared to come in first. Because he liked me second.

"I always meant to ask you and Chris to come to Cambridge. When today is over could we try to get to know each other better?"

I nod and suddenly see something to be glad about. I never tell him but I sometimes do what doctors say because I hear the friend. I'll write this down tonight to remind me for a moment I felt glad. The glads will add up even when the sad won't let me count. The glad was thinking Lucy held a part of Chris I didn't, something we could share. Because I need as many parts as I can find to keep him whole.

I feel my face draw half a smile, see Lucy draw the other half. She draws another face as mother comes towards us, a patient one.

The gossip focused on the shadows we were dressed in black for, eating cake they couldn't eat. Today our presence toned it down, the volume would be turned up tomorrow. Questions no one dared ask us. Why Paul's family had not come to the funeral? Why my mother barely spoke to me? Why I was living in the doctor's house? The questions would go round in circles fading to a dot... If the villagers talked inside their shops and houses, in the end they loved their doctor too much for talk to spread too far. They believed whatever he told them. Paul was the outsider after all, the sea a serial killer. The police returned to town. The newspapers said his sisters were too distraught to comment, no one told them that his widow was too distraught to leave the house or why her daughter never went back there.

Paul's body was never found. The sea had stayed on our side and kept the bargain silent. Silently I wished a bargain could be made to take the baby too.

I used to draw this house inside my head when I needed somewhere I could flee to. The upside down house I had always envied Robert was mine now too. It had never mattered less. It felt like being given back the doll with the blue satin dress that Chris had stolen when I was thirteen and going to show it to him to find him dead and see the doll grow every day. The baby's kicks reminded me of the bargain I had made to cause all this, the bargain I was carrying I could drop but never break. The house reminded me that everything was upside down without Chris and nothing I could do would overturn that.

The doctor had agreed with mother that I could stay as long as that was what I wanted. Part of me had wanted her to fight to get me back. A little part of me had wanted someone there who would remember parts of Chris that Robert and his father couldn't. What difference would it make when the differences were too big to forget? I made a deal to start to call the doctor David, made a deal with David that I would eat a little more each day. He said that wants came back and deals would do for now. We made a deal that I could sleep in Robert's room or he in mine. He said we ended up together anyway, we might as well start off there. When Robert found me messing up the bed I hadn't slept in it was the first time he'd laughed since Chris had died. He said his dad would leave us to make our own beds, knew that only deals with leeway worked. I knew his father hoped by pushing us together we would stick. He knew I needed Robert, knew that Robert needed me, that right now wants were trumped by needs. The last thing I had wanted was to mark my sixteenth birthday. That morning I sat down for breakfast, caught the scent and smiled. The table was a sun of yellow roses.

When Robert held me close he wanted me to turn to him, he wanted me to let him feel the baby moving, ask me what it felt like when it did. The only place I felt safe now was in his arms. I never told him I felt like a cocoon the baby grew in, once it didn't need me I would be a husk. I couldn't tell him that the house was just a keep, that no knight kept Paul out. What good were walls when wolves were in your head? I knew what turning turned into, knew that love could not be shaped by fear. I turned the other way and couldn't tell him why. I woke one morning finding him not there. He moved into my room.

His father was too wise to try to mend a rift that trying might widen. It was easier to talk about the baby, easier to believe that something new would fill the gap. We tossed names back and forth like peace offerings, picking colours for the nursery like flowers on olive branches. Carefully we built a bridge. We never talked about the baby's father till the day his father told us we were acting just like children, running out of time to write a story people would accept. He said belief was less important, if we planned to stay here when the baby came she had to be accepted. What we told the village soon would matter. When I found him on his own I asked him why he always called the baby she. He said he simply liked reminding fathers-to-be that daughters could be too.

We tried to think which story would be best, not easiest to tell or true but possible to understand. The baby must be Robert's not Paul's. I knew that Robert wanted this. A baby with his name would be a vow, would tie our hands in knots so tight untying them would cut us all for as the baby grew the tie would too. I countered this by knowing we were already tied, in ties of chain, the lies had alloyed into steel, the links we'd forged to keep the baby safe must keep us all safe. Naming Paul the father would reveal too much if someone saw the links. How did you decide which version of a story you should tell? You picked the one that people would prefer to hear, the one a child could grow beside, the one you hoped would hurt the least. We decided that the doctor would tell people the truth: I couldn't stay here now that Chris was never coming back and yet would never leave. We needed somewhere I could grow without the questions growing too, a place to set a different story. Cambridge would have no pictures of him, Cambridge would have Lucy. We decided when I was ready I would go there for a week and stay if Lucy didn't change her mind. In the end I didn't go, I ran.

Someone To Turn Back To

July, 1975

In the moments when you wake you are between two worlds, you may slip either way. You can wish it, fight it, not choose it or compel it. Once you are gripped by one world you are locked out of the other. But you belong to both. If I belong anywhere it feels like in-between. I am not even sure sometimes which one I'd choose.

It feels like playing hide and seek and finding that the game is real and hiding more than being found. It feels like seeking knowing who you're looking for is hidden somewhere you can never reach – except in dreams and nightmares, for Chris is part of both. What I tell no one is that Paul is too and that I look for him, as tangled as I was before the telling pulled me out. I remember telling Robert fear and darkness are not twins and know this is true. They are not twins but they are partners. I know now that love and hate are too. I hate Paul for a hundred reasons. None will count in the world that borders this. I love Paul because I can't escape the path we made in darkness; I love Chris more because the paths were made in sunlight too. It doesn't matter if they only take me there at night. I would rather have the nightmare, freeze the lifetime we were fighting to the surface, than be warm where he is cold, slipping from his guard to rooms and things that only prove him gone.

I can sit here half the day if they go out. Days cut in half so easily. I may say goodbye, I may just let them go. I may have things I say I'll do and never do them. I may say nothing then do something I never tell them. They will not spot the difference. It is not hard to miss, for it makes none. I am a trespasser in dreams, an eavesdropper in reality. In dreams there is nothing I can take or keep, in reality there is nothing that I want.

I stand upon the balcony, the sky so endless, I grip the rail and feel like paper that letting go will blow away. The clouds have shapes that make me want to hide. I can't believe I used to sit and watch them, can't believe I ever made them islands. The girl who used to lie and make the grass a sea is scared of green now, scared of strangers, scared of laughter. I am not her, she is not me. Unless I swim.

I know they'll never understand what draws me here, why I will swim where Chris was drowned. Or if they guess they keep it as a guess and not a know. I do the same, the knowing will not fill the spaces. I am jigsaw, nothing holding me together, nothing they can do to glue me back. There are too many pieces only Chris and I have pictures of when whole. I think of what my father said about reflections, how mirrors make us feel that we are real. My brother's face had been my mirror, my face his. He was nowhere, everywhere reflected only me. I make their world the dream and swim to Chris.

In the dream I feel him slide inside the covers, feel his skin is bare and match my skin to his. I let him seek, discover where I hide, exploring, swimming till we pull each other underwater, till I guide him to me, flicker in the jolt of joining flowing on his face. He moves to feel me catch him, moving deeper, filling me until it feels like falling, till suddenly one movement sends us flying to a bottom so far down that touching it we shatter knowing nowhere else will we be whole again. We hold each other till the pieces hold together, as whole as love can be once it's been made.

That is why I go there, without him nowhere else I feel complete. The trouble is I fall apart each time I have to leave because he can't. I break the surface feeling my shell break as I see the sky and swim the in-between until the water gets so shallow that I have to stop, imagining he is willing me to push my feet into the sand and wade until the sea runs out. Inside my shell I feel too soft to stand. I always do because I feel him watching. Telling me I am the one who's real.

I don't remember anything being different the day I stopped believing him. I remember wading back so empty I lay down on the sand and let the waves wash over me and wished they'd take me with them till they numbed me, numbed the wish as well. The tide went out and left me there to dry. I dimly thought I should go back. I tried to stand but cold had turned muscle into wood. I fell back down and used what strength was left to burrow in the sand. I felt the breeze become a wind, the time the lap of waves, the falling sky. The clouds were made of eiderdown. I let thoughts come and go until they had no sense or shape. The sand was swallowing me. I woke up back in bed and heard my name and squeezed my eyes shut. I felt the baby feebly kick and knew that it was stronger.

May was June. Days were pictures through the windows when I bothered looking. Dinner was a salad with some kind of sliced meat I assumed was ham but could be almost anything when nothing tasted right. I could see them watching me or rather watching what I ate. I saw the doctor look at Robert knowing what the look meant.

It meant "It's better coming from me." He was wrong.

"Grace you're not eating enough."

"For me or for the baby? Does it matter what I want? Or feel?"

"Of course it does." he said.

"Tell me then. Tell me what I want right now? Get it right and I will clear the plate and ask for more."

"What happens if I get it wrong?" he asks and masks a smile.

"I haven't worked that out yet." I snap.

"Just dad or me as well?" Robert asks.

"Oh join in if he needs help." I bait.

The doctor takes his time to answer.

"Angry. Obviously."

"That's the façade. What's underneath?" I dig.

"Sad, lonely."

"Only layers," I say.

"I don't like playing games with feelings," David says. "If we're even doing it we've got it wrong. Can you tell us instead?"

I feel it as I drag the words out. "Nothing...Empty.. Like I thought I was real and instead I'm made of plastic like a doll. With a little doll inside. But that's the one that's real. And it's because of it I'm not."

Robert gets up, to comfort me. I freeze him there.

"I remember stopping eating after dad died. And when I ate, it was for Chris. But he's not here. I don't want to eat or drink or care. I just want him."

"Can you think of one thing, anything, that would be better than this Grace? Anything you want, even a little bit, even if want is too big a word?"

"I don't know. I didn't even know I was going to say that. I didn't even know it was inside," I say. I focus on him, can't look at Robert.

"… Then it proves something was. Just feel, don't think, then say it."

I try. It feels like falling through myself and pulling something tiny out.

"Lucy."

I look at the numbers as I copy them. Strange how so many makes it feel so faraway. The writing doesn't feel like mine. I dial before I change my mind. I hear it ring and when she answers start to cry.

David said we'd drive to Cambridge, Back then the railway lines between went anyway but A to B. The morning sun was warm, When Robert kissed me on the cheek I knew my leaving was a leaving behind to him. His father deftly steered away from this. I watched the scenery rippling by, slipping in and out of focus till I let it go to sleep. I woke and tried to stretch and wondered if the baby stretched when I did. He handed me a pack of toffees.

"Are we -"

"Nearly there?" he smiled. "About ten miles now. There aren't many signposts, Cambridge doesn't need them. People plan to come here, don't just come by chance."

"What's wrong?" His voice had caught, a needle sticking on a record.

"I never planned to not come back. I told myself when Nesta died one day I would. I'd think of taking Robert, it always stayed a thought."

"But when your parents died?" I ventured.

"They moved to Norwich after we got married. Trouble with the neighbours." He tried to joke. I remembered Nesta's father hadn't planned on her marrying the neighbour's son.

"Why now then? Robert could have brought me."

"He offered. He would have tried to talk you into visiting not staying. He's good at talking into. I knew you needed out. You need a woman now. To talk, not in or out, just talk. To teach you how to giggle, be sixteen."

"Then I'll thank you now," I said and meant it, seeing giggles had a price.

"There was another reason. Norwich has no medical school. Robert has applied to study here. He should find out by Friday. So today's a practice run for me. A coming back."

I turn to the window but know he's seen it hurts. I know how important becoming a doctor is to Robert. By not telling me himself is he telling me I'm not important to him anymore or that he isn't important enough to me?

I don't have to ask how nearly there we are. The outskirts turn brighter, richer, gold and green and honey, red and lime and emerald. The buildings are not built but sculptured, the streets laid out, not left to happen. They look like pictures in a fairytale. It makes me want to walk and be a part of it.

"Why are there so many bicycles?" I ask, as he brakes suddenly to avoid hitting one, the person responsible flashing us a smile and riding on.

"So many students. This is nothing, out of term time. But most people here have bicycles, cycling is easier than driving. Tell you what - let's take the scenic route. Lucy's street isn't far now."

I can't think of anything to say. All of it is scenic.

"This bit along the river is where I used to walk with Nesta. It's called The Backs."

"Why?"

"Because it's the backs of the colleges, the most important ones anyway. If you walk along here you can cross the bridges, or just stand on top and watch the punters."

I gave up. I had no idea what he meant but asking questions was making me feel lost. He seemed to know where he was going, cutting off and slowing down.

"This is Madingley Road. Lucy said to look for number 27."

He changes gear to a crawl then stops. Not because the house says twenty-seven, because Lucy is running down the drive.

"Perfect timing David. Here before the rabble. And how was the chauffeur Grace?"

I say fine. My shyness has come back and Lucy doesn't look like Lucy here. Her short skirt suits her. The sky blue with the matching T shirt makes her legs look long and gold, makes me feel pale and fat.

"Come through and have tea in the garden. Leave the suitcases for now. You can see the house later. I've given you a front bedroom Grace. You'll be cooler. I remember carrying Jake in summer. At five months I felt so hot I couldn't sleep."

The way she says a front bedroom makes me wonder just how many there are. Automatically following her we take the path around the house into the garden where she leads us to an oval table big enough for six at least. The sun is dancing, bringing everything to life except for me. I sink into the nearest chair. The table is teak, the cushions on the chairs cream with raspberry stripes. Lucy tells David to sit down too. She says she'll bring the tea and disappears before my eyes catch up.

"I would have offered to help if I wasn't scared she might have told me off!" He whispers. "She seems different here, as if she likes her own way best."

"I don't think I feel scared, more looked after." I whisper back.

I'd like to explore the garden but I'm too tired to move so I sit and look around. The tallest trees are taller than the house. In the top half an island of lawn is surrounded by deep borders, colours flowing into well-trained rainbows. In the bottom half the garden has been left to its own devices, getting lost and running wild. In one tree I can spy a swing.

A fortnight later I am sitting on the swing half tempted to give in and try it, half worried it won't take my weight.

"Dare you!"

The voice is Jake's, the cousin I had never met until two weeks ago, the eldest one of Lucy's rabble. Fiona I had barely seen so far. Because we were the same age I had hoped she'd like me. Now I was beginning to think she didn't. Thomas being ten liked everyone. The voice emerges from the fruit cage. Jake follows, carrying a basket of raspberries. I suspect the first lot are in his stomach.

"Go on Grace, you know you want to! If you break my swing I promise I'll forgive you." he teases, grinning.

Jake looks like Edward, his father. Taller already though, with hair and eyes the colour of treacle toffee. Always eating, always laughing, charming when he wants to be, trouble when he gets the chance. I liked Jake but getting to know him made me sad as well. It made me wonder if without the trouble of looking after me Chris would have been like Jake, made me miss the parts of Chris I'd never get to know. I couldn't tell Jake this, just like I couldn't tell Lucy why I couldn't sleep in the front bedroom. Pink would always have secrets. Other things couldn't be secret. Like a baby due in October or why that secret must be kept here till it couldn't be kept anymore.

"Jake," He looks up from the basket. "Does the baby make Fiona uncomfortable?"

For once he looks serious.

"The baby isn't inside Fiona. It's you this happened to. You can't get away from that. Or stop it happening. Fiona likes to be the centre of attention. That's all Grace."

"I'm sorry you never met Chris. I think you could have been friends."

"I did meet him. Once. With dad. We went for lunch in Norwich."

I wait for him to tell me more. My look becomes a question. When he meets my eyes he looks too careful. Like Robert when he's thinking whether thoughts are better in or out.

"I'm not sure about the friends with Chris and me."

"Why not?" I accuse. Why does it matter now? As if Chris is listening.

"Brothers and sisters don't have to like each other. Love comes first. I love my sister because she's my sister. But we wouldn't really be friends. Chris reminded me of Fiona. Only happy being number one. Always having to come first."

"I never minded being second."

"That's like saying you don't mind not being good at tennis when you've never tried. You care about something taken away, not what you never had. I think we could be friends though. If you let me remind you how to swing!" He put the basket down and pushed till I was swinging by myself without feeling that I was.

I found out the house had been built by Edward's father who had given it to Edward when Thomas was born. There were two living rooms, the second called the morning room, the other called the television room because it was the only room that Lucy would allow one in. We spent the evenings there when it got too cold to sit outside. The kitchen and the dining room looked out upon the garden. Edward had a study he rarely used because he said it only made work feel like work. I discovered there were eight bedrooms. When I managed to tell Lucy the pink bedroom made me feel homesick she simply nodded and said the roof bedroom would be ideal if I could manage the stairs. She took me up to show me. Stretching out my breath I climbed the narrow staircase I would have bounded up a few months before. She slowed her pace to mine and waited at the top. She opened the door and held it letting me go first. I looked and let my eyes play hide and seek, the room was like a magic box designed to perfectly fit inside the roof. A window set above the bed let the sun fall through. I could imagine waking up would be like swimming in the sky.

"You wouldn't need to use the stairs at night. It even has a bathroom," Lucy said, pointing to a door I'd thought was just a cupboard.

"The walls could do with freshening up. For now when you finish your painting of the garden you can hang it here and have a roof garden!"

"If it's good enough." I said.

"Grace, you say that and I hear your mother. Cambridge is for finding out how good you are. Try painting over her and listen to yourself. Now shall we get my lazy son to bring your things up here?"

Dr Jolly had left a prescription for a walk each day. He had said it would make the labour easier. Unconvinced and tired of everything revolving round an alien that would change my world forever I found a new excuse whenever Lucy tracked me down. She began to set a time at breakfast, making up a picnic, planning where we'd go. I found out the strange canoes were punts, the punters were the people who were paid to punt or the ones stupid enough to think a pole would get you anywhere but in the river. Watching from the bridges I could see what Lucy meant: the professional punters looked like Adonis and glided past like gondoliers, the beginners looked like Pooh Bear navigating with a giant Pooh stick. I soon knew each bridge by name: the Bridge of Sighs an echo of its Venice cousin, the Mathematical Bridge and the myths surrounding its construction as convoluted as it was. I found out the college gardens were the perfect place to have a picnic if you could get past the guard dogs trained to chase you to the front entrance. Lucy's charm tamed them instead. Inside the gardens romped in the midsummer heat, the roses tangling with each other, phlox and Japanese anemones white as snow. The silver grass would catch the sun, the feathers burnished into copper. Topiary shaped into bears and peacocks made strange companions when I woke forgetting where I was. I fell asleep like falling in a sea of flowers, slowly floating my way back. Lucy brought a book and dipped in and out of it till I woke up.

I found I could get lost in Cambridge, switching off my thoughts. When Lucy had things to do I felt my way alone. The ancient streets were soothing, alleyways that led to nowhere with any memories at all, quadrangles where I sat and drew the buildings that enclosed me, never capturing their perfection, succumbing when they captured me, safe beneath a lid of cloudless blue.

Robert phoned at precisely eight sixteen once a week. What began as reassuring started feeling sad when every week the talk ran out before the clock hands even got to eight thirty. He had been given a place at Jesus College as he had wanted. He said he'd come and visit soon to look around the college and I could be his guide in Cambridge, we'd have time to talk, I almost asked if time would be more than sixteen minutes, if we'd find more than sixteen words. Soon didn't seem too keen to come. Soon visit came alone but never seemed to care how long it took to get here. I tried to say I missed him, miss was just a word, it had no shape or feeling, nothing forced it out. I couldn't shape a lie instead. He asked about the baby, if he or she was kicking yet, if I was feeling tired, if I'd thought of any names. The next week when the words were echoes I threw them back and fired more. Yes, it was kicking, kicking hard like I'd kick him if he was here. Yes, I was tired, tired of talking about the baby and no I hadn't thought of any names for something that I didn't want but I could think of plenty names for him. If he ever bothered coming. Then I slammed the phone down and ran upstairs as if there was no baby. Gulping in air I felt the tears an inch away, the bed a step away. I was about to close the gaps when I heard the footsteps on the stairs and heard the knock then turned away. Before it came again I heard the door push open.

"Is it safe in here?" Lucy said.

"Will you go away if I say no?" I pasted on a smile.

"No, probably not. So we might as well sit down." She shut the door and sat down on the bed. I felt too heavy to keep on standing so I sank beside her.

"I'm guessing that was either Robert or his father. From where I came in."

"Where did you come in?"

"In time for kick. The kicking him." She smiled, the smile I recognised now. The smile was the one she used with Fiona, meaning all the things I guessed a mother said when she didn't know what might come tumbling out. It always hurt to see and yet I couldn't pull myself away. Fiona always did though and Lucy would go to find my uncle. And I would feel left out and all the things I felt inside but couldn't say. Because I knew what could come out. I felt it stirring now.

I sat and wondered how much was safe to say.

"It was Robert. If I talk to his dad at least he asks how I am. Robert asks about the baby so much I feel like passing it the phone." Lucy smiles.

"Sorry Grace. I know it isn't funny."

"Yes it is. Once I could have said the same to him and he'd have laughed. We fight all the time now. What makes me so angry is I know why he's doing it. I was surprised he phoned at all tonight. I wonder if he almost didn't."

"What makes you say that?"

"Oh, he always phones at sixteen minutes past the hour. Tonight it rang at twenty past. It's silly really. Just a habit. It goes up a minute on my birthday. It was our way of knowing the other one was phoning."

"Edward and I used to have a code like that as well." I want to ask her what it was but see a shadow cross her face.

"I meant why you thought he might not phone?" she asks.

I can't see a way not to tell without making it seem bigger.

"Last week I said something horrible. I didn't mean it, he said the wrong thing and I was angry but that's no excuse." I haven't even told her yet and I am telling lies because I'd meant every word and he'd been all too right.

"He asked straight out if I was missing him. I said I was still too empty to have space for missing anyone but Chris. I should have said it was a different kind of missing, and if he'd left it there I would have, except he said he was tired of Chris still coming first." I glance at her and hope she'll interrupt. I remember Lucy is used to Fiona spinning straw to gold so I give up trying.

"I said Chris would always come first at being dead. That if he wanted me to miss him that much I was sure Chris would swap places. That was when he hung up on me."

Lucy doesn't look shocked as much as puzzled. "But Grace, you're bound to miss Chris. Miss is too small a word for what it must be like. I miss Jake when he goes back to school but if anything happened..." She shudders. "Surely Robert understands that."

"Robert knows better than anyone how much I miss Chris but he doesn't know how to talk about it. Because in a way what I said was true. Chris will always come first by being dead and Robert can't compete with that. So he talks about the baby instead. And I get tired of that."

"I hardly know him but at the funeral Robert watched you all the time. He's shielding you from something that could ruin him. So he must really care for you. But you've been here six weeks and I don't have a clue what he means to you. Before all this happened what did you feel for him?"

I can tell her half the truth and she'll see half of me. But lies will be the other half, the half I'll see in every mirror if I do.

"I never had a chance to find out. I always stood him next to Chris. The more I felt for Chris the further off that got. I'd punish Chris by pulling Robert back. But what I let Paul do was worse. Because Paul wouldn't care if I saw Robert, what he did later rubbed him out. And sometimes I wanted him to. He didn't always make me." I glance at her, ashamed.

"You trusted him Grace. He used that to get closer. When you're halfway between a girl and a woman being close to someone feels the most important thing of all. He used that too."

"Robert used to be my best friend. He was the closest thing to a boyfriend you can have when most of what you say is lies and most of what you do is just an act. Because if you told the truth or stopped pretending anything you said or did would hurt them more. The trouble is the lies don't ever stop and you keep on and on pretending. You don't know what else to do."

"I used to do exactly what you're doing now Grace." She says it slowly as if she's testing something out.

"What bit?" I smile but I'm acting.

"The bit you do when you don't want to be in your body anymore. The only bit you can do. Because bits is all you are. So you say you not I or me because it makes you somebody else while you stand and watch it happen. I lied to my boyfriend as well."

"But Edward must have forgiven you."

"I don't mean Edward. It was your father I lied to. That was why I didn't marry him. Because I would have had to tell the truth and it gets too big to tell."

"When does it get small enough to tell?"

"I'm not sure it does. But you get stronger and time pushes it further away. I guess when you can let him be a ghost. Paul still feels real to you. My father has been a ghost for long enough to keep him there. Provided I stay here."

"Your father?"

"Yes. My father. I wish that I could call him something else. But I can't. So I became the someone else instead."

"But mother always said you were his favourite?"

"I was. Favourite to love and favourite to hurt. He didn't do what Paul did, He never touched me that way. He never left any bruises either. He knew lots of other ways."

"My mother never noticed if there were bruises. But Paul was careful where he left them. Not that it mattered when she barely looked at me."

"I did try once to tell my mother. He'd cut six inches off my hair while I was asleep. He told her it was just a punishment for serving in the shop and not tying it back. She didn't want to know how often he punished me or what he did. She was too scared he'd punish her. My father was an iron God to her and my sister, a tin god to me. He was a grocer who had aimed too high and missed the mark. He served and hated everyone he served. Behind the scenes we were expected to serve him. I should have told your father but my father made me feel so helpless everyone else seemed powerless. I also knew Lawrence would never leave Sea Palling.

"Was that why you didn't marry him?"

"I didn't marry him because I didn't love him. Edward was my best friend's cousin. We met at her engagement party. He asked if he could call me, I wrote the number on my napkin thinking he would leave it on the table. He phoned the very next day. I told your father knowing I had broken our engagement with a napkin, knowing it was right even if Edward and I were wrong. We were engaged within a month. I never told him we planned to live in Norwich. After the storm Norwich wasn't far enough away."

"Mother wouldn't talk about the storm. Father told me there are some things you can't put into words because the pictures are too loud. I know now he was right." I said bitterly.

"Her story's different from mine. And I had Edward to write a new one with. That might be the same for you. Why not try seeing Robert here?"

How do I tell her I don't want a story Chris can't be in? How can I say the person I'm really angry with is the one I never show it to? Because I used to be his shadow and now he's mine, I have no shape without him, no body that belongs to me. I was a shape Paul filled too long.

I try to let out something. Like turning on a tap not turning all the way. "I keep expecting to wake up and Chris will tell me this was all a nightmare. Nothing's real without him. Especially not me. The only time I feel real is when I paint and I can't paint myself."

"What if there's another way of painting yourself? Like chameleons do. Where you change by changing places? You don't reinvent the colours, you absorb them. You don't have to change by growing, you can change by fitting. Like I did. Like you could if you stayed."

"You mean stay here in Cambridge? But..."

"Not just in Cambridge, here with us."

"Live here? Not go back home?"

"I was hoping this could be your home and we'd become your family."

"But Edward..."

"He would be delighted. We've talked about it."

"Fiona?" I said doubtfully

"Would come around to it. I had to talk to you first. Will you think about it, Grace? If Robert's right for you he'll be here anyway, you can take your time to find that out. Because if you change the scenery the whole play changes. You can make a whole new you. By being somewhere different." She smiles and reaches for my hair and lifts a lock she curls round her finger, letting go to watch me sweep the strands behind my ear... And suddenly she's Paul. Telling me I can be anyone I want to be. Before he set fire to my wants and left me made of holes. When Lucy says goodnight I escape beneath the quilt and grip my dark.

By day I could be in a dream, I cannot put it into words. It is the way I feel when I am walking in corridors of trees that reach to touch my hand, the shadows all seem friendly, nothing happens here that didn't happen yesterday, that will not be the same tomorrow, a place where everything is set in place, and everything has symmetry, everything is beautiful. Everything can stay like this if I stay. The castles can be real, the pavements can be solid. I have to decide if I have run away for good.

Jake takes me punting, stopping near the ice-cream shop. He ties the punt up and dashes off. He reappears with three cones sprinkled with moon dust. Laughing I take the chocolate one.

"I thought I was eating for two Jake. And how did you know what I wanted?"

"They can sell fifty flavours and you'll still have what you have at home. The mint-choc-chip is good here though. I'm starting the baby on vanilla!" He eats the baby's first and doesn't notice I'm drizzling mine with tears.

I ring Robert that night and keep it simple. All I say is summer's almost over, this time next year we'll have to think in threes and two comes first. He simply asks when.

I wish he'd hurry up. I'm in the garden eating breakfast, most of it still on the plate. He promised he'd be here by noon and now it's one. I'd hoped it would be warm enough for punting and it is so all the punts will go. The telephone is ringing. When it stops I suppose Lucy must have answered it. Edward left an hour ago to visit his parents, taking my belligerent cousins with him. I look up when I hear her footsteps. Only they sound wrong. When she looks at me her face is wrong but set, a captain's in a storm.

"Robert's in hospital. He's in a coma Grace. His father's asking if you'll come."

Edward told me what he had to as he drove to Norwich. Only afterwards I realised how carefully he'd steered, avoiding false reassurances, focusing on optimism while explaining to me what a coma was. He said the brain put up a roadblock keeping Robert sleeping while the doctors watched for any danger signs, the coma was the brain's way of diverting all the traffic so it could begin repairing itself. By the time we got there I knew the biggest danger was the coma if it carried on, a tunnel with less chance of coming out the longer you stayed in, a sleep without the guarantee of waking up. I stood inside the lift and told myself I couldn't lose him too and knew I could.

Robert came out the tunnel as I slept on a chair. I woke up and heard his father's voice, relief a rearrangement of the clouds upon his face. I was allowed to sit beside his bed in the intensive care room and soon adopted the soothing tones the nurses used to speak to him until they gently led him back to sleep. Dr Jolly swapped places with me till the evening then said the night shift was a father's job. Edward had booked rooms in the nearest hotel. He asked if he could check me and the baby over, telling me he was my doctor and my uncle now.

"All fine Grace. But you both need sleep. There might be few hills in Norfolk but Robert will find them all and some will feel like mountains on the course this takes. Recovering from a head injury is an expedition first and then a journey. If you're planning to go with him there's no other way but as a team. And something's telling me you'll be a visitor to Cambridge. Sometimes our minds are made up for us."

It is the last Saturday in September and I am sitting waiting for Lucy in the cafe, wondering if Cambridge was a dream or if Sea Palling has been made into an arcade game. Everything looks the same and is so different underneath. I am home, it doesn't feel like home, Robert's home and doesn't act like Robert. By now the story in the village is that I ran away to Cambridge too scared to tell him I was pregnant, Robert crashing when he went to get me back. His father broke the news of both together so the accident hit the front page. It was hard to see a baby as a scandal when the father was in and out of hospital, hard to ask about a wedding when the would be groom was still confusing rings and doughnuts. When he gets tired words play hide and seek and jokes need subtitles. Robert is supposed to have at least one nap a day now he's home. I know at least one nap will never happen if he's left alone, will turn to television the moment he has heard me shut the door, I know because he will forget to turn it off and I'll go back to find it blaring through the house to turn it down and find him in the kitchen burning toast or looking in the wrong cupboards for the same thing he'll complain has disappeared again. The doctors said we have to gently feedback his mistakes or else he'll keep on making them, we have to give the thing its name to peel it from his tongue or it will stay stuck. The doctors don't have to listen when he snaps back and can't explain why swear words flow like sonnets. Robert doesn't see the differences we spot, how he plays Monopoly as if the money's real, real money disappears so fast his father spent a week in jail for telling Robert to remember which is which.

Edward says the signs are good, that Robert will recover but some days are more snakes than ladders. It feels more like a yellow brick road where you find courage along the way, for swear words are not spells for new brains. Cambridge has agreed to hold his place a year. The doctors told us it takes time for roads to get diverted back inside your brain and Robert's brain is young enough to make new roads.

I sometimes wonder what's so bad about forgetting, I could make a list of all the stuff that crawls inside my head and lose it. I wish that I could write a different story and believe it true, like Robert when he says the car in front appeared from nowhere, leaving him with nowhere to go but the wrong side of the road. I wouldn't have to know the car in front had been on that stretch of road for half an hour. But wishes should be saved for when we need them most, not wishing for a crystal ball.

Lucy comes every week and sometimes Jake comes too at weekends. Jake's more patient with Robert than I am. I go to him when no one gets there first. The baby feels so big it's squeezing me out: I've lost my breath and Robert's lost the biscuits. The Robert I knew before the accident would be asking how I'm feeling, if I'm frightened, saying all the right things, chasing all the wrong thoughts out of my head. It feels as if his head can only cope with his own thoughts now. When Lucy goes I wish I'd gone too.

I feel the baby pushing down as if it's coming now and all the others say is that my body will take over when it's time. How can I say the thing that scares me most isn't how I'll get the baby out but the space I'm left with when its gone?

"Sorry Grace." She looks carefully at me. "Have people been asking too many questions while you've been waiting?"

"Only how many weeks I have to go. Then they say I don't look big enough." I try to smile.

Dr Jolly had kept the dates as vague as possible, helped by the fact that they were. He had told me late October, the villagers November. So I guess by then I'll be enormous.

"I really am sorry. I made the mistake of going to see your mother first."

"Did she ask about me?" The words were out before I could stop them.

"No Grace," Lucy said quietly. "It isn't really you. It isn't as simple as that."

"How simple can it be? I killed Chris. He killed Paul for me. So I did really. Do you know what she hates most? The way we lured him in. That he thought I was trying to kill myself and it mattered. That he couldn't swim and still went in to save me. Because I mattered more than her," I said viciously.

"All of that is probably true. You have every right to be angry with her. She always loved Chris more. She put Paul first as well, she should have seen what he was doing, should have looked at you. But you have a choice Grace."

"That's why I'm angry. I don't have choices. I have to live when Chris is dead. I have to have this baby."

"I don't mean that kind of choice. You could do what she couldn't. Really look at her. Try to understand."

"Why? You said it Lucy. She doesn't even care enough to ask about me, remember I'm alive. What more do I need to understand?"

"What makes her how she is, who she is. It might not stop you hating her. It won't take away the anger. Feelings are a bit like babies. They weigh you down, fill you up. They kick and punch and wake when you're asleep. But understanding is like gas and air. It cuts the pain."

"How do I understand when she won't talk?"

"You find someone else who knows the story. A sister."

The sun was bright, the sky still blue, the clouds marshmallows. But Lucy saw a different picture, painting it she took me there. She told me of the day the sea began to boil while they were sleeping, how the tide changed its mind and drove the waves across the dunes and up Beach Road, how the menfolk ran from house to house to warn them, how the day stayed dark as night, they sat around the table like figures in a doll's house as the sea sluiced in the door, until the sky caved in and the sea was muddy soup that froze all will to move. She told me how her father said they had to get upstairs and how she sat beside my mother on the bed as her mother shrank back to a child, how he made a rope from bedsheets, told my mother to climb out the window to look for something she could tie it to, how well he knew she'd go because he was asking her for help not her sister, punishing Lucy for the ring she twisted on her finger like a talisman, how one by one they clambered to the roof and huddled there like birds while all the buildings melted into cardboard, started toppling like dominoes.

"I should have tied that rope. Your mother was pregnant and I was the only one who knew, the only one she'd trusted to admit he only had a first name to her.

"What was it?"

"I never really listened to remember. I was selfish. I let my sister get dressed up to meet a stranger, dresses he wouldn't even see the colour of, makeup I was glad to lend her so I didn't have to look at me. I guess he was a tourist seeking entertainment for a fortnight like they all do then one night don't show up. I was the real one who let her down. I was engaged with a wedding in the spring. I had my escape route planned."

"Where was Edward?"

"Safe in London. Too far away to help or even know how bad it was. It gets worse Grace."

"Because you went away?"

"Because I left her drowning. My father knew my mother couldn't swim but knew she'd jump before she'd stay up there alone. The house was shuddering around us like an animal. He shouted "Now!" I hit the water, felt it swallow me and swam not knowing up from down. I fought to reach the air and it was colder than the water. I looked for them and saw your mother struggling, I heard my father's voice and swam to catch it up. I shouted for him, a shout came back but not an echo. I saw him look around and saw what he saw, turned away before she pulled me back. He dragged me to the edge and someone threw a blanket round me.

"And he went back for mother?"

"I tried to tell myself he would have if someone hadn't been halfway there. Just like I told myself I was too scared when I couldn't see my mother. Lies show through no matter how you wrap them up. Your father was the someone, he was the strongest swimmer in the lifeboat crew. I saw him force the sea back out and thought he was too late. Perhaps he was. There's more than one way you can drown. You never really get the sea out."

"But you were at their wedding?"

"My mother wasn't. She was drowned. The sea will take the weakest. Or are they? They jump when they will fall, try to swim when they have no idea how. Your father asked me hoping we could share the space she left. All it did was make us islands. Causeways need the tide to shift. They take a while to build."

"Aren't causeways much like bridges? Because I don't see mother building any bridges Lucy."

"Causeway means a path of stone. You take a risk in crossing, have to know the tides."

"Suppose the causeway lets the ghosts across? Would my father save her now?"

"Yes, I truly think he would."

"Knowing what she let Paul do? That Chris is more a ghost each day? Would you sit here with your father telling him it's all alright now? Truly Lucy? You ran away remember? You put a sea a hundred miles wide between you and what he did."

"And I came back for you Grace. I take the risk of getting stuck each time I come here, see him sitting listening now. It floods back everything he did and throws back who I was. I take that path for you, for Robert, so you don't have to run away. But don't pretend you never want to."

I suddenly remember a different table, a storm that fit inside a teacup, yellow roses in a vase.

"Lucy can we try something? To stop this storm at least?"

I ask her to swap seats and tell her when we do we will become each other, see and feel as if we are inside each other. If we can't imagine we can ask a question but we have to try hard first.

"Is this by any chance an upside down house game?" she smiles.

"It puts things the right way up."

I walk along the road and pick up flotsam Lucy cannot touch except when she's asleep, I sit upon her bed and hear him marching up the stairs, I feel the scissors chewing through my hair. I tell myself that hair can't hurt but in the morning it hurts more. I feel the shells he scattered in her bed and told her would be snails if she took them out. I ask her questions knowing all the ones I make her ask along with mine. Could she have stopped him? Should she have told him she deserved it and know the lie was worse than any snail? And most of all I feel the sea in every space I thought I had, a river I can never stop. Because it isn't the things he means to hurt that hurt the most. He can hit you, humiliate you, freeze you with his silence, stab your mind with words until he owns that too but you will only find the worst bruises when he's gone. It is the trail of things that you believed were crumbs. You will learn to steer around them if you can but words become tattoos. As Lucy drinks it I smell it, taste it, hear Paul laughing, hear me asking why it can't taste nicer, hear him say it can if I pretend it's something else. When he told me the real name all I remember is him spelling it. The word just soaked like water into sand. Paul always called it lemonade. But there are many its, too many things will trip you up. The pink roses in Lucy's garden I changed to yellow in my painting, the cigarettes I can't bear the smell of, the candy floss I can't eat. The snares lie in the shallow soil of what were normal things and normal words. The safest places are the places they will never look. I guess why Lucy left, it was her way to punish him. I guess a ghost can follow you. The bedroom in the roof is Lucy's second bedroom, the one she climbs to when the storm returns, when nowhere but the roof feels safe, when grey shows through the bluest sky. I have to stay because the roses are still pink underneath. All scenery does is paint over the top. I need the grey to hide in, a sky the seals can fly in, I need to swim between two worlds even if I have to run on sand to get there. I have to turn back to me for no one else can find me.

You will forget how long the hiding places took to find, how many things you turned into until you try to turn back. It feels like coming out of the water with no idea where you left your clothes, like they don't fit when you put them on. I go to hospital for checkups shying from a glance, an animal pacing in a human zoo. But listening to the heartbeat I felt soothed. I lay in bed and found it without meaning to. One night when hunger forced me upstairs I discovered Robert had become nocturnal too. The fridge hunts began to synchronise. We'd sit in the kitchen eating ice-cream in the dark.

"Would you have come back if I hadn't crashed?" The question drops but only sounds as if it's come from nowhere, when words don't count he doesn't have to pay attention, these ones have been waiting, stirring ice-cream into custard.

"Yes, I think I would. It would have taken longer, I was completely lost. I needed somewhere I could cry and nobody to keep the volume down for, nobody to try to switch the channel. I don't want to hurt you but I left for you and stayed for me. I didn't fit in Cambridge,

Cambridge drew me in. I didn't tell you Lucy wanted me to stay for good. I was trying to decide."

"You didn't have to tell me, that's what hurt. You might not have fit at first but you were changing. I could hear it down the phone. Each time I talked to you it seemed I faded more."

"I had to go away before I could come back. Like a picture you see better when it's just a picture. Or a bridge you stand on knowing you can choose which way you cross. I had to go to see how big I'd be without you."

"Well that sure worked. Is the bridge still standing!"

"It was yesterday. I meant the beach bridge. You can stand on top and look at everywhere you know or see the road and know if you just take it everything will change. I thought if I could see both ways I'd know which one to choose."

"I can't imagine how, but that made you decide to stay?"

"No, it didn't. I got too cold and bought some fish and chips and then came home. And realised home could never be anywhere else." I say home and know it's just a word till you are there the way a kiss is nothing till your lips meet and everything when they do.

It was the last Saturday in November when Robert heard me. He woke in my room, hearing cries from his. Not missing Chris cries, not nightmare cries. I never even heard him coming in. He held my hand and shouted for his father while I squeezed so hard he gasped each time I did. He told his father how far apart the contractions were. His father looked at him and didn't have to ask me. Robert could stay, I wouldn't drop his hand.

She came as dawn was breaking, when if you are born here you will learn to tell the moment sea and sky begin to melt apart. We called her Nesta as her grandfather had agreed. As her father would have understood.

When I think of Chris I see and hear him, smell and taste him, feel him there as if he is a part of me. It means the pain will not die until I do because the pictures will not run out. Robert's father says we dream to keep a door ajar. There are nights when Robert wakes to hold me sobbing when ajar won't budge. The door into the nightmare opens day and night and pulls me in like quicksand. I somehow know the nightmare is the price I pay to keep the dream. They share a causeway.

I think of him as often as I loved him, I miss him, knowing missing is a sea. It will never run dry, it will drown me if I let it, so I let it spitting out the salt and tasting what is sweet. I think back to the day I almost caught him up and know that even made of sand our steps were set in stone. He was bound to run and I was bound to follow, he to set the pace and I to set the distance he could go before I drew him back. All running did was set a fire, all chasing did was light it. Distance only fanned the flames. I am left with a dream, a family, a path that goes both ways. And myself. Because to go back and forwards you have to know where you belong. Or you'll get stuck.

I have a sky to paint a thousand colours. If my sky is sometimes hard to tell apart from sea I let it blur. I turn the clouds to smoke and leave the wind to stub a hole. I sometimes put a candle in it. So that I can blow it out. I have a photograph of Paul I never look at. It is the one Chris took when they had built a snowman in the garden, he could be smiling at mother in the kitchen or me as I am running down the path. I don't know why I have to make it me or maybe I don't want to. I keep it buried in a drawer. I can't say what he was to me or I to him. I can paint him black with every word I choose and all of them will turn to grey. I can fill an empty page with words I cannot write and still hear every one. What is a story but an imprint? Whether you are Goldilocks or Grace it is a trail. You start at the beginning and don't know where you're going half the time, don't know who you'll meet along the way. I remember Lucy telling me the people in your story were like actors in a play. If someone plays so big a part you cannot cast them out then they are there because they taught you something. Paul taught me love must do more than cast a spell: it has to worm its way into your heart before it can belong there. So I guess he stole a corner.

Some evenings the sun is an amber circle, a painted jigsaw piece that joins the sea to the sky. Sensation overwhelms me. Here I am strong and the sea fills me. Back there I am weak, fighting shadows. I look and Paul is never here. But I know that Chris is. I whisper to him. I swim underwater until my need for air is strong enough to drown the urge to let the water fill the space he used to fill.

I would like to say I take fewer risks now in the water but I still swim too far out, dive much too deep, ignore the warning flags. I tempt the sea as if I barter, offer up my body in exchange for his. Then I remember he would never have wanted that; he would want me free.

One thing counts in this grey liquid land. Stay afloat. Keep moving to keep from freezing. Stay strong as you push through the water. Break the rules and you are lost. One choice. Swim or sink. It is never as simple as it sounds.

Then I look at the position of the sun and know it's time to come out. Half wet, I pull my clothes on and race the wind back home. I push the door open where it sticks and call his name. To see him smile, to know that I am there. Sometimes stars trace a different path from those we wished on. Sometimes they are neither hot nor cold: they smoulder, wait. The sky must turn completely dark before you see them shine. I hear our daughter laughing somewhere upstairs. Robert saw the child instead of the reflection, knowing that for Chris I'd keep on swimming. When the waves calmed I saw he loved her. When the sun came back I took her from his arms and loved her too.

I know my mother loves her in a way she never could love me, I know this from the way that Nesta will not sleep without the doll she gave her, how she dresses Alice up to go to see her grandmother every Friday, from the pictures Nesta draws of the house I've never seen. But I'm not looking at the house but at the colours, at the twigs she draws for hands and how they join.

Robert persuaded me to let my mother see her saying she had lost too many people to deserve to lose one as a punishment when Nesta would be punished too. I wonder if I deserve him when he's always waiting for me. A year before I said I loved him; two years before he could begin his doctors training, three years more for the village to have two doctors. He always tells me that only I am counting. I ask him why he waits for the answer to a question he asks so often the wind can whisper it. He smiles and says he told me he would never walk away so he has to wait for me to catch him up. Now I know I have. I know that to take his hand I have to let Chris go. Tonight I will imagine him standing on the balcony urging me to ask and daring Robert to say anything but yes.

If I imagine him everywhere, an eavesdropper to everything I do, it will blend to somewhere and – sometimes – he will become the one I tell things to when no one else will do.

I will never catch him up. He will walk in my footprints yet they will trace each path he left. In the end all we do is trail a finger in the sand, then hear the sigh or thunder of the waves as we walk away. But not too far.

Epilogue

Stepping Stones

January, 1975

It was the last Saturday in January, the last train from Norwich that afternoon. The train was late as usual. It begins to rain. My mother and stepfather are in Cambridge. My stepfather had laughed, blatantly kissed me, sarcastically saying he supposed I would prefer to meet my brother on my own. I push my way between the passengers, mostly shoppers, running home with shiny paper bags. I wait upon the platform too relieved he's coming to be angry that we only have tonight. I have not seen Chris since November: Christmas pantomime without him, January drifts of days that piled on top of one another, pages turning backwards not forwards. In those empty days I looked at my mother, wanting to tell her the truth, not knowing what it was. I had recognised that a part of me was not blameless; even as Paul stole inside me, I had kept as a talisman the thought of stealing something from her. I feel the thought between my fingers, let it join the litter on the platform. I shiver, spinning round, the cold air sucked in as the train arrives. I spy him standing by the window of the door, impatient to reach the handle, push it down. A smile is leaping at the edges of my face. I want to hold it back, pretend I do not care. I turn and let him find me. The figures slipping past me blur. Then footsteps stop, his hands are on my shoulders, breath upon my hair. I stand and feel the warmth of his hands blot out the imprint of the fingers only I can see. Paul has not touched me for four weeks yet still I feel him. I have to find the words to tell Chris the truth while I am me.

When we reach the taxi rank it is empty. The shoppers have taken all the taxis. Wisps of twilight trace around us, charcoal scribbles. Rain is sequins that street lamps toss upon the ground.

"Let's not go back yet, Chris," I say.

He looks at me. "Where do you want to go, Grace?"

I catch his hand, tuck mine inside his glove. "Anywhere," I plead.

"How about dinner, then? There's a hotel at the bottom of this road. I've been in there with Robert a few times. They should be serving food in the bar now."

"I'm not old enough yet," I remind him.

"Pull your hair around your face, then. It's always dark in there."

We melt into the rain and do not run. The hotel is framed against the seafront, the windows stained by the rosy glow of light inside. We climb the stairs and step into the hallway, shaking off the rain. Chris finds the bar, I drink it in. The walls and carpet are red to match the velvet seats, the lights are ornaments, the fire is real, the smell of molten pine. I smile at him. As usual he is right, in this light I could easily be older. Easily be somebody else.

We find a seat by the window, share a menu, pick at random. Silence draws us back together, spinning a cocoon. If I try hard enough I can forget the rest. I will ask nothing about his world, he will ask nothing about the one he left behind, until the one we create is the only one that matters. It always was. It just grows smaller every time.

The room is warm, the food the waitress brings she takes away untouched. Time slides like sand, too fast to squeeze the feelings into words. I drink the lemonade and give up trying, feel him take the glass out of my hand. A gentle tap on my shoulder, followed by another, more insistent, bring me out of sleep. My brother's face is close to mine.

As if I made it out of papier mâché, a hundred younger versions smile below his smile.

"Grace, look outside."

I lift my head as if he holds the strings.

"It's snowing," I say happily.

"It's also closing time. The rain will have frozen. No taxi will dare those roads. I bet Paul would if we rang though. He drives like he's on ice anyway!"

"No, don't." I cover up the panic. "I mean it's not fair. Too dangerous."

I can see him thinking, know there is only one option, wait for him to say it.

"We could get a room here. If I have enough money. Wait while I go to reception. I'll find out what they charge. If we can stay, then I'll phone mother."

Paul will be furious if we spend the night here. Suddenly I don't care what that costs me later. I'm tired of fear. I see his face, his anger turn to hunger, sated into smiles. I make the pictures freeze-frame, blink.

I smile at the barman and order another drink while I wait for Chris, finish it and try to stay awake. I feel him whisper through my hair, the way he does when no one else is meant to hear.

"Stop looking like it's past your bedtime. I got the cheapest room they have. That guy on reception doesn't care who we are as long as you look eighteen. But if the manager appears he'll want proof and we'll get thrown out!"

I laugh and see the barman lift his head. Chris smiles a conspirator's smile. I see him miming 'sister'. I play along and almost get away with it until I knock my glass over. I put out my hand to pick it up. He grips my arm.

"Please tell me this is a joke and that was lemonade..." It's half a growl, nowhere near a plea. His arm locks around me steering me along the hall. He pulls me into a stairwell.

"What the hell are you doing Grace? I leave you for five minutes and you're ordering a drink! What was it?"

"Mostly lemonade" I look at him and add the rest, "and vodka."

"Why?"

"I don't know really. To see if I could?"

The arm relaxes. When it drops I want it back. It must show on my face. He starts to draw a smile on my mouth as I used to do to him when I was ten. It's half a smile. It's nowhere near ten. His finger curves across my lips to stop as if intrigued to find they open, parting them again as if to find out why, I see his lips move and hold my breath and kiss him. It feels like kissing glass, as if there is a wall between us. Suddenly I know what's missing. Pulling him close I tell him to imagine we are on the beach at night and when his eyes shut the kiss is different, like drinking lemonade then drinking lemonade and vodka. I move my lips on his until he finds me, opening my mouth to let him make me lost. I press against him and feel him answer me, confused and hurt when suddenly he pushes me away. Then I hear the footsteps, see the barman walking past. He drawls something I cannot catch then laughs. I look at Chris as the echoes fade.

"What – did – he – say?" I breathe.

I can't decide if he is shocked or breathless.

"He said 'I wish my sister kissed like that', " my brother mimics.

"Am I really that good at kissing?" I tease.

"You have the benefit of no comparison group." I puzzle over this but sense he won't explain.

"How did you guess about the drink?"

"Because I still see through you like glass." I wish that still was true.

"Was mother cross?" I ask to change the subject.

"She'd gone to bed. Paul said goodnight, said you need the sleep. He's right. You look exhausted." I cut Paul's words out. He cannot touch me here.

The room seems a long way away. I follow blindly, letting corridors and stairs unwind. Chris finds the keyhole, twists and pushes free the door. He leaves the light off, the room is bathed in moonlight from the window. Immediately I run to look, the moon stares back, a face made up in silver. Snow falls like balls of cotton wool. The sea is glass behind the esplanade, the sky is ivory black, a mine of stars. The crazy golf is calm and shadows skate along the promenade. Below the grass is edged in frost, the pavements gleam and snow is blossom in the flower-beds. The room is in the eaves, so high up I look down and street-lamps shrink to candles, cars are fondant toys. I breathe in, breathing out to watch it float away as mist. Chris laughs softly at my face, the child he knows. Here I can pretend to be her. This is the first hotel room I will sleep in: a wardrobe, a spindly chair, a double bed. I sink onto it, undressing to my underwear. This room is just a box. I can be who I might have been. I can be Grace tonight, forgetting all the reasons why she disappeared. I slide inside the quilt, no need to burrow underneath, no nightmares hang upon the walls. I needn't check the door, the lock will make the box a safe. I try to hold the feeling, sleep turns the key.

I wake and jump, relieved to see my brother's eyes, not Paul's. Warm stars, not cold. He is sitting fully clothed beside me, watching me. Like a guard.

"Chris, you must be freezing. Do you remember when you used to stay awake when I had nightmares? You used to say that nothing could get past your guard. I woke and saw you there and you looked just the same: like you were guarding me."

I wait for him to smile. Instead he sighs.

"I'm not guarding you Grace. I'm guarding me. Against you. Against everything I feel and everything I could feel if I let you slip past."

"Then why did you kiss me back tonight? Where was your guard that night on the beach?"

"Did you never wonder why I left, Grace? I'm trying not to feel something I know is wrong or want something I'll never have. That doesn't stop me wanting it or wondering what it would feel like."

"Does right or wrong matter here? For us? I learned to walk because you walked away, to swim underwater when you disappeared. Must I find out that wanting someone feels like playing hide and seek? Without it being you?"

I move his hand across my breast and steal his mouth. I feel his fingers slip inside my bra, pulling it aside to move his mouth there, tasting me till I cry his name. As if a spell is broken he pushes me away.

"Now do you see why it matters, Grace? We'll always be playing hide and seek. All you'll ever have to do is say my name and I will see my sister. All I'll have to do is hear you say it to be your brother."

"Then I won't be hiding. I'll be lost," I whisper. His face says he doesn't understand. If I count to a thousand, the words won't come out to explain. I hide in the pillow and know tomorrow he'll go back to school and I'll go back to Paul. I pull the covers over my head and wait until I think he is asleep before I start to cry.

Dreams protect us from the truth. The dream was real once. It is the version that is left after I cut out what I cannot bear remembering. The version closest to the truth is the hardest one to tell.

I start to cry and hear him say my name. When I do not answer he pulls the covers off my head. I turn my face into the pillow, feel him stroke my hair. I feel the longing in his hands, know how longing grows if it is stretched. I sit up and let the covers fall.

"You used to dress me, Chris. If you undress me will you still see a sister?"

"Don't, Grace." He pleads.

I touch his lips and watch it stain his eyes.

"Just once. So we never have to wonder what it would have felt like. So we know."

Kissing we undress each other, throwing clothes and covers on the floor. I let him seek, discover where I hide, exploring, swimming till we pull each other underwater, till I guide him deeper, quicken in the jolt of joining flowing on his face. He moves to feel me catch him, moving deeper, filling me until it feels like falling, till suddenly one movement sends me flying to a bottom so far down that touching it I shatter, knowing nowhere else will I be whole again. I open my eyes and catch his face as knowing cracks it. I hold him till the pieces hold together, as whole as love can be once it's been made.

I wake, my head still swimming, kissing him to wake him too.

"Let's get dressed and go downstairs for breakfast. Go for a walk in the snow. Work out the rest later."

"Work out what, Grace? I have to go back to school. You have to go home."

"Then last night didn't matter? You can carry on as if nothing happened?" I feel as if he's hit me.

"Last night was once. Tell me what was meant to happen? What did you think we would do then? Live happily ever after? If once isn't right how can there be an after?"

"I'm really sorry, Chris. I must have got so carried away last night I didn't hear you asking what the plan was." He glares at me.

"When I woke up I would have said that once had turned to once upon a time, as if a story was beginning. In stories if you love someone you're meant to make wrong right, do anything you have to. Slay a dragon, solve a riddle. But if all you can do is ask me questions then you're making love the riddle. Not solving it. Slaying it."

"Who do we tell this story to? How would we find words they'd understand ? We'll be the dragons. I'm not brave enough to fight that, Grace."

"Then go back to school. I fight monsters you don't even see."

My eyes are dry. They won't be later. But later isn't now. I will pretend this doesn't hurt if it's the last thing I pretend. I go into the bathroom, get dressed and don't look in the mirror. It will tell me nothing's broken on the outside when inside everything is smashed.

When I come out I sit upon the bed and stuff the few things that I have inside my bag, aware he's watching me, too fragile still to look at him. The hairbrush drops onto the floor. I bend to pick it up and so does he. I cannot see it, all I see is his hand but as I reach for it he snatches it away. I want to grab the bag and stuff the hurt inside as well but the urge to look at him is stronger. When I look he's facing away from me. Furious I drop my head and see the hairbrush. Then it's flying at his head. For once my aim is perfect. Touching his head he turns and stares as if to check it came from me.

"Have you gone mad?"

"Nothing you can cure, Chris. Why? Did it hurt?"

"Did it help?"

"It made you see me."

"I always see you, Grace. When I wake. When I go to sleep. I've undressed you in my head so many times I can't imagine looking at anyone else."

"Then why?"

"Because that beginning was always going to happen, sometime, somewhere. But I can't see the middle and the end. It becomes two separate stories."

I sit and feel the pain sink in and know no matter how deep I swim it will always be deeper.

"Grace?" He sounds wary.

"I know I have no right to ask you this but what about Robert? He wants to see you. I was supposed to talk to you this weekend and find out why you keep putting him off."

"So that's why you found the time to see me?" I bait. "Well, now you can go back and tell him why you forgot to talk to me. That you lost track of time. Inside me."

"You know you don't mean that. You couldn't hurt Robert like that."

"I am hurting, Robert. Just not that way. Don't worry, you're not the reason."

"Can you tell me, not for Robert?"

"I can tell you for me. I don't ever want to end up like mother and father. Hurting each other, disappointing each other, melting down what little love is left to turn to hate. So I leave Robert where he is: not as close as he would like to be but far away from where I'd hurt him."

"I can't see that happening. You and Robert want the same things. The same places, even the same food. You like your houses upside down and your beaches in the rain. Even from my balcony I see how much he loves you."

I keep my thoughts my own, they sound too selfish. I love Robert's smile, the way it makes me smile back. I love his house, that I can lie in bed without checking the door and tuck the noises in. I love his father catching tears in roses. But I have to love Robert more than all those things.

"I sometimes wonder if I wasn't me which one of us you'd pick. If you met us both as strangers I think it would be him."

"I'm not a doll you can give away, Chris," I flare.

"And he'll never treat you like one. But I'll never love you like he does. Remember how upset you were when you thought I didn't like your bridesmaids dress? The perfume I gave you that day?"

"When you said I looked like a flower?"

"That did come from me, and I meant it. But then you asked me where he was. I'd read your letter, you'd described the dress to him, said you missed him. I was jealous. So I teased you about the colours. Worst of all, I lied. The perfume was from him."

"Then you never really lied. It's your smell I want." I will fight until there's nothing left to lose.

I walk him to the station through the blur of snow. We stand upon the platform, use the cold to numb us. If I don't ask him when the train is coming he won't check the timetable. Time will run out soon enough. If I don't reach for his hand I will not beg him to stay. I know the only way to keep him is to tell him how much once will cost me. I know why I am looking at the snow and he is looking at the rails. No matter what our faces say we have to make them masks until they stick. He turns to face me and nothing but his eyes are real. They beg me to forget, to lock the face he showed me last night somewhere with no reflections. I look at him and silence seals a pact. For words will glue us to these moments, tear the past apart. We must pretend to be the people in each other's lives that we were meant to be. We have to write a whole new set of lines for the brother and sister we would have been if who we are had not got in the way. I stop myself from asking how we begin to do all that and why they are right and we are wrong. I have to let him go. Till all the other nights turn last night to a dream.

I hear the train sweep through the snow and when it stops I let him climb aboard and as it slides away I see the window frame the picture I will never paint. He is waving like he always does when he cannot turn goodbye to good. And lying. Robert knows I only like perfume on flowers. Chris is telling me the truth he cannot say. In his dreams he does not love me as a sister; when he looks at me he will always love the sister more.

Some things slip past your guard. Nesta is Chris's daughter. She is Robert's more. A father is who you love, who guards your journey through that childhood kingdom. That is how it should be. She will draw herself first, see her own reflection. Even if her eyes are topaz blue.

I will spend a lifetime skipping pages, slipping on the face of truth my kiss revealed, the face I draw in dreams, the face the sea rubbed smooth, each face my memory paints. I never land upon the one I want, the one he'd wear today. In time we find the pages safe to stand on and make them stepping stones.